SHELBY FOOTE

Love in a Dry Season

Although he now makes his home in Memphis,
Tennessee, Shelby Foote comes from a long line of
Mississippians. He was born in Greenville, Missis-
sippi, and attended school there until he entered the
University of North Carolina. During World War II
he served in the European theater as a captain of field
artillery. He has written six novels: *Tournament,
Follow Me Down, Love in a Dry Season, Shiloh, Jordan
County*, and *September September*. He was awarded
three Guggenheim fellowships during the course
of writing his monumental three-volume history,
The Civil War: A Narrative.

ALSO BY
SHELBY FOOTE

Tournament
Follow Me Down
Shiloh
Jordan County
September September

The Civil War: A Narrative
VOLUME I. *Fort Sumter to Perryville*
VOLUME II. *Fredericksburg to Meridian*
VOLUME III. *Red River to Appomattox*

LOVE
IN A DRY
SEASON

by SHELBY FOOTE

VINTAGE BOOKS
A DIVISION OF RANDOM HOUSE, INC.
NEW YORK

First Vintage Books Edition, June 1992

*Lyrics from the Jelly Roll Morton songs "Don't Leave Me Here" and
"Mamie's Blues," copyright by Tempo-Music Publishing Company,
Washington, D.C., and used with their permission.
Lyrics from the song "Empty Bed Blues," by J. C. Johnson,
copyright 1928 and 1947 by J. C. Johnson,
and used with his permission.*

Library of Congress Cataloging-in-Publication Data
Foote, Shelby.
Love in a dry season / Shelby Foote. / 1st Vintage Books ed.
p.   cm.
ISBN 0-679-73618-2
I. Title.
PS3511.0348L68   1992
813'.54—dc20   91-50722
CIP

Manufactured in the United States of America
10   9   8   7   6   5   4   3   2   1

CONTENTS

ONE

1. The Barcrofts

Major Malcolm Barcroft was sixty-seven when he died, the last male of his line. Accompanied as it was by word of his daughter's peculiar reaction, the announcement of his death caused people to remember many things about his life which they otherwise might have forgotten, as is usually the way in the formality of getting a man of property buried and awaiting the reading of his will. He was an institution in Bristol, one of the final representatives of what the town had progressed beyond. Winter and summer he wore dark suits and pleated-bosom shirts with a pearl stud and plain gold cuff links and a snub bow tie. When he stood alone or walked about for his evening constitutional he gave an impression of height and stiffness — 'high-stomached,' Negroes called him; but when he was juxtaposed among other men you saw that he was not really tall and that his shoulders were even a bit stooped. He wore a rimless pince-nez from which a length of fine chain dropped like a golden cobweb to a spring button at his left lapel. His mustache and roached hair were iron-gray, and his nose was like a blade between flat cheeks, sallow from recurrent malaria, and burning brown eyes. Lightly grizzled, his eyebrows were tufted at their outer ends, giving him a somewhat Mephistophelian air. This was belied, however, by a soft voice and a courteous old-world manner.

3

He was born in Reconstruction times, 1873, two months after his father, who had been a Confederate officer and had come home one-armed from the war, was killed in a scuffle over a ballot box with one of Governor Ames' imported election officials. Reared by his mother and a maiden aunt, Malcolm was wilful and impetuous and domineering, until the two women, taking the advice of an uncle, gave it up and packed him off to military school in Tennessee. There he found interests worth his talents, studies of campaigns more complex than those involved in outwitting two admiring but rather terrified female relations, and he settled down with unexpected seriousness. He was impatient during vacations at home, reading military biographies, Jomini and Badeau, for which he drew sketchmaps to follow the battles and entered his objections in the margins, usually with exclamation points and cross-references to sustain him. He cultivated the habit of saying, "Good, good," as Stonewall Jackson was said to have done, and of raising one hand palm forward from time to time, also as Jackson was said to have done — to implore divine guidance, according to some, or merely to slow the flow of blood and thereby ease the throb of the wound he had taken at First Manassas, according to others. Malcolm took all this quite seriously, and if it sometimes had its ridiculous aspect, he at least was never conscious of it.

In his final year at the Tennessee school he was appointed cadet captain and had decided definitely on an Army career. His life seemed to stretch out before him in agreeable vistas, brilliant forays on the frontier, punctuated with periods of tedious but glittering staff duty in Washington, and perhaps — if the Germans and Spaniards continued to bluster — a real war to lodge his name in the history books, or at least in the tactics manuals. To these last he brought an enthusiasm and appreciation which some young men his age were devoting to Keats. He found them exciting, and not only for their subject matter — the language itself enchanted him. The mission of the infantry in attack, as defined by the text: "to close

4

with the enemy and destroy him," had a wild, triumphant, almost lyric beauty, while the mission of the infantry in defense: "to maintain the integrity of the position," was nothing less than the finest phrase in literature. His scalp would tingle when he read such things; the hair on his neck would bristle.

But just three weeks before commencement exercises he received a letter in which the family stationery was puckered with little blisters where his mother's tears had dried. The gentleman left in charge of his father's estate — a lawyer, a friend of the family — had absconded ("gone to Texas," the letter said) with what little was left after hopeful but feverish mismanagement. So when the final dress parade was over Cadet Captain Barcroft packed his trunk, folding in the gaudy uniforms with the unblooded sword and the paper-backed texts, of which no future edition would bear his name, and came home to Bristol to enter his bachelor uncle's cotton office. He renounced the dream of pomp and glory, the study of evolutions of the line and the finer points of precedence, and undertook the study of staple values and fluctuations in the cotton market.

Within three years he had learned the business well enough to permit his uncle to relax, and within another three years the uncle retired. If Malcolm's income was not sufficient to make him the catch of the town, at least his family background and his earnest manner after his mother's misfortune made people consider it hardly more than he deserved when he became engaged to the only daughter of a wealthy retired planter. After a wedding still remembered in the Delta for the tubs of champagne punch and the fine gowns of the bride and bridesmaids, Mr and Mrs Barcroft sailed from New Orleans on a Mediterranean tour. Halfway up the Italian boot they were recalled by the death of the father-in-law, and a year later, when the legal smoke had cleared, the young husband found himself in possession of just under half a million dollars in good securities and his wife had borne him a child.

They named her Florence, for that was the city they had most looked forward to visiting; they were in a coach on the way there, reading of Florentine splendor and intrigue in their red-bound Murray, when the cablegram overtook them. Malcolm Barcroft now had everything he could ask for, except the very one thing he wanted most: a male heir. However, the disappointment at the child's being a daughter was offset somewhat by the assurance — doubly welcome since his wife was far from robust — that there was no question of barrenness.

When the second child was born he was in Panama Beach, Florida, commanding a company in the Second Mississippi Volunteers, the former Mississippi Rifles who, arrayed in a V by their colonel, Jefferson Davis, had pierced the Mexican center at Buena Vista fifty years ago. His early dream of martial fame had been offered him again and he had taken it. In point of fact, however, there was little glory. The war ended before his regiment embarked, and though there were casualties in numbers large enough to compare with the bloodiest of campaigns, embalmed beef was no enemy to reflect glory on the men who fought it — no man brags of a battle when the field was his own gut. In 1899 he received his majority and was mustered out to come home to his wife and children.

This second child was a girl too; they gave her her mother's name, Amanda. Two days after the major arrived the doctor took him aside. "This birth was even harder than the first," he said, an old man who retained a diffident, apologetic manner despite forty years spent attending the ills of half the county. "I dont advise that Mrs Barcroft bear another child."

Less than a year later the third was born. Major Barcroft walked the corridor for two days, back and forth, passing and repassing the door of the room where his wife lay wailing and whimpering. On the second night, however, the wailing stopped; it stopped quite suddenly, and the nurse came out and told him she was dead. The major glared at her. "Did you save the child?"

"It's a son," she said.

That was when his eyes first misted with tears: he had waited for this — so that they appeared to be not so much tears of grieving as of triumph. For a moment he considered calling the boy Hezekiah; that was the name of the dead father-in-law. Then he put the thought aside; it had been a notion of his wife's, who had always been a bit off her mind in the final stages of pregnancy anyhow. He called him Malcolm, the name of the firstborn male Barcroft for five generations now. And they lived, the four of them, father and daughters and baby son, in the big gray house which the father-in-law had built five years ago for his daughter to move into when she and her husband returned from the grand-tour honeymoon. It was in the fashionable part of town, with four large oaks across the front. Angular, wooden, Neovictorian, it loomed among clapboard cottages and two-story stucco 'mansions,' dwarfing them. Gingerbread trim, tacked to the eaves and mansard windows, gave the house an incongruous aspect, at once lightsome and clumsy, like an elephant dancing.

Major Barcroft left the girls to the care of their nurse, but himself undertook the raising of his son. The boy resembled his mother, with parchment-colored skin, soft violet eyes, and a head too large for his body. In time he developed a finicky, effeminate manner — a bit of shell in his soft-boiled egg at breakfast would upset his stomach for the balance of the day. Better than anything he liked to be alone in a far corner with a pair of his dead mother's scissors, clipping the bright flimsy illustrations from magazines. He was nervous and excitable; if anyone spoke to him harshly he became ill. On his sixth birthday the major gave him a Shetland pony, but he was afraid of it. When his father tried to persuade him to sit in the saddle he began to back away, and when the major finally lost patience and lifted him to place him on the pony's back, he kicked and screamed and then began to vomit and had to be put to bed.

After this Major Barcroft tried other ways. He bought a crate of lead soldiers, miniature warriors done to scale, each with its musket or saber. There were all the accompanying impedimenta of armies, cannons and wagons with horses to draw them, headquarters tents, ambulances, and field kitchens. He had the crate taken into the parlor and unpacked it there, not caring how much excelsior cluttered the carpet and furniture as he lifted out the figures one at a time. "See this one? He's a general. Look at his stars." When he had unpacked them all, he arrayed them for a grand review, then turned to Malcolm and said earnestly, "Thats your army, son. What do you think of it?"

"It's nice, papa."

"Nice — " Major Barcroft looked at him. Malcolm was not nearly as enthusiastic as his father had expected him to be. "Wait," he said, turning back to the soldiers; "I'll show you how to play with them."

He built two opposing ridges with sofa pillows and chalked a wavering line on the carpet between them. "Thats the Rappahannock. This is the town of Fredericksburg, on this side. Those hills over there are Stafford Heights and they belong to Burnside." He dropped to his knees, arranging the soldiers and cannons so that they faced each other across the little valley. "These hills on this side the river are Marye's Heights. They belong to General Lee — this is the hill where he stood and watched the battle. 'It is well that war is so terrible; we should grow too fond of it.' He said that standing on this little hill. All right. Longstreet was up there and Stonewall Jackson down here. Your grandpapa was with General Barksdale in the town, shooting to keep old Burnside's men from crossing on their pontoons."

The major went on with it, scrambling about on hands and knees, moving the soldiers. He demonstrated Pelham's gallant resistance with two of the miniature fieldpieces and became highly excited as he staged the Federal advances, leaving windrows of slain lead soldiers behind on every charge. Then, as he moved the survivors forward for their third assault against Longstreet's sunken road, reproducing the deep, throaty roar of the Yank attackers and the high, fanatic scream of the Rebel defenders, he turned to say something to Malcolm. He had become so absorbed in the tactics of Fredericksburg, shifting the troops, emplacing the artillery, he had almost forgotten that the demonstration was intended for his son.

At first he did not see him. Then he caught sight of the boy behind a chair. Malcolm had not even followed the battle; he had taken two of the horses from General Pendleton's artillery park and was concentrating on making them lope around a chair leg in a decidedly unmilitary manner. The major rose, brushing the knees of his trousers and shaking his head, and left the room without saying anything further. He was too angry to trust himself to speak.

For the next five years Major Barcroft divided his time between his cotton office and his son, doing all he could to change the boy from what he was to what he, the major, wanted him to be. And he had some success. He got him onto the pony, for one thing: taught him to ride with his legs straight, dragoon style, without posting — Malcolm even became fond of it. Though the major was discouraged to see that he treated the animal more like a pet kitten than a horse, it gave him real satisfaction to see his son's large head jogging steadily above his narrow shoulders as he rode the streets of Bristol on the round-barreled little stiff-kneed Shetland pony.

On Malcolm's eleventh birthday his father gave him a case of shells and a 410-gauge shotgun, a fine hammerless model, a Parker, with a chased design of partridges and ducks at the breech and his name embossed on a silver plate set into the cut-down stock. The major took him onto the levee south of town and taught him to shoot, setting up bottles and cans and paper cartons for targets. At first he was gun-shy, flinching at the prospect of the kick; but soon he began to get over it, and at length, within a month of the day he first fired the gun, he began to put an occasional pellet into the target.

It was summer, and the major encouraged him to take the gun into the fields by himself. Sometimes Malcolm and the boy next door would go together, taking turns setting up targets and shooting. One morning in July they set out together, and two hours later the other boy came running back. He was crying, and at first they could not get him to tell what had happened. Then, between sobs, he told them. They found the gun where he had dropped it as he ran, and fifteen yards away, lying across the barbed wire fence on which he had been hanging the target, they found Major Barcroft's son with the back of his big head blown off.

Florence and Amanda — Miss Flaunts and Miss Manda, their nurse called them — did not go to the public school; they went to St Mercedes Academy, the parochial school at the Catholic convent, where the teachers were called Sister, never Maam. Other Protestant children were there, most of them from the same neighborhood, for the public school was not considered 'nice.' The years progressed like floats at carnival, a succession of bright hair ribbons and crisp dresses worn with ribbed stockings and button-top shoes. Florence was called "the pretty one" and Amanda was called "the smart one," though both adjectives were applied in a sense comparative strictly between the two of them. Less politely, but by the same token, Florence might have been known as 'the slow one' and Amanda as 'the plain one.' This last, however, was never done, and indeed there was little unpleasantness in their lives beyond the rough cloth their nurse used when she scrubbed their knees and elbows for Sunday school, the calomel which the doctor measured on his knife blade, and the occasional small pink bottles of medicine that he left when the sisters fell victim to grippe or whooping cough or chicken pox — for they were subject to all the ills of childhood. One terrible week they had mumps, and that was the worst.

Malcolm's death came at a time when they were just beginning to be invited to ice cream parties. It frightened them.
After the funeral they lay side by side in Florence's big tester
bed, rigid with the same unspoken memory of how their
brother had looked in his gray casket set on trestles in the parlor, the way his hands had been crossed on his breast to show
his clean fingernails bitten neatly to the quick, the thumbs like
little clubs because he had sucked them. He might have been
just lying there, about to sit up and speak, except that the smile
was not like Malcolm's smile at all and the man had propped
his head unnaturally on the pillow to hide where he was hurt.

Amanda said, "How long do they stay the same — in the
ground I mean, before they begin to change?"

"Hush," Florence said. She was the older.

But what frightened them even more was their father's face.
It showed through the succeeding months, at once stern and
unyielding and yet at the same time ravaged — a surface whose
changes could be remarked only in details, a certain redness
rimming the eyes, a tremor at lip or eyelid in moments when
he thought himself unobserved. Florence and Amanda watched.
Before this time, grief had been merely a word in the speller.
Now they knew its image.

For two months after the funeral the girls did not leave the
house except for church or Sunday school. In the hours of
gathering dusk and early darkness they would hear children
from adjacent houses playing on lawns and sidewalks, the
abrupt bursts of laughter which meant that a joke had been
played, or, worse, the sudden periods of quiet which might
mean almost anything. From their upstairs bedroom window
Florence and Amanda would hear the others, children of families death had not touched, playing Spin-the-Bottle or Clap-In
Clap-Out, new games somehow connected with kissing and
introduced since their retirement, their imposed period of
mourning. They would look at each other in the glimmer from
the arc light in the street below, their faces neat pale ovals
empty of everything, even regret, and they could feel in the
room — not quite tangible, but no less real for that, like an

odor of sachet or musty velvet — the presence of the dead brother.

"Has he changed yet, in the ground?"

"Hush, Amanda. Hush."

But later she did not need to ask. For he came to her in her dreams, and he was changed indeed; she hardly knew him. Then she did know him and she was frightened worse than she had ever been in her life. She went and got in bed with Florence, hugging her back. But when she told her sister what she had seen, Florence said she must never tell a living soul about it. People would think they were haunted.

Late in September, the day after they returned to the convent, Amanda stayed behind in the classroom during the first half of the recess period, doing her afternoon homework. When she came down the steps she saw a group of girls clustered at the far end of the playground, by the swings. Those on the outside of the circle were straining on tiptoe, their hands on the shoulders of the girls in front, and occasionally one would give a little jump for a better glimpse, causing her curls to toss on the collar of her middy. From the top of the steps Amanda could see Sister Ursula in the center; she was bending over something. Then the girls gave back, opening a lane, and Sister Ursula came running, her narrow black shoes flicking from under the skirts of her habit. She carried someone in her arms, and when Amanda saw the long yellow hair streaming almost to the Sister's knees she knew it was Florence.

They laid her on the couch in the Mother Superior's office and then the priest came, Father Koestler, red-faced and flustered, and after a while the doctor arrived with his satchel. Florence could not catch her breath. She had been swinging on the exercise bar, a girl said who was peeping round the others in the doorway, and suddenly she had stopped and could not breathe. Her nostrils were ringed with white and her eyes bulged with terror. The doctor said Asthma, a terrible word, and when she was better he took her home in his buggy and carried her up the veranda steps. This was 1912. It was twenty-six years before she came down them again, and that time she was carried too.

It changed their way of life, their outlook. They lived apart, removed from a world they had only begun to know. Major Barcroft hired the high school principal, Mr Rosenbach, to come every schoolday afternoon from four to six-thirty and give them private lessons, with an additional four hours on Saturday mornings. Professor Frozen Back, he was called, a German with a soft brown beard and inward-slanting teeth; his stiff Prussian carriage made him appear almost deformed, and on his watch chain he wore seals that clanked like a miniature saber. His public school pupils could testify to his zeal with the birch, though of course he never punished the Barcroft girls. He never had to, for they were terrified and never gave him cause; they knew their lessons perfectly and sat as still as mice all the time he was with them. "Very good, young ladies," he would say at the end of a session. "Very good indeed." Then he would take his hat and be gone, and the sisters would sigh and look at each other, smiling trembly smiles of nervous relief.

That was the way they grew up in the big gray house on Lamar Street, where hitching posts and carriage blocks were being removed as traffic hazards, and filling stations and curb markets were already beginning to encroach. The clapboard cottages would disappear overnight, like palaces in the Arabian Nights, and the stucco mansions would come down in clouds of dust, workers swarming over them with the disinterested rapacity of locusts in a Biblical curse. It was no longer the best residential section; their neighbors were migrating east of town to escape the soot and whistles of the new box factory and the incessant gramophones of the wives of men who worked there. Mrs Esther Sturgis, an old lady in a wheelchair — soon to be known as "the Mother of Bristol" — was subdividing her plantation east of town, and those who could afford it were buying lots and building new-style houses beyond the silver twin-thread sweep of the C & B. So now, seated by their window in the darkness, the Barcroft girls had more to overhear than the ice cream parties and kissing games. Weekend nights were filled with music, throbbing drum and wailing horns muted by the sliding feet of dancers at the Elysian Club three blocks away, and while sleepless townspeople would toss and curse, or lie quiet and regret, the sisters would imagine they could identify, by the shrill empty cachinnation and even by the sliding feet, their former schoolmates and neighbors, one by one.

Soon afterwards, however, Florence stopped sharing the second-story bedroom with Amanda. Her choking fits continued, and under the doctor's orders to avoid the stairs, she moved into the downstairs front parlor, a high dim room, musty from disuse and cluttered with velvet drapes, dark gold-framed paintings, cumbersome furniture, and ornate wall-paper with birds stenciled on it like no birds that ever flew. Their mother had furnished it; this had been her favorite room. It was where Major Barcroft had fought the Battle of Fredericksburg in small, as well as where Malcolm had been displayed in his gray steel box. Florence called it her bedroom, but there was no bed in it. She spent her nights in a chair, a patented model with an adjustable back and a pull-out for her feet, because she believed she would choke unless her head and shoulders were propped higher than the rest of her body. The room was made airtight for her fumigations, calked with folded newspapers at jambs and sashes. Yet even above the reek of camphor and burning sulphur there was always a rancid odor of unwashed female flesh. She feared death by drowning; one of her attacks might come while she was bathing, and her modesty would not permit anyone, not even her sister, to be in the room with her at such a time.

She claimed she never slept: "Not really. I just rest my eyes every morning about two," but Amanda would be wakened almost nightly by her screams. She had nightmares of clammy nets and snakes and galloping horses, smothering her, constricting her, running her down. In consequence, her appearance was affected. No one, even by the old limited comparison, called her "the pretty one" now. She had begun to get fat, in a flaccid, dropsical way. Her skin was stretched tight over her cheekbones and at the backs of her hands, which were curiously rounded. There were little folds, like the flap of an envelope, at the outward corners of her eyes. All that was left of her restricted claim to beauty was her long yellow hair, now finer and longer and yellower than ever. Hanging over the back of her Morris chair so that it almost trailed the floor, it had the rich sheen of cornsilk when the ears begin to tassel. She was very proud of her hair and would call attention to it by complaining that it bothered her, especially in hot weather. "I declare," she would say; "I declare this old hair of mine is about to drive me crazy. There's so much *of* it!"

Major Barcroft would come to her room for a half-hour visit every evening. Florence was afraid of him; he so obviously represented the outside world against which she had built her barricade. But she would try to keep from showing this — she would chatter pleasantly about nothing at all. During the summer after she passed her twentieth year, the long hot summer of 1918, she complained especially about her hair, holding the thick limp pale gold weight of it away from her neck, and the major would listen testily. He despised boasting, never having needed to boast himself; most of all he despised any pretense that was meant to cover boasting. He would listen impatiently while she complained about her hair and held it out for his and Amanda's admiration.

He had been kept from a third chance at glory by a heart murmur which he had never suspected until he reported for his physical examination the year before. All through the period of skittish 'armed' neutrality he chafed at the delay; his hate for President Wilson was an intensely personal thing. As soon as war was declared he got his papers together and went to New Orleans to volunteer for active service. He was forty-four — they would probably give him a desk job; but he figured that, once he was in uniform, he could manage to get himself assigned to duty with troops in the field. Everything went well until at last he stood in the line of applicants, each with his shirt in his hands, queued up before a medical officer who thumped their torsos and listened to their chests. With most of them he made short work: a couple of thumps, a moment of auscultation, then a pat on the shoulder: "Youll do. Next!" But when Major Barcroft stood before him the doctor listened, paused, listened again more carefully, and finally said, "Wait over there, please."

One man was already waiting. By the time the doctor had finished with the queue two others had joined them. "I didnt think I'd make it," one of them said. "But I'm glad I tried." He was middle-aged, with a dyed mustache waxed to needle points. None of the rest of them said anything. They avoided looking at each other's faces, like candidates blackballed from some exclusive club.

After a more thorough examination the medical officer told Major Barcroft, "It's not anything really serious. Just a murmur. But you see you could keel over at any time, under severe exertion. And we cant take those chances." He spoke as if the Army belonged to him, and he had a hearty professional manner, a personable young man whose patients had mostly been women. The major glared at him, as if the doctor were somehow responsible for the murmuring heart. Then he put his shirt on, walked to the station where he had checked his bag, and took the train back to Bristol. Rejected, dejected, he watched the scenery slide past the Pullman window.

He did not mention the incident, but all during the war his manner was short with everyone. Thus one night when Florence was complaining about her hair he looked at her with a peculiar intentness. "Does it really bother you so much?"

"Oh yes, papa. Look." She held it out from her shoulders on the pretext of keeping cool.

He watched her, the pince-nez glinting. It was late July and Chateau-Thierry had been fought — the papers were full of it. "Sam Marino can fix that for you," he said. Sam Marino was his barber. "Would you like that?"

"Ah no, papa," Amanda said.

Florence was frightened but she continued her farce. "It really is warm," she said uneasily.

"Then I'll tell him to come tomorrow night." The major looked from one to the other, still with that peculiar intentness, as if he expected them to protest. But neither of the sisters said anything.

Next evening, as the three of them sat together, no one mentioned the barber. From time to time, however, Major Barcroft would take out his watch, look at it, then put it back in his pocket and clear his throat. At last there was a rap at the front door. Amanda started to rise, but her father put out one hand; "I'll get it," he said. When he had left the room Florence sat watching her hands in her lap, head bowed, eyes almost closed, as if she were praying.

Sam Marino followed Major Barcroft into the room. Carrying a small black satchel which resembled a surgeon's instrument case, he paused just inside the door. "Evening, ladies," he said, short and dark, a Sicilian with a neat but large mustache and an air of suppressed joviality. He bowed to each of them in turn. Amanda nodded but Florence remained in her attitude of prayer.

"Here's your new client, Sam," the major said.

The barber put his bag on a chair. "Ach, what a pity," he said. He made a gesture of despair: "Such fine hair you seldom see," then another of resignation: "But it makes business."

"It bothers her," Major Barcroft said. "It makes her hot." He watched her with the peculiar intentness of the night before, but the lamplight made his glasses opaque and they could not see his eyes. "Dont it, Florence?"

She kept her eyes down. "Yes, papa."

"But if youd rather keep it, we can tell Mr Marino it was all a mistake. Are you sure it bothers you so much?"

"Yes, papa."

"Youre sure you want to get rid of it?"

"Yes, papa." She kept her eyes down.

Now that the scene had progressed this far, the major began to have qualms. Intending to give her a lesson on the evils of pretense, he had thought she would back down, would admit her falseness when faced with the actual loss of her hair. But now that he saw she had no intention of admitting any such thing, he was almost sorry he had begun it. For now it was a contest: either he would relent or she would recant or she would lose her hair, and it had gone too far now to be anything but the last of these three — discipline had come to resemble cruelty. Yet at the same time he was rather proud of her determination; it showed the stock she came from. He stepped forward: "All right, Sam," and outlined the style of the haircut with the tip of one finger.

Sam Marino took his shears and a fine-tooth comb and a pair of clippers from the satchel, and while Florence sat perfectly motionless, her gaze fixed on the opposite wall, he cropped her long yellow hair as her father had indicated. Glinting coldly, the shears snicked along the line of her jaw and two short curves of hair sprang forward, projecting like spikes on both sides of her mouth. He combed her top hair forward so that it curtained her face, and then as he moved the shears across her forehead, clipping neat Dutch bangs, hair tumbled onto her hands in her lap and they saw that her eyes were filled with tears. The barber worked fast; he felt that something was wrong about this house, some tension he could sense but not define. He snicked the shears rapidly at the back of her head, great skeins of hair cascading to the floor, and then he ran the clippers up her neck.

Though Amanda still had to come downstairs and sit with her, holding her hand and comforting her till dawn paled the windowpanes behind the draperies, Florence's nightmares were no longer of nets and snakes and wild-maned horses. These were replaced by quiet dreams in which the violence was not actual but implied, not kinetic but potential: of a small room, a sort of cell whose walls are hung with shears and clippers and other tools, vaguely obstetric, and Sam Marino is there with his black satchel. Up to this point there is no terror, for the barber is not threatening her; he is merely there. But she feels a dim uneasiness, a sense of another presence, someone who intends to hurt her. Timidly she begins to look about the cell, turning her head to glance over her shoulders. Half her mind wonders what she will see, but the other half already knows. This disturbs her; this is part of the terror. How can I be two people? she thinks; how can I know and not-know? Then she sees him, her father, sitting in a far corner. His legs are crossed and he swings one brightly polished boot tip. For a moment terror chokes her; she cannot breathe. But when he rises and comes toward her, his face growing larger, she finds her breath and begins to scream. Her cries fill the cell, growing shriller as he comes nearer, and she feels a hand upon her arm and hears a voice she knows — and always it was Amanda holding her hand, saying "It's all right, Florence. Shh: I'm here: I'm with you. Shh," and the terrible dream-shapes were gone at last, back into whatever darkness they had emerged from; there was only Amanda with her.

She had always been afraid of her father — in her early girl-hood when he had no time for anything but his business and his son, in the time of mourning when he presented across the dining room table the stern and ravaged face of sorrow, and in the years of the great war when he believed himself robbed of his last chance at glory. But now, as a result of her nightmares and other imagined horrors, she would go rigid with fear whenever she heard his step on the veranda, the street door coming open, and then the sound of his feet in the hall, halting beside the hat rack and then coming on. As he approached the door she would stop breathing; she would clutch at the arms of her chair until he had passed and she heard him climb the stairs.

There was no chance of happening on him; she never saw him unless he came to her. For now she never left her room. She even had her meals sent in and ate from a tray, propped in the patented chair. She wore a series of violently flowered wrappers — seven of them, named for the days of the week — black lisle stockings, the seams awry, and bottle-green carpet slippers that became shapeless within two hours of the first wearing. Twice a week Major Barcroft would visit the close, rank chamber, watching her shrink back in the chair. He never stayed long, and as the years passed he came even less often. Sometimes there was more than a week between visits. But Florence never got over her terror, the particular quality of which was obvious — the whole time he was with her she sat with her knees pressed close together, like a woman in fear of assault. Her hair was kept short; she preferred it that way, and Sam Marino returned four times a year for 'trims.' He brought no terror into her dreams, however: it was as if he had had no share in the original operation. "The night papa cut my hair," she would say; she dated everything from that, after the manner of women who had more serious — anyhow bloodier — operations, or after the manner of the old people of her childhood, who dated everything from the year the stars fell.

She had two interests. One was the Memphis paper, the one that came down on the evening train, with lurid headlines and pictures of bank robbers and gentlemen riders and beauty contest winners in one-piece sleeveless bathing suits. She read it column by column from left to right and page by page from front to back, picking up the continuations as she came to them, moving inch by inch down the newsprint, through congressional debates and legal notices and want-ads, with the grim unflagging headlong perseverance of a mole burrowing in loose earth. Theory and problems did not interest her (editorials, for instance, passed from her memory as soon as she had read them) but she acquired a host of facts — she knew all the journalistic celebrities by their first names, including the various husbands of Peggy Joyce and the wives of Tommy

Manville. The newspaper brought the outside world to her, and she preferred that world to be as different as possible from the one she knew.

Her other interest was sewing. She spent her daylight hours stitching flower designs on quilted satin. Folded into envelopes, they were handkerchief cases; left unfolded, they were samplers. Each Christmas she wrapped the year's production in holly paper, individually, and sent them to women she had known as girls a decade back, most of whom were mothers now though she always addressed the packages with their maiden names, looking up their addresses in an old phone book she had saved. A receiver would unwrap the gift and spend five minutes in speculative contemplation — it was too fine for a tea cosy and too thick for framing — and then give up and pack it away in a cedar chest. Ten and fifteen years later, when her daughter would lift it from the stale confusion of yellowed lace and dance cards, asking what it could be, the mother would pause for a moment, the tip of one forefinger at the corner of her mouth, and then: "Why, I dont rightly know, darling," she would say. "It's something poor Florry Barcroft sent me, years ago."

These two occupations filled her ordinary days. But the first Sunday of every month was an extraordinary day, with two events neatly separated by two oclock dinner. Soon after noon the rector came, Mr Clinkscales, with his rosy cheeks and pleasant manner, bearing under his arm a calfskin case containing the utensils and the bread and wine for Communion. He walked with a limp, the result of breaking his ankle long ago — he was making a genuflection and when he straightened up, stepping backward, he fell off the dais; the break had knit improperly and now he walked with a rolling gait like a seafaring man. He improvised an altar in front of the Morris chair, and there he administered Communion. Florence took the wafer greedily. While it dissolved on the back of her tongue, digested almost before it was even swallowed, the words of the ritual seemed to float in the air about her head:

*Take and eat this in remembrance that Christ died for thee,
and feed on him in thy heart by faith, with thanksgiving.* She
stretched her neck eagerly for the cup, and while the wine
fumes set her brain reeling, the words had a particular beauty:
*Drink this in remembrance that Christ's blood was shed for
thee, and be thankful.* Thus transported, she remembered the
half-naked man nailed to the wall of the church beside the
altar, and she fed on him in her heart and drank his blood.
When Amanda came into the room after seeing Mr Clinkscales
to the door, she always found her sister sitting with her hands
folded in her lap and her eyes would be filled with tears of
happiness.

Later that afternoon the doctor arrived — Dr Clinton, who,
though already well past middle-age, was rather dandified, af-
fecting stand-up collars and pepper-and-salt jackets with bel-
lows pockets and the belt sewed on. He spent half an hour
with Florence, talking symptoms in a guarded manner and
making a perfunctory examination. Then he went to the rear
of the house, to the small downstairs room that was called the
office, for a consultation with Major Barcroft. Whether this
was for professional attention or to report on the condition of
the invalid daughter or perhaps merely social, the sisters did
not know. However, they ruled out the last possibility — their
father was never 'social' — and soon they ruled out the first
as well; for when the doctor left the room he put his instrument
case on a hall table just outside the parlor door.

It was Florence who discovered about the instrument case.
On a November Sunday, a chill drizzly day three years after
the barber's first visit — Sam Marino came back four times a
year, in March and June, September and December; he was
always punctual, arriving the first Monday in each of those
months, and Florence no longer feared him; he was one of her
'visitors' now, along with the rector and the doctor — Amanda
came into the room in time to see her sister make a sudden
furtive motion, hiding something beneath the newspaper in
her lap. Then she looked closer and saw a glint of metal and

a length of rubber tubing. "Now, Florence," she said quietly. "You'd better put that back before he leaves. He'll need it, you know."

Florence was flushed with excitement. "I was going to put it back. I always do." There were two bright spots on her cheeks, like rouge. She paused. Then she said, with the forthright manner of one who has considered and made a decision: "I found out something. Do you want to hear it?"

"Hear what?"

"Listen." She gave Amanda the stethoscope. "Listen to yours first," she said. "Then mine." She bent forward with an air of conspiracy, hands clasped under her chin, and said eagerly, "Oh Amanda, it's the strangest thing! Just listen." She showed her younger sister how to wear the instrument with the ear hooks pointed forward and even how to place the listening cone. "No, no," she said authoritatively. "It's not way over on the left. They just tell you that. It's in the middle, almost. Listen." She reached out and shifted the cone. Then Amanda heard it: her own heart, like a tomtom, going *Bump. Kibump. Kibump. Kibump* with a steady, viscous, pumping sound, the rhythm of her blood. Watching, Florence smiled. "Now listen to mine," she said, pressing the cone to her own breast. Amanda leaned forward, hearing her sister's heart: *Kibump. Ki-kikibump. Bump. Kikibump*: a terrifying sound. The tomtom had gone all wrong, as if a madman were beating a mad rhythm.

"See there?" Florence said proudly. Her cheeks were flushed. "Isn't it just the strangest thing?"

So now Amanda knew; whenever she looked at her sister she knew. Something alien and dread had entered their lives. It was as if a third person were present now whenever they were together: Florence was never alone. From this day, in the dim hot airless room, close and fetid as a winter den in which a wolf had recently littered, while Florence sat by the window pulling bright thread through hoops of quilted satin, her back hunched as she leaned toward the light, her short hair spiked forward in two abrupt, vicious curves against her jaws,

Amanda felt the presence of death poised like an actor in the wings of a theater, disinterestedly awaiting his cue to repeat a performance he has played too many times.

For Florence there was no relief, no other life, no other atmosphere; but Amanda had outside duties. Three times a day she left the house. First in the morning, soon after the major had gone, she went to do the marketing, carrying a basket over her arm. Then in the afternoon, at five oclock when slanting sunlight threw long shadows on the pavement, she would walk to Cotton Row to meet her father. And finally, after supper, she went for her seven oclock constitutional, a half-hour stroll which the major prescribed (for her, not himself: he never went) to 'settle' the evening meal.

The five oclock outing was the one that put her most in the public eye, for she and her father would walk together homeward through the quiet downtown streets while others were still waiting for five-thirty, quitting-time. At fifty Major Barcroft had the septuagenary dignity, the stiff, sway-backed carriage, the grizzled hair and slightly tufted eyebrows he was to take to the grave. Townspeople would watch them — the middle-aged old man who maintained an air of inward contemplation, as if he somehow had managed to swallow a cannonball, and the young daughter who was as drab, as deferential as a hired companion not too sure of holding her job, aged, too, beyond her years, whose air, though not contemplative, was as removed as her father's — and there would be a ripple of comment following their passage, like the bubble and foam of a wake:

"There they go, the high-and-mighty Barcrofts."

"Thats quality, man."

"Quality. You can have it."

This was spoken not so much in pity as in judgment, and not so much in judgment as in triumph. They could forgive him his reverses, the sorrows that crowded his life, but they could not forgive him his reported million dollars and his highborn insularity. They, or others like them, had watched him all his life, and when trouble came they resented that he did not call for help. They would have preferred it so; they would have enjoyed watching him run shrieking into the street with his hands in the air: 'Help me! Help me! My affliction is more than I can bear.' In that case they might even have gone to help and comfort him. But as it was, their eyes were hostile as they watched him pass.

"Punch him with something sharp," they said; "what would run out? Ice water."

Amanda and the major did not so much as glance to the right or left. They went past like figures in a tableau moving slowly along the pale sidewalk dappled with low-angled, watery sunlight and the shadows of leaves. Young men among the watchers would nudge each other:

"There's your chance."

"My chance at what?"

"At a million dollars, man. What else?"

"Hm. No thanks. It's not enough, considering what goes with it."

But there was someone who thought it was enough, who weighed it carefully, point against point, made his decision quickly, and believed himself fortunate that no one had done so before him. There was a suitor on the way.

2. Jeff and Amy

Briartree, the Tarfeller plantation down on Lake Jordan —
what was left of it, anyhow — went to Amy Carruthers when
her aunt, Miss Bertha Tarfeller, died intestate. "Miss Birdy
should have known better than to die like that," people said.
She had been principal of the Ithaca school for almost a generation; Miss Birdy they called her, and though it had mostly been
forgotten by now, she had had one love affair in her life. In
1890, when she was eighteen, she was left lonely in the house
after her older sister married a young lawyer visiting a classmate on the lake and moved to North Carolina: whereupon
Bertha took up with a professional gambler. No one knew how
they became acquainted, though she was the one suspected of
having made the overture; such horseback rendezvous appealed
to her romantic nature — which later took a milder form; she
was poetess laureate of Jordan County in her later years. An
anonymous letter informed her mother, who told her husband,
Bertha's father, that he would have to do something about it.
"There is a thing you must do," she said, a tall broad-shouldered
woman with fierce eyes. "A gambler and a loose man has de-
filed your daughter."

Cass Tarfeller had never done anything about anything.
Vapid and congenial, he lived on land inherited from his father, who had been a man of convictions and decisions, one of

the original settlers of the region. But this time, goaded by his wife, Tarfeller did something — the one action in his life that was out-of-character. He wrote a challenge to the gambler, Downs Macready: *I will shoot you on site if I see you Tuesday when I come down town & I mean it.* But Tuesday when he went to Ithaca, wearing his father's horse pistol, Macready shot him with a Henry .44 repeater, twice in the belly and once through the chest. Tarfeller crumpled and lay in the hot white August dust, stained but not even bloody, as if even the dignity of bleeding were denied him in his belated assumption of a heritage for which he had never been fit. Macready in turn was shot by a man named Bart, a planter friend of Tarfeller's, who himself was wounded but recovered.

So then the widow and her daughter lived alone at Briartree, the mother brooding, reliving the scene in the lower hall immediately after the shooting, when a messenger came from Ithaca and told them her husband was dead, along with the gambler, and Bertha turned on her with a face like a tragedy mask, accusing her: "*You* killed him, and Downs as well; you killed them both! I'll hate you forever!"

"I didnt kill them," Mrs Tarfeller said, shrinking back; she raised one hand in protest, palm outward in front of her face as if to protect herself from a blow. Within a dozen years she had brooded her way into an asylum, where during the years until she died she would approach a total stranger on the grounds; "I didnt kill them," she would say, holding out her hands, and the stranger would be frightened; for though by then she was harmless, she still had the broad shoulders and fierce eyes.

At the time of her commitment the older daughter and her lawyer husband came down from Carolina for a division of the estate. He was honest enough as lawyers go; it was Bertha herself who insisted on taking the house and eighty surrounding acres as her share. The Carolina couple took the rest, the fifteen hundred acres of cotton land, which they sold to the first bidder at a price outrageously low. The low price did not matter, however, for the lawyer lost the money in the market crash of 1907. He would have lost a larger amount with the same facility. That was his luck all his life.

Bertha was left lonelier than ever in the big house, without even her mother to hate. She moved to Ithaca, took a room in a boarding house, and began teaching school. That was 1902. She rented the house and the eighty acres, using the income to send what she called 'deserving' pupils to college (most of whom disappointed her completely, being spoiled by this one taste of easy money) except a bit she held back to finance the publishing of her biannual books of poetry, selections culled from the poems which now began appearing one a week in the Bristol *Clarion*. Since there was no spare money for repairs, the house deteriorated. At last it was almost a ruin, occupied by the kind of people who rent eighty acres for a year or so, not caring what manner of residence is included, and then move on. When you opened the gate, rusty plowpoints strung on haywire for a counterweight would shriek and jangle, and as you passed down the double row of mule-gnawed cedars toward the house, three or four flop-eared hounds would come belling from under the gallery and razorbacks foraging in what had been the rosebeds would turn and look at you and someone in a barrel-stave hammock swung between two of the cedars would ask what you wanted, not bothering to sit upright to ask it. Inside, conditions were worse; dust was everywhere and the tenants had been using the woodwork for kindling. Early in the Twenties the ladies of the Bristol Garden Club voted to buy the house and restore it as a showplace. They sent a delegation to the Ithaca school and Miss Birdy came to the door, her hair untidy and chalkdust on her dress. "Oh I couldnt do that," she said when they had made their offer. "My people are all buried there, you know." Six years later, when she died, they were disappointed that she had not left it to the garden club in her will, though in fact she left no will at all. They shook their heads. "She should have known better than to die like that, being a teacher and all."

That was 1927, the year of the great flood, and Amy Carruthers, daughter of the Carolina sister, was the only surviving member of the family; her parents had died of Spanish influenza during the war, within a week of each other. The following April, soon after the anniversary of the day the levee broke, she came to Mississippi with her husband (he was also her cousin; Carruthers was her maiden as well as her married name) to look over the property, see what she had inherited. They obviously had money, or anyhow one of them did, for they came in a car considerably longer than any Bristol had ever seen — pearl-gray, with almond lights, fenders like wings on the upbeat, and a baggage rack at the rear: a town car with a glass partition between the back and front seats, the chauffeur sitting out in the weather, sweating in his winter livery, for it had still been almost chilly when they left Carolina two days ago. This was the year when Southern voters, mostly Baptist, were confounded by having to choose between a Republican and a Democrat who not only was believed to be under the thumb of Rome but who also announced for Repeal, and they felt betrayed.

Its rear protruding almost to the center line of Marshall Avenue so that people out for their Sunday rides had to detour around it, the long gray car stopped first at the Kandy Kitchen, and the Negro carhop who went out to the curb to take their order — two glasses of ice "shaved dry, it has to be dry," two lemons, and the sugar bowl — came back with his eyes stretched perfectly round. "They got them a bar in the back of that thing," he said. Several people left their cherry phosphates and Green Rivers on the marble counter, walked by the car, glancing more or less casually into the back, and it was true: the woman was mixing Tom Collinses with a long-handled silver spoon. The chauffeur watched them but neither the woman nor the man appeared to notice their curiosity. They went back into the Kandy Kitchen and resumed their places at the counter, sipping their soft drinks and shaking their heads. Early afternoon of an April Sunday, and here were people drinking on the sabbath streets — at a time, mind you, when Bristol husbands were still forbidding their wives to smoke in public.

The woman was in her middle twenties and she wore a sort of tennis dress that shouted Money almost as loudly as the car did, sleeveless and V neck, of a semi-transparent material, chiffon or crêpe-de-Chine or maybe georgette, which allowed the pink of her nipples to show through. She not only wore no brassiere, she obviously wore no undergarment of any description. There was nothing of modesty about her. Not that she was flaunting herself; that was what was so outlandish about it (for this was the late Twenties; plenty of women were dressing almost as scantily); she appeared not even to know the watchers were there. Her hair was brown with streaks of sunburnt yellow, bobbed just a little longer than ponjola, and her skin was tanned to the smooth, soft tint of café au lait. She moved slowly, after the manner of the inherently lazy, not so much as if she had no energy, but as if she were conserving it for something she really cared about — bed, most men would say, for there was a strong suggestion of such about her, like an aura. Her mouth was lipsticked savagely, no prim cupid's bow, and there was a faint saddle of freckles across the bridge of her nose.

She finished mixing the drinks, stirring them until they were frosted over, then touched the back of the man's hand with the cold wet bottom of one of the glasses. He hesitated, then turned his hand palm-up and took the drink. He did not look at her or even turn his head in her direction. "Mud," she said, watching him, and he lifted the glass with something less than a flourish; "Mud," he said. The chauffeur continued to sweat beneath the wheel.

The man appeared to be younger than the woman, perhaps by a couple of years. He too was tanned, though not as dark, and he had a hale, athletic look, wearing a white, open-neck shirt and lightweight gray flannel trousers, buckskin shoes with red rubber soles, and a wrist watch that had no crystal.

His hair was crew cut, like a furry skullcap golden in the sunlight. He had that same economy of motion the woman had, but in his case it did not seem to be based on indolence or conservation; it seemed rather to proceed from the caution of a hostage among enemies. The features of his face were small, occupying a scant one-third of the front of his head, as if a hand had squeezed them forward without doing them any individual damage. His mouth was small, its corners barely extending beyond the wings of his nose, though the lower lip was full and rather pendulous; from time to time he gripped it with his upper teeth, which were small and sharp and very white. His eyes were light gray, peculiarly fixed.

When they had finished their drinks and the carhop returned, the woman asked him the way to Lake Jordan. He told her, turning his eyes this way and that, in every direction except toward the front of her dress. She tipped him fifty cents. "Yas maam!" he said and his teeth were as white as his eyeballs. The car backed almost to the opposite curb, swung left, a long gray curve (actually the metal seemed to bend) and then was gone. "Who could they be, asking the way to Lake Jordan?" the watchers said to each other, ranked along the marble counter of the Kandy Kitchen.

They were Amy and Jeff Carruthers and they rode south out of Bristol, gravel chattering under the upswept fenders. After a while the man said suddenly, "Whats it like?" Amy glanced out at the fields.

"Cotton. Everywhere nothing but cotton."

"Young?"

"Just little green lines. People plowing. Niggers."

"Ah," he said, and did not speak again. His reserve was like a wall to hide behind.

It was thirty miles. After a while: "There's water," Amy said; the lake was sparkling in the sunlight. The car turned left, moving down the eastern shore behind a screen of cypresses just beginning to bud with tender green along the paleness of their boughs. Jeff said nothing.

31

They asked again at a service station and the attendant, a young man almost startlingly handsome, told them how to find the Tarfeller place. Another two miles, he said, and described the gate. He had trouble with his eyes, the same as the Negro carhop had had, except that he did not deny himself, and his confusion showed in his voice. Jeff turned his head at the sound; Amy watched him. "Drive on, Edward," she said. Then she said to her husband: "You neednt have bothered; he was ugly as sin. There!" she cried, leaning forward. "By that gate." The car pulled up, tires growling in the gravel, and the dust cloud they had been trailing caught up with and blanketed them. Then it settled and Amy sat looking at the house. "My God," she said. "It's haunted. It's bound to be. And to think thats where they got me." Jeff said nothing. The chauffeur sat sweating dark halfmoons at his armpits.

She meant that she had been conceived here, an only child born after twelve years of marriage. Searching through her mother's diaries, she had discovered — or at any rate, folding down her fingers, had computed — that she had been conceived at Briartree when her parents came down for a division of the property at the time when her grandmother lost her mind. Returning to the place appealed to her as a sort of pilgrimage to hallowed ground, the blind seed swimming home. Maybe I'll die here, she thought, for though she did not really believe in death — her own — she was superstitious and even sentimental to a degree.

"Want to get out with me?"

"All right," Jeff said.

She got out first, then he with his hand on her wrist. "Careful through here," she said. When she pushed the gate ajar, the plowpoints slid along the wire and clattered. They passed through, then walked up the lane with its double row of cedars toward the house, Jeff still with his hand on Amy's wrist and a bit in front, so that an uninformed observer would have said that he was the one who was doing the leading, the guiding.

"Oh Jeff, Jeff," she said after a time. "You wouldnt believe how lost, how lonely it is."

Last year's tenants had left when the flood came, and when the flood went down had not returned. No one was living in the house; nothing had been done to clear away the ravages of high water. Vines and weeds were everywhere. A six-inch deposit of silt covered the floors of the lower story, baked almost as hard as concrete though it had a fine powdery surface that shifted and stirred with the slightest breath of air. Fractional chocolate bands on the walls of the house, paling in ratio to their distance from the ground, marked the receding stages of the flood. There was no sound, no motion. An old hound, sway-backed, gaunt, half blind — part Walker and part Redbone and part stray — came from under the gallery, stood for a moment looking at them, blinking its milky eyes in the filtered sunlight, then turned and crawled back out of sight. Amy did not mention this (dogs were a taboo subject just now) but she gave a running description of the place: "Columns. One of them's down. A carriage house — all run down too. Oh Lord, Jeff, what a sight. We're miles from nowhere. Miles. A person might as well be buried as here. What an inheritance: it's just my luck."

She said these things in a natural, offhand manner, but she watched Jeff's face as she said them — particularly when she said, "Miles from nowhere. A person might as well be buried" — and she appeared satisfied with his reaction. Then she went on.

"You can see how beautiful it used to be and of course it could be restored. But who would live here, miles from nowhere?" She paused and watched him, afraid that she was overdoing it.

"You," he said, breaking the silence, and at first she was afraid that he had outsmarted her, had seen through the pretense. But he said it in a somewhat threatening tone — which reassured her.

"Ha!" she cried, imitating a laugh.

They continued their tour of inspection, Amy doing the talking, Jeff the listening. "All right," he said at last. He stood stock-still, holding onto her wrist. "You can cut the sales talk. I'll do it."

"Do what?"

He turned his face, as if he were looking at her. "Who you think youre fooling?" he said harshly. Then he cursed her, the words coming fast like slaps, all the while holding her tightly by the wrist. Sunlight glittered golden in the furry skullcap as he nodded in time with the words. Then he stopped; he stopped quite suddenly. "Lets get back to the car," he said, waiting for her to move.

They rode north on the gravel, which made a steady tinkling against the rims. "Did you really think you were really fooling me?" He smiled as he said it. Amy was smiling too by now, but she managed to keep all evidence of it out of her reply:

"All right, we'll have it your way. Dont we always?"

They rode through Bristol again, then up to Memphis, where they made arrangements with an architect and a landscape gardener for the restoration of Briartree.

△

The money was tobacco money, not from the growing end but the manufacturing; they were from Winston-Salem, and there was plenty of it. Even Jeff who was a younger son (as Amy's father had been, in the days before the increased popularity of cigarettes boosted the fortune) could look forward to something over a million in his own name after three brothers by his father's first wife had got theirs. It had come in time to give him all the advantages: expensive Virginia prep schools — two of them, for he had been expelled from one when a snooping proctor found in his locker a collection of pornographic comic books such as daycoach butchers used to sell — enough spending money to attract the companions he really cared about, and later a succession of high-seated runabouts and out-of-season weekends at the beach. His mother was his father's second wife. She had been governess to the first three sons and a carnal relationship had existed between her and her employer for years. The first wife was an invalid; she never got up from her last childbed, and when she finally died the governess blackmailed old Carruthers into marriage, though in fact it was not so much that her threats frightened him — nothing ever really frightened him — as it was that she caught him off guard, while he was grieving: for he had loved the first wife very much, in spite of his infidelities with the governess. ("At least I dont go chasing outside the house," he had said to himself with satisfaction, where another might have said, with equal satisfaction, 'At least I dont betray her here in the house.') The governess had little time to enjoy her success, however, for she died in her second pregnancy, during their second year of marriage. The old man's third wife was a Broadway showgirl; he met her while he was up there doing the town, celebrating the death of the governess. A dewy-eyed Norwegian from the Minnesota prairies, who cultivated an air of innocence, she taped her breasts to make them jut and later resorted to paraffin injections. She raised Jeff, having no child of her own. He called her *mama* — accent on the second syllable; it was all the French she had.

Though Amy was almost three years older than Jeff (she was born in February 1903, he in November 1905) she was the daughter of Jeff's father's younger brother, who had gone into law and found a wife on a Christmas visit down to Mississippi. She was an only child. Then her mother and father died, both practically at once during the influenza epidemic two months before the Armistice, and Amy came to live with her uncle, Jeff's father, what time she was not at one or another of the girls' schools she attended through girlhood and youth: which meant, in effect, that she spent summers at the country place near Myrtle Beach. She resembled her mother — and indirectly, though she had never seen her, her Aunt Bertha — thin and intense, with a pouting mouth and a wealth of hair. Like Jeff, she had been expelled from school: twice in fact, though never for any such reason as he had been. It was merely that she was insubordinate on the slightest provocation, and sometimes with no provocation at all; every teacher was an enemy per se. Her mother died, then one week later her father, and all through that last week he asked the same question, as if now at last, on his deathbed, some sense of responsibility had caught up with him: "My God, what will happen to Amy?" He took his brother's hand, looking up from the hospital bed; they had never really been friends. "Look out for her, Josh, will you? Will you, Josh?" He kept asking that, even after the brother said he would, and then he died.

Amy came to Myrtle Beach the following summer. She was sixteen; Jeff was thirteen, and at night he would hide in the shrubbery, watching her and her beaus in the side porch swing. It was better than the comic books, and sometimes strangely like them, though a good deal more grim and without the exaggerations. He would crouch there, watching, and at length the lover would disengage himself, would come down the steps, sometimes to within touching distance of Jeff in the shrubbery, and with one heel dig a shallow trench in the sand to bury the contraceptive, which glistened rather sickeningly in the moonlight before it was covered. That continued, and Jeff was always there to watch. Then one night her date telephoned to say he couldnt come — he had to drive his mother down to Charleston; someone was sick or something. It sounded suspiciously pat to Amy. She was angry enough for any enormity.

So Jeff took his place in the swing. He had studied well, watching the others; his movements were bold and selfassertive up to a point. Then at the critical moment he panicked; he was terrified; he even began to weep; "Hold me! Hold me!" he cried. Then it was over and he was amazed: Was that all there was to it? Then gradually he became conscious of a sort of animal chuckling near his ear. She was laughing at him: had been laughing all along, he realized. And he was horribly ashamed.

He never got over it. But afterwards, through the remaining years of school and college, when he looked back on that summer it was not the brief period spent in his cousin's arms that he remembered with most pleasure. After all, her manner had been more that of a riding instructor than a lover, let alone a maiden in submission. What he remembered mainly, what he dwelt on, were those drawn-out moments when he crouched in the shrubbery and watched her with the others. It seemed to him that at such times he could enjoy his pleasure with a greater clarity, his mind being less clouded by emotion.

There were other summers at Myrtle Beach, but he was never admitted to such intimacy again; there were not even any more performances in the swing. For she had reformed — as far as he could tell. Still, they were together every summer, sharing the same house, and this had its consequences. He would stand in the hall outside the bathroom door, listening to the splash of water, the flop of a soapy washcloth. The keyhole was blocked by the key on the other side, though Amy never turned it. Two summers later he mustered the courage to enter. Her breasts and belly were dazzling white in contrast to her arms and legs and shoulders. "You squirt," she said, standing beside the tub and holding the towel limp at her side, not bothering to raise it. He stood looking and suddenly she moved; she moved quite fast. She struck him with one of her foster mother's reducing devices, a plaited rolling-pin, and he fell back. "Squirt!" he heard her shout through the slammed door. However, despite the violence, it seemed to Jeff that she sounded more amused than outraged, and even then she did not turn the key.

That was what bothered him most: the fact that she seemed to encourage his advances, and even granted him certain liberties, up to the point at which she turned on him with violence or laughter. He did not know which was worse, the chuckling or the blows; there was something terribly unmanly about being on the receiving end of either. But he looked forward to a time when he could repay her, could laugh at her or strike her as he saw fit. Thus marriage was already in his mind.

Next year he entered the state university at Chapel Hill. It seemed a shame to waste all that expensive and exclusive prep school training on such a democratic institution, but he really had no choice. All the Carruthers men had gone there, beginning with the grandfather who was the founder of the fortune. He worked his way through, this patriarch who later had his portrait hung over the mantel in the baronial living room, wearing a morning coat and a stand-up collar, and had a coat of arms designed and cut in stone above the driveway entrance; he worked his way through, waiting on tables in the dining hall and making beds in the dormitory at twenty cents a bed a week. Given the time and place, North Carolina in the early Eighties, he had little trouble deciding on a career. He went into tobacco, the marketing of it. In later days, when he was on the rise, a classmate would hear his name and say with a smirk, "Josh Carruthers? I remember him. He used to make up my bed every day in Old East." Afterwards, when he had power and this remark got back to him, together with the names of the men who made it, he ruined some of them financially, though generally they never suspected why.

Jeff, however, waited on no tables and made no beds, not even his own. He went a good fraternity and became a football hero — this last in spite of the fact that he had never been 'athletic,' had not enjoyed the beach games that were a part of summer vacations, had not gone out for any sport in either of the prep schools, and in fact had avoided exertion in all its forms. Football was a manifestation of the fury and frustration that grew out of the annual three months spent near Myrtle Beach in the same house with Amy, crouching outside the bathroom door, hearing the splashing water, the flopping washcloth, or standing on the porch in the gathering dusk and watching her ride off with a series of young men in topless roadsters, or lying in bed, tense and wide-eyed, waiting until the small hours when the roadster's tires would whisper in the driveway sand and stop beneath the porte-cochere, directly under his window, where he would hear them talking in low voices or, worse, silent; then they would kiss again and say good night and she would come upstairs with her shoes in her hand and enter the adjoining room, from which he would hear the rustle of her clothes coming off and the sighing complaint of the bedsprings as she lay down, relaxed for sleep. It added up to more than he could bear. Every September he brought the memory of all this to Chapel Hill and tried to work it off on the football field, to take it out on the opposing team, both in the weekday scrimmages and in the Saturday games. What he lacked in weight (it was not until his senior year that he reached a hundred and fifty pounds) he made up for in fury and a nonregard for injuries. He was clever enough at finding gaps, but when there was none to plunge through, he hit the line as if bent on self-destruction, breaking the chain of flesh. Then he would be into the clear, the spectators a mass of tossing arms and pennants in the grandstand roaring his name. For a moment there would be an illusion of freedom, an elation at having found release. But then, the touchdown made, the furor in the grandstand having subsided except for the sharp occasional cries like the yapping of dogs on a scent, he would find himself in line for another kickoff and it was all to do over again, the chain of flesh relinked.

His father was delighted (but not surprised; he saw his son's football prowess as a demonstration of qualities inherited from his mother, the second wife, the governess) — delighted so much that he gave him a Bearcat roadster to go with the coonskin coat Jeff bought himself. He was Somebody on the campus; other students would stop on the paths, strolling classward, and look at him; he was pointed out, and he did his fraternity no end of good. He even suspected a change in Amy. She had made one among the cheering mass of grandstand faces, had heard them roar his name (it was also hers) and maybe even had swelled the chorus herself, though he rather doubted this last. When she came down for weekends with other men, Jeff sometimes thought he saw her watching him with different eyes — not tender, but anyhow different — and he thought perhaps his time had come; he could declare himself. But then it would be summer again, the long hot days, and he would lie in the close, familiar darkness, monklike on his narrow bed, hearing her under the porte-cochere with other men, her bare feet on the stairs, the rustle of her clothes as they came off . . . and his nerve would fail. Wearing his new dignity, his aura of football and the cheering throng, he more than ever feared a scene that would end in submission to ridicule or violence.

His education was rounded off with a year at Harvard Business School, during which the most memorable times were weekends in New York. Jeff would load his car on a Friday and drive down, crowded to the fenders with young men like himself, ex-athletes mostly with over-developed chests and heavy thighs, spending (like him) a final year of youth before entering their fathers' businesses, taking their places at desks where their bellies and pectoral muscles would sag with the accumulating years of idleness. Their favorite club was Luba's, down in the Village, a gathering place for fairies and lesbians and people who came to watch them. At the climax of the floorshow a fair-skinned two-hundred-pound man stood on tiptoe, arms outstretched, wearing a g-string and a silk-lined cape and a smile that was like a grimace under the spotlight. The young ex-athletes, Jeff among them, would sit at a small round table, bulging a bit in the dinner jackets which a year away from the football field had already made too tight at the waists and armpits, pounding derision with little wooden mallets and sneering at the performers, who responded with glances that somehow managed to combine contempt and longing, insult and invitation. "You better watch out," a girl said once from an adjoining table. "Theyll put the hoot on you." "The what?" "The hoot. They point their fingers at you and recite some kind of poem, and that makes you one too." The young men laughed their disbelief. But it gave them pause; they were more guarded in their jeering from then on.

The year at Harvard completed, Jeff got his reward: a six-month tour of Europe, of which the highlight was seeing Josephine Baker dance in a costume of brown skin and bananas. Coming back, he engaged in a shipboard romance with a Boston girl who was making her debut next year — a frail blonde with thin arms and legs and prominent collar bones, accompanied by her mother and father; her father was a judge. She had a precise manner of speech, indulging in no elisions or contractions. Her final *g*s seemed emphasized, as they always do when anyone bothers to pronounce them. Her muscles, though slight, were long, inherited off the Mayflower. Jeff thought perhaps he was in love — the frailty was what did it. But on the final night she slipped out of her cabin and he had her in a deck chair with their clothes on. It was abrupt and fumbling, really painful, and when it was over she wept on his shoulder, smearing lipstick on his collar. "Oh gracious oh goodness. Oh gracious oh goodness," she sobbed. And he thought, My God — comparing her to Amy. Next morning he went ashore in a hurry and never saw her again, though two years later he heard that she had married a young political figure, the Republican white hope up in that rocky end of the country.

By then, however, he had troubles of his own. He came back to Carolina bent on marriage. Amy was all there ever was or ever would be, and he knew it. He waited a week, again at the summer place near Myrtle Beach. Then he asked her, holding his breath while waiting for her answer. They were alone in the side porch swing, for it was naptime; sunlight was dazzling on the sand, the contraceptive graveyard. "Marry me," he said. He waited.

"All right," she said. He let his breath escape: Was that all there was to it? Then he went to ask his father.

But his father objected, an old man still spry, with an oversized nose and a tuft of white hair like a crested cockatoo. "Dammit, boy, she's your cousin. Do you think we're mountain people?"

"In England they do it."

"This aint England."

"Anyhow —"

He meant it; the old man saw that. And besides, his step-mother — the ex-Follies star, who by now had resorted to the paraffin injections — was wildly jealous of Amy. So old Carruthers said all right; anything to keep the peace. The wedding, in June of 1927, was the largest in Winston-Salem's social history. Among the groomsmen two were boys Jeff had watched in the side porch swing with Amy at Myrtle Beach eight summers back.

The quarrels began almost immediately. A month of marriage taught Jeff things about himself he had never suspected, some of which he continued to deny even to himself. And his sense of inadequacy took the usual form — he became violently jealous. Yet, paradoxically, he did not in truth object to Amy's infidelity; he desired it in fact, provided she would let him watch. But how could he tell her that? All this time, too, he was trying to learn the tobacco market and worrying about his self-respect. He began to think that all his life, no matter where he turned, he would be required to carry more than he could bear. At any rate, though he never succeeded in laughing at her, as she had done (and continued to do) at him, he fulfilled at least half of what he had predicted he would do when they were married; he beat her. The trouble was, she fought back. And ably, too: for she would snatch up any weapon that was handy, a table lamp, the nail scissors, one of her sharp-heeled shoes, an open box of dusting powder, and once her rubber douche bag. With Amy thus accoutered, husband and wife were about evenly matched.

This continued, hammer and tongs. It even got worse. Then one night something happened. They were at the country club; there was a dance; a quarrel had been building up all evening.

Jeff was sitting at their table, watching Amy on the opposite side of the room as she danced with a man named Perkins, a bachelor. He could not see them clearly — other couples kept coming between — but he saw that the man had his knee between her knees and she was enjoying it, answering the pressure. Then they turned and he saw too that Perkins had his fingertips inside her placket, which might or might not have been accidental. Jeff got up and went toward them, weaving among the intervening couples. Within touching distance he stood and watched them; they had their eyes shut, hardly moving. Several other couples stopped and watched them too, amused, anticipant. Then Jeff took hold of Amy's arm and jerked. She whirled and faced him; Perkins stood his ground for a moment before fading into the crowd. "Get your coat," Jeff said. He turned and looked at the watchers. Like Perkins they stood for a moment, thinking of the Carruthers money, the football prowess, the sanctity of marriage; then, like Perkins too, they faded back, resuming the rhythmic shuffle and weave that passed for dancing in the latter half of 1927. "Get your coat," Jeff said again.

She went. Usually she was defiant, especially when there were witnesses, but now she went. Jeff waited at the door. "Better put that on," he said gruffly when she emerged from the powder room carrying her coat across her arm; it was October, the first cold snap. But she said nothing. She marched past him with her chin in the air and led the way down the gravel walk. In the car she sat far over, nursing the coat on her lap.

The roadster came out of the drive already speeding. He had made one conciliatory gesture by advising her to put the coat on; she had rejected this, and now he was ready for a fight. Somehow, in his mind, the rejection had put her even further in the wrong. "You!" she said once; that was all. He was pulling up a slope behind a truck, approaching a blind curve and chafing at the delay. At last, his patience gone, he jerked left on the steering wheel and started around the truck. He turned his head, beginning the recital he had rehearsed: "You think I didnt see what he was doing? Perkins? You think I'm blind?"

"Look out," Amy said.

She said it casually, matter-of-factly, so that by the time he turned his head it was too late. A bus had emerged from around the curve and was bearing down on them. Jeff accelerated to clear the truck, cut hard right again, and almost made it. There was a click at the rear; they hardly felt the shock as the bumpers met. The roadster swung left, then right, careening, and plunged through a low white fence rimming the lip of a bluff. It all happened faster than their minds could register the succession of events, and yet there was a sensation of slow-motion. The splintered ends of palings floated past like the ends of a breasted ribbon, and suddenly the windshield held an enormous jagged star.

Amy never lost consciousness, though there was a gap of amazement that almost amounted to that. Her mind clearing, she discovered that she had wet her pants — which, after an initial pang of disgust, was a relief; at first she had thought it was blood. Then she saw Jeff. "Jeff," she said. There was a gash on his forehead running back into his hair; the rear vision mirror had hit him. A shard of glass protruded from his temple, as neat and bloodless as if it had been driven there by a craftsman with a mallet. Then she glanced up and saw the truck driver standing at the crest of the low bluff. "Anybody hurt down there?" he asked. He bent forward, peering cautiously; his tone was almost conversational. Amy began to whimper.

Jeff woke in darkness and slept again. Next time he woke he could hear someone breathing beside the bed. The room was dark. He put his hand to his head and there was gauze and adhesive tape wherever he touched; the whole top half of his head was in a sack. "Who's there?" he said. A voice said it was his nurse. He slept again, and again he woke in utter darkness. For a moment he was panicky—no night was ever this long. Then he remembered the bandage. "What have they done to me?" he asked. That afternoon the nurse left the room, was gone five minutes, and returned to find Jeff sitting bolt upright in bed, the bandage turned up on his forehead. "Is it dark in here or what?" he cried, shifting his eyes this way and that in the brilliant sunlight as the nurse hurried toward him. "Whats she done? Whats she done to me?"

The nurse called the doctor, who came and prescribed a sedative; that was all he could do now that the operation had shown what had happened. It was as he had told Jeff's father. The sliver of windshield glass, as long and sharp as a knitting needle, had penetrated deep into the brain. There the optical nerves had crossed, and there they had been cut.

Two weeks later they brought him home. At first he claimed he saw moving lights but that was his imagination at work. Amy had been there all this time, nursing a sprained ankle. Though she never blamed herself for what had happened, she felt sorry for him. He looked pathetic with the short spikes of new hair growing around his scars and he had that strangely combined expression of anguish and aloofness peculiar to the blind. She did what she could; she had never been half this tender, and in bed now it was she who made the advances. But there was no response, no resurrection of the flesh. "It's not any fun in the dark," he said, and she saw his eyes brimming with tears that glistened in the moonlight. She really felt sorry for him — even she. For what could be more pitiful than a voyeur in the dark?

So Briartree was restored and in late July, three months after their first visit, Jeff and Amy returned in the long gray towncar, followed this time by two vans of furniture and a station wagon of servants. They bypassed Bristol, came straight south from Memphis to Lake Jordan, just short of two hundred miles by the winding gravel — it was almost as far by road then as by river — and took up residence in the carriage house, which had been converted into the servants quarters and garage. The architect and the landscape gardener were well along with their work by then, and within another six weeks Jeff and Amy were settled in the big house. It was grander now than it had been in all its original glory, for the appearance of ruin and desolation had been mostly a matter of dust and grime and incidental vandalism, surface damage; missing banisters, for instance, burnt for kindling by a generation of transients, were easily replaced. Fundamentally the house was as sound as it had been back in '57 when it was built by the first Tarfeller. Its walls were of slave-made brick, sixteen inches thick; the oak flooring was still good. "Listen to that," the architect would say, rapping his knuckles against a lath or stringer. "They really knew how to build them in those days." Amy would smile, proud and possessive. For her the house was a sort of talisman, a fulfillment of her destiny; she clung to that figure of the blind seed swimming home.

She had received word of her inheritance the week after Jeff returned from the hospital, back in November of the year before—her aunt had died in September. Within the following four or five months a combination of things made her want to go there. In addition to the sentimental, superstitious, purely romantic aspects, there were practical considerations. For one thing, her affair with Perkins had reached full swing and now was on the wane, at least as far as Amy was concerned. A month after the accident she went downtown shopping; she parked and Perkins was passing. He came off the sidewalk. His face was serious, grim, and he put one foot on the running-board, leaning forward with his hands on the door: "How's Jeff?" She looked at him, remembering the way he had faded into the crowd. "Slide over," he said. For another moment she looked at him, still not answering. Then she slid over and he opened the door and sat beneath the wheel, simultaneously disengaging the clutch, putting the gears in reverse, and whirring the starter. He had a fifth interest in a shooting lodge, deserted now, and that was where they went; they went there often. Within six weeks, however, he was not only getting tiresome, he was getting insistently tiresome.

There was that consideration. Then too, and this was as romantic as the others, Briartree was the only thing she had ever really owned. Everything else had more or less been lent her; so it seemed. But this was hers, earned by blood, the only good she ever got from being kin to her mother. Partly, too, she wanted a change of scene — not only from Perkins, who wouldnt discourage, but from everything; she felt that her life had reached a new, important stage, a turning-point. Also there was the incident of the dog.

It had been a Christmas present from Jeff's father, a Seeing-Eye Shepherd bitch, a little lighter than fawn, long-muzzled with upright ears and dark brown eyes flecked with gold. She took, if not a dislike for, then at any rate an indifference to Jeff, though like all animals she was immediately fond of Amy. Jeff would rise from his chair, and the dog, curled on the rug at Amy's feet, would watch him, moving nothing but her eyes. He would snap his fingers but she would not stir until Amy spoke to her, whereupon she would get up and allow Jeff to take hold of her harness. Then Amy returned one day — from an assignation with Perkins — to find the two of them in the library, the bitch on one side of the room, sprawled dead though there was no blood, and Jeff on the other, crouched half under a table, panting wild-eyed, bleeding, and weeping hysterically.

As soon as they had been left alone, Jeff and the bitch, he had snapped his fingers at her and she had not come, though he could hear her breathing at the other end of the room. Finally, in his anger, when he located her he grasped her by the throat, his thumbs on her larynx. That was when he realized he had gone too far. She yelped and her hackles rose, and when he gripped her tighter she snapped and struggled, her teeth raking his forearms. There was nothing he could do but tighten his grip, for by then he was afraid to let her go. She bit at his wrists and forearms and raked at his thighs with her claws. For a moment both were frozen; they posed, eyes close, the corners of the dog's mouth pulled back in a grin, the blind man's face depicting a combination of terror and exaltation. Then it was over. He loosened his hold; she was dead. Unnerved, he retired to the far side of the room, crawled half under the table, and began to weep, mingling his tears with the blood on his wrists and arms. "Damn you!" Amy shouted, kneeling beside the dog. "Oh damn you; wouldnt I know it?" And he had no defense; he remembered the exaltation as well as the terror.

From childhood theirs had been a strange relationship. Jeff operated by plan, by calculation, subterfuge; but Amy went solely by instinct. She had known from the start how he felt, and even what his feelings would lead him to. But she never planned ahead; she was never feverish over any outcome; she had never schemed to snare him, not even that one time when she allowed him a substitute's position in the swing. It was all by instinct. This gave her a certain advantage in the war of nerves their courtship mainly was. During the final two years before marriage, the years he spent at Harvard and in Europe, she had been ready for him to speak; she had even wondered a bit why he delayed. Then as soon as he spoke, asking her to marry him — early afternoon, sunlight dazzling the side yard sand, and he blurted it out like a challenge; he addressed her in exactly the tone he would have used to address another man: 'Step out in the alley and fight' — she accepted, as she had known she would do, though still without calculation; she took things as they came. The attraction was not so much his money as it was her desire that there be no change in her life, though of course the money was part of that, along with the summers at Myrtle Beach. Marriage with anyone but Jeff would have meant a wrench, and that was what she most avoided. Inertia held her, prime and secondary.

But the death of the dog made a change. She truly resented her husband now — not with any real intensity, but to a degree — which she had never done before, not when she had found that her bride-bed was to have its circus aspect, nor even when, after the accident, she found herself harnessed with a blind man. This last even had its advantages; she could tell herself she was 'sticking by him,' and it was especially advantageous when something like the Perkins affair came up. But the dog, the death of the dog: "That was a horrible thing to do!"

"She attacked me — " It was true; in a way it was true. She had fought back, and he had thought she would attack him if he loosened his grip. Amy did not believe him, however.

"You!"

So their relationship entered a new phase, characterized by enmity round the clock. True, they had fought all along — there had been the gladiatorial contests in which she would snatch up any handy weapon to even the odds. But that sort of combat was almost a sporting thing: it seemed the natural way to close their arguments, just as war is said to be an extension of politics, statecraft. Now it was deadly, with a to-the-finish aspect, and for the first time she began to plan ahead, to calculate. More and more her mind turned to Briartree, her inheritance. She knew Jeff also wanted to get away: get *her* away. Besides, Perkins was truly impossible by now, laying hands on her in the same room with Jeff, who turned his eyes this way and that and seemed to prick up his ears at the squeak of kisses. So Amy made plans for the first time, knowing that the point to emphasize was the deadness of the plantation in Mississippi, the notion that he was retiring her from the world.

They made the trip in April and she moved according to plan. "How lost, how lonely," she said. And Jeff was taken in,

49

even though he saw through it; she had calculated well. They
returned in July to supervise the final stages of restoration,
and now they were living there, the house in all its new glory
surpassing the old. She was the mistress, the chatelaine — 'Old
Miss': successor to those other women, dead a generation
now, who ran this house (and others like it, up and down the
lake) with efficiency at hand like a muleskinner's whip, who
wore clothes that gave inch for inch as much covering as
armor and yet were able, laced and stayed as they were, not
only to be willowy and tender but also to bear large numbers
of children and raise them according to a formula whereby
life was simple because indecision did not cloud it. Amy was
mistress and Jeff was master — 'Mars Jeff' he would have
been called, back in the days of the men he superseded, men
who settled the land at the time of Dancing Rabbit and
worked it and built the houses scattered along the cypress-
screened shores of Lake Jordan, living their lives with a
singleness of purpose, save for the temporary distractions of
poker and hunting and whiskey, like priests whose cult was
cotton. The house was neither the oldest nor the largest,
but it was the one in best condition now. It was the grandest.
Carruthers money, personified by the architect, the landscape
gardener, the Carolina servants, had made it the showplace of
the lake.

Soon they joined the Bristol Country Club, where they made
one among the couples at the regular weekend dances. Jeff
had bridled against joining; he wanted no part of it, either
'back home' (meaning Carolina) or here in the Delta. But
Amy, turning on him, flung out in anger: "After all I gave
up for you — "

"For me!" He pursed his small fat mouth.

" — Coming down to this God-forsaken back end of the
country, this *no*where . . ."

"For me! And what did I give up for you?"

They paused. Blind, he glared at her and she drew back.
He said coldly, "Where would I be now and what would I

be doing if you hadnt been cavorting on the dance floor with that Perkins?"

"I told you to look out," she muttered defensively. "I *said* that bus was coming round the curve." She shouted, attempting to regain the offensive: "But no, oh no; you had to — " But he cut her off.

"*Me!*" he cried. "For *me!*"

They joined, however. As always, Amy had her way while seeming to yield. "All right: have it your way. Dont we always?"

Saturday and Sunday nights the long gray car would be parked among Fords and Chevrolets, as if it had littered or spawned on the gravel quay beside the club. Inside, the five-man Negro band pumped jazz — *Button Up Your Overcoat* and *I'll Get By* and *That's My Weakness Now*, interspersed with numbers that had been living before and would be living after: *San* and *Tiger Rag* and *High Society* — while the planters and bankers, the doctors and lawyers, the cotton men and merchants made a show of accompanying each other's wives through the intricacies of the Charleston, the Black Bottom, the Barney Google, or else backed off and watched one of the women take a solo break, improvising, bobbing and weaving, wetting her thumbs and rolling her eyes, ritualistic, clinging desperately to the tail end of the jazz age — so desperately, so frantically indeed, that a person looking back upon that time might almost believe they had foreseen the depression and Roosevelt and another war and were dancing thus, Cassandra-like, in a frenzy of despair.

Jeff and Amy were part of this, though never in the sense that the natives were. They were not indigenous: they were outlanders, 'foreigners,' distinguished by a sort of upcountry cosmopolitan glaze which permitted them to mingle but not merge. Even their drinking habits set them apart. Deltans drank only corn and Coca-Cola; gin was *per*fume, scotch had a burnt-stick taste. They would watch with wry expressions while Amy blended her weird concoctions, pink ladies and

Collinses and whiskey sours, and those who tried one, finally persuaded, would sip and shudder and set the glass aside: "Thanks" — mildly outraged, smirking — "I'll stick to burrbon."

There were other differences. Jeff's blindness, for instance, was an awkward thing to be around. He would turn his eyes from speaker to speaker, twitching his absurdly small, fat mouth; then suddenly he would retreat into himself, almost as if he had thrown a switch or had sound-proof flaps on his ears like a bat, and the voices would be left addressing emptiness; they would trail off and the people would look at one another, embarrassed, ill at ease. There was also that aura of money, of gilt-edged stocks and expensive prep and boarding schools; there were the various barriers which separate the well-off from the rich and the rich from the very rich. Though these were never forgotten, they were sometimes ignored. Given enough whiskey, people sometimes managed to say We, including Jeff and Amy, without self-consciousness. Whatever camaraderie was possible was enjoyed.

This was especially true at the Briartree parties. Within a month of the restoration they supplied the highlight of every Delta season. A glance through the files of the Bristol *Clarion* would show each of them occupying more Society space than any other two functions, not excepting the Christmas cotillion or the Easter Revellers dance: *Mr and Mrs Jefferson T. Carruthers entertained at "Briartree," their lovely Lake Jordan plantation home, last Tuesday evening*, and so on for two galleys, concluding with the guest list, which ran as long again, a sort of roll-call of the elite. The musicians, the caterers, the decorators, all came up from New Orleans or down from Memphis. Whiskey and gin and brandy were racked inexhaustibly on the sideboard and on occasional tables; the lawn was hung with Japanese lanterns, twinkling above the guests and caterer's men. Jeff and Amy wore formal attire, as indeed about half their guests did, Jeff posing in the entrance hall (where Bertha Tarfeller had turned on her mother, forty years ago) beside a long refectory table with two brass lamps, one hand thumb-deep in his jacket pocket, the manicured thumbnail making a pink glister against the 'midnight' blue, and Amy moving among her guests, passing from group to group, never pausing at any one group for long at a time. This was what she had wanted, and now she had it.

Yet it had already begun to pall before the end of the year. The trouble was the people, she told herself. The women were vacuous, flighty, really absurd. And the men: the men were boring. They were planters — or they imitated planters, which was worse — too bluff, too hale, too muscular, too sunburnt, talking cotton and niggers, niggers and cotton, as vacuous as the women. In her boredom Amy began to think that she had outgeneraled herself, maneuvering Jeff into coming down here to live. If she could have seen a bit into the future, however, she might have taken heart. Someone who would change all this was arriving even now.

3. Harley Drew

He was a tall slim young man in his middle thirties, with a red face and a straw-colored mustache, 'buyer' for a St Louis cotton trust. Not that he actually bought anything: they just called him that. He had pale, light blue, depthless eyes and a prominent jaw and his hair was parted carefully in the middle to show a line of scalp as neat and precise as if it had been run with a transit. In strong sunlight his eyebrows and lashes were invisible, which gave him a rather blank expression, like that of a face etched on a billiard ball, but in shadow they showed white and distinguished against his ruddy complexion. In rural communities of the cotton country where his business now for the first time took him, wearing urban-cut imitation tweed in contrast to the villatic duck and seersucker of the men with whom he dealt, Drew stood out — like the oldtime professional gamblers in their flowing broadcloth and tall hats, their sideburns and heavy watch chains, their aura of Chance — with an emphasized smartness which the men might view askance but which their women were apt to call romantic.

He came to Bristol in early November of 1928. It was a good crop year, following the flood which in turn had followed seasons of postwar panic when the price had fluctuated from high to low, ranging the scale like a dizzy soprano; but now it was leveling off, his employers told him, speaking with that particularly hard-headed optimism of money men. He was scheduled to be in town three days, going from door to door along the block of one-story office buildings known as Cotton Row, sitting for an hour or two in each, talking crops and the market, especially the market, always with a suggestion of inside information in the tone of his voice and the deepness of his reticence — especially the reticence. There was no real business to attend to, no orders for him to solicit or even confirm: his job was to lend a personal touch to contracts already closed. In a trade which considered the warm handshake as integral a part of a transaction as the dotted line, Drew supplied the handshake, the vital oil for the smaller gears of the big machine. The fact that clients viewed him a bit askance was to his credit: the company wanted him that way, remote and rather mysterious, representative of the twilight world of finance, an emissary of power, as different from the run of men as if he had been an agent from Mars or heaven or even hell. Personable, urbane, with his city tweeds, his removed and somewhat condescending affability, he had been selected for the job. The natural friendliness behind the sheen suggested that behind the façade of high finance the company also had a heart of gold — as indeed it had, though in another sense.

However, for all his natural manner, he had not come by it naturally. The war gave him his chance, as it gave so many others, though it was to his credit that he recognized and took it. Drafted in Youngstown, Ohio, where he had clerked in a downtown shoe store (— that at least had been done on his own; he had refused to follow his father and brothers into the steel-mill labor gang) he went overseas with an early contingent, a corporal, and finished the war with a DSC and a commission. He spent two years in Europe after the finish: six frost-bitten months fighting the Bolsheviki, six months getting over it, and a year with the army of occupation back in Germany, during which he experienced for the first time the leisured life and the social distinction due a handsome and decorated officer of a victorious army. Then he came home for discharge. In a ten-day poker game on the ship he won eight thousand dollars. So when he was mustered out he took a three-year vacation — "to look round," he said, for he had no real plan. There was only one thing of which he was completely certain, and this was that he was not going back to the shoe store in Ohio.

As it turned out, he was not going back to Ohio at all. He spent his first thousand dollars on clothes and another five hundred on accessories; the rest he planned to spread over the three-year 'look round.' He even drew up a tentative budget, a future expense account — at least he began it. But he had not gone far, the pencil poised above the pad, before he discovered that his knowledge of the life he was about to lead was too limited for him even to estimate its cost; so he gave that up and satisfied himself with a resolve to watch his pennies. In point of fact it proved less expensive than he had imagined. Skimped breakfasts and counter lunches made dinners in elegant surroundings possible at a cost not much higher than for an average three meals. Two days of walking, though hard on shoe leather, enabled him to take a cab on the third and flattened his wallet little more than three days of riding the bus or elevated. He was learning; this was all preparatory, though he could not have said just what it was preparatory to.

After a year in New York, mingling with glittery women and starch-bosomed men in theater lobbies and midtown restaurants — always as an observer, never as a participant in any real meaning of the word; if they so much as looked in his direction (at first at least) he turned away with a start, like a peeping tom detected — he began to write to army friends. He had an address book in which he had them listed more or less in order of eligibility, with a complicated scoring system of dots and circles and stars. And when their replies suggested that he "come see us," he would pack his thousand-dollar wardrobe in his expensive pigskin luggage and go visiting.

Now that he saw them at close quarters, the ensconced ones he envied, rather than from the periphery of their circles in public places, he admired them more extravagantly than ever: not for their personalities or their 'wit' or their general charm, but simply for the life they led. Now that he had seen them in their informality, in their off-hours so to speak, out of the public glare, he believed that he could lead the same life even better; certainly he could lead it with more appreciation of its satisfactions, since he had another life to compare it to. Mainly, though, he watched without conjecture; he watched and imitated, cultivating their air of boredom and disdain in the face of what was really the wildest excitement. He did well at it. Sooner or later, however, in conversation with them there arose the question he had come to fear; they wanted to know what he 'did.' In time he learned to avoid the question, to break off the exchange when he felt the question about to loom — he became expert at detecting this — or to sidestep it with a laugh. After all, he could not tell them the truth; he could not say, "I float." But he knew he would have to find a way to answer it before he could feel at home among them.

As a house guest in St Louis he got a chance. His host, a cotton broker whose son had been killed in Drew's platoon, offered him a job — something none of them had done before. Drew thanked him and said he would consider it. Then he put it out of his mind and moved on, continuing the round of visits. This was toward the close of the third year; he was approaching the postgraduate phase, still without any definite plan, and it was beginning to get a little stale. Six months later, while he was on a goose hunt up in Canada, his mail caught up with him. Among the letters — invitations in answer to notes he had written, a few old bills, and such — was a month-old bank statement showing a balance of two hundred and eleven dollars. He threw the mail into the campfire, bank statement, bills, invitations and all, and when he got back to town he wrote to the cotton broker. Then, without delaying for an answer, he took the first train for St Louis.

They gave him a desk at the home office and a list of reference books. He spent his office hours checking invoices and in his spare time he studied the books, learning the business. Before long he could quote prices on the New Orleans exchange, from the 190 record high of September, 1864, to the 4¾ record low of November, 1898. He became familiar with the life cycle of the boll weevil and read of Nicholas Biddle's financial maneuvers with an excitement he had not known since the paperback Deadwood Dicks and Nick Carters of his Middle Western boyhood. This took up most of his time, yet the other was not altogether abandoned. He stayed in touch with highlife mainly through once-a-week dinners with his employer, an old man with trembling hands and a damp, rosy mouth that was shaped like a kiss.

Soon, though, he began to dread these evenings. Invariably they progressed toward a point at which his host would lead him apart, usually into his study, where he would mix drinks and set out Havanas and question Drew about his son and the war. Drew barely remembered the boy; he had come as a replacement, terribly frightened, had lasted less than a week before being sent back to the aid station with a bullet wound in his foot — self-inflicted, the medics said — and had died there of gangrene.

"Tell about Leo," his host would say, watching him over the rim of his drink and nursing the lengthening ash of his cigar.

"Well: he joined us in October, as you know . . ."

And as he told it, attributing to the boy every heroism that had been credited to a soldier in his battalion, Drew would watch his employer's eyes mist over, the trembling in his hands grow worse; the drink would slosh, the ashes spill, and Drew would continue: "One time down around Perle Capelle . . ." His voice was like a phonograph and he was listening too, surprised at what came out, thinking behind the drone of talk, telling himself that he was no scoundrel, that the old man was asking to be lied to, and the end was the justification of the means. But no matter how he lied, misattributed and finally invented, the father was insatiable. Drew was his protégé, and next week he would be led apart, the drinks mixed, cigars lighted, and: "Tell about Leo," his host would say, already trembling.

When he had been at the desk for a little more than a year they sent him out on the road. After two seasons in the Texas area, they called him back to the home office and told him he had passed — the Texans had liked him; his apprenticeship was over, and now he was to receive his reward. They sent him to the Yazoo-Mississippi delta, land of the long staple and big money. Coming south out of Memphis, first past the Chickasaw Bluffs and then through a region of broad flat fields, the air scented and hazed with wood-smoke, Drew watched the big, remote plantation houses slide past the daycoach window like a magic lantern show of baronial splendor. Three years of work had made him understand that even with the best of luck, the greatest ability, he would get what he wanted only after years of effort, protégé or not. But he had kept his goal in mind; he had not lost his eye for the main chance.

"Bristol!" the conductor cried, coming straddle-legged down the aisle, swinging his hands from seat to seat and balancing like a tightwire artist to counteract the buck and sway of the wheels on the old roadbed. The train took just under seven hours to make the hundred and fifty miles — which was why it was called the Cannonball, in inverse ratio to the compliment implied. Drew took his bag from the overhead rack. "Bristol!" the conductor cried again, jaws apart, as he passed through the windowed door toward the Jim Crow car ahead; "All out for — " and the door slammed shut behind him.

Major Barcroft's office was the largest on Cotton Row. Drew had been warned in St Louis that the major was a crotchety but valuable client, so as soon as he had checked in at the hotel and had bathed and dressed, he went to call on him. "In Bristol see Major Malcolm Barcroft first," they had told him. "He'll expect it and so will all the others. That way no one's offended. And mind you: dont call him Mister. Call him Major."

It was late afternoon of a soft, summery November day, the town somnolent with the lull preceding closing-time. Clerks and proprietors drowsed on sidewalk chairs, their heads turning slowly in unison as Drew passed, bland eyes following him along the street. Major Barcroft was not in his office; the bookkeeper, who was late-middle-aged and wore a thick green isinglass eyeshade and bombazine sleeve protectors, said that he had stepped down the Row for a minute and would be back. Drew sat talking with the bookkeeper till the major came in. Then he rose and introduced himself: "Harley Drew. I believe the company wrote you I was coming: Anson-Grimm." He put his hand out, stiff as a board, the thumb raised high, and the major touched it, noncommittal, watching from under his grizzled, tufted eyebrows. It was not actually a handshake, but it was as close as these two ever came to one.

Ten minutes later Major Barcroft looked sharply past Drew's shoulder toward the door. His pince-nez glittered, the rimless lenses opaque on both sides of his narrow nose and beneath the high pale forehead, the roach of hair. Then he glanced at the clock, stood up, and closed his rolltop desk. He locked it, tested the catch, lifted his hat from the antler rack, and addressed Drew with an abrupt, peremptory nod: "Good day, sir."

Drew rose, surprised and even awkward; it always came as a shock when anyone showed signs of not liking him. As the major came past, he turned and saw a young woman standing in the doorway. She was dressed in gray, with swatches of lace at her wrists and throat. Beneath the felt hat her hair, pulled so severely over her ears that the lobes protruded, was screwed into a tight knot at the base of her skull. Her eyes were a curious violet color and her face was unnaturally pale, as if she had not quite — or at best had just — recovered from a long illness.

"Evening, papa," she said. Her voice was low.

"Amanda," Major Barcroft said.

And that was all. She did not look at Drew. He watched them walk away, the major stiff and straight, his narrow shoulders drawn back so far that they made a crease in his coat between his shoulder blades, and Amanda slim and willowy beside him, almost as tall as her father. Dismounting from his high stool, the bookkeeper peeled off his sleeve protectors and tossed them onto the desk, where they lay like the cast skins of two snub blacksnakes. The sun was low; its rays came almost level through the window, throwing a green half-circle down the bookkeeper's face until he removed the eyeshade and laid it alongside the bombazine snakeskins.

Drew stood in the doorway. "Has she been sick?" he said, not turning his head.

"That was Amanda," the bookkeeper said. He was locking his desk, imitating the major. "Youre thinking about the other one."

"Other one?"

"The other sister: Florence. Or dont you know? They keep her shut up in the attic or something; it's kind of a secret." He finished locking the desk, testing the catch as the major had done. "She aint got all her marbles. So Ive heard."

"Oh?"

"Yair. They slide her meals under the door. Thats what folks say; I dont know. There used to be a lot of talk, but it kind of simmered down."

"Oh," Drew said. He said it as if he were not really attending, as if he had had to choose between looking and listening, and had chosen looking. Major Barcroft and Amanda were a block away by now, but Drew still stood and watched them; he had not turned to look at the bookkeeper. "Is that all, just the two daughters?"

"Well — there was a son, a peculiar little fellow, but he got his head blowed off one day a good while back. That was, lets see, fifteen years ago. Or was it sixteen? Sixteen. And the mother, of course, the major's wife: she died when the boy was born. There's just those three is all thats left of the high and mighty Barcrofts." The bookkeeper watched him, quizzical and amused, faintly risible, as he pulled on his coat and fastened a patented black bow tie between the points of his celluloid collar, a crisper version of the major's. "But dont be getting notions," he said, moving toward the door. "It aint worth it."

"I suppose not," Drew said absent-mindedly. He was still watching; he was watching and thinking — it really came that fast. The bookkeeper laughed, for the first time out loud, and Drew turned from the doorway, puzzled. Then he laughed too. "I suppose not," he said.

Next morning he made two calls, both of them brief, and then went for a walk around the town. The weather had held, Indian summer attenuated, still balmy after the mid-October cold snap. Trees kept their hectic leaves, like flames in the wind, awaiting the ultimate turning of the year, the rainstorm that would strip them and bring winter overnight. There was a sense of urgency in the air, the hesitant strain of a slowing wheel trying for one final revolution, the false, pregnant calm of dynamite fused and waiting for the shock. It was Saturday, the downtown curbings lined with country people wearing stiff, mailorder clothes, men and women mostly gaunt, and tow-headed stairstepped children whose cheeks bulged with the walnut-sized spheres of hard candy called wining balls. Negroes clustered on the sidewalks of the two blocks nearest the levee. Here were the cheaper clothing stores, and from time to time a clerk would appear in a doorway, peering hooknosed and sinister out of an almost cavernous gloom, and invite them to enter, singly or in groups. If none of the Negroes stirred the clerk would come out, take one of them by the arm, and lead him inside with a show of good-natured cajolery. "I ask you, feel the quality of that goods," those on the sidewalk would hear the clerk telling his captive. "Cheap at half the price, a downright walkaway bargain I give you my word." And presently the victim would emerge, looking sheepish, carrying in both hands a paper-wrapped bundle hastily tied with string, and the clerk would come out behind him, pausing in the doorway to select another customer. Drew watched, amazed by what he thought at first was exploitation of the ignorant. He had not been watching long, however, before he recognized it for what it was: a two-way game, a contest. The baiting was being done as much from one direction as the other, and the end result was the same, no matter how it was reached; the Negroes had the merchandise, the merchants had the money.

Turning away from the business district, he walked toward a residential section where housewives in summery dresses stood at windows or on porches, brooms arrested on the back-swing or the follow-through, and watched him pass. Sometimes he walked fast; sometimes he strolled; sometimes he loitered, watching the squirrels romp and frisk in the trees and along the lightwires. When at length the barbered lawns and natty bungalows gave way to the grassless, packed-dirt yards and the squat unpainted boxlike cabins of factory workers, Drew turned back toward the hotel, a four-story building whose sign he saw every now and again through gaps in the sear and red and yellow leaves.

Though Amanda was nearly a block away when he first saw her, he recognized her almost immediately, a slim gray figure leaning slightly sideways to balance the weight of a market basket. Drew quickened his step. Within ten feet of her he stopped and removed his hat with a gesture that was almost but not quite a flourish. "Good morning, Miss Barcroft," he said brightly, smiling above the hat which he held with both hands, upside-down, displaying the shiny satin of its lining; a fragrance as of heliotrope rose from it. He introduced himself with a shallow bow: "Harley Drew, and pleased to make your acquaintance. I'm a business friend of your father's."

She seemed frightened. When he took hold of the handle of the basket she gripped it tighter for a moment. Then their hands touched and she let go. "It's only another block," she said, covering with her other hand the one that had held the basket, the one he had touched; it was as if she were hiding the evidence of a kiss.

But he did the talking. "I like this town," he said. "I really do. It's so much better than the ones back home." He paused, smiling down at her from under the halo of his hat brim. "Back home means Missouri: St Louis." Then he waited for her to speak, like an experienced actor cuing an amateur.

"Everyone says how nice it is" — still hiding her right hand with her left " — but I dont know; I never saw any others."

"Ah," he said, combining sympathy and regret.

Now they were at the big gray house, which soared and loomed with its gingerbread trim and rococo cupolas. They turned in and Amanda stopped at the foot of the steps, holding out her hand for the market basket. They faced each other, scarcely a foot apart, and she could see the individual hairs of his mustache, the curve of his nostrils. "Thank you for helping me, Mr — "

"Drew," he said promptly. "Harley Drew."

She was flustered at his nearness as well as at having forgotten his name so soon, but in taking hold of the basket she remembered to grip the handle at one side: that way their hands did not touch. Though she had not quite recovered from her fright, he believed her eyes were softer. "Thank you for helping me — Mr Drew."

"Glad to, maam." He raised his hat with that same gesture, just short of a flourish. He was smiling and sunlight, filtered through the leaves of the four oaks in front of the house, lent his mustache the color of old gold. "I intend to see you again, with your permission. I'll be here several days."

She went up the steps almost at a run. Drew watched for a moment, then turned and walked away. Twenty yards down the sidewalk he stopped to light a cigarette. Then he glanced back over his shoulder, still holding the cupped flame, and saw Amanda standing in the doorway, watching him. This surprised him but he soon recovered; he smiled, removed the cigarette from his mouth, and was about to raise his hat again. But when she saw him looking back, she stepped quickly into the house and closed the door.

That was Saturday. Next morning he waited for her across the street from the church; he had meant to attend the service but he was late. He went into a restaurant and drank coffee, sitting at the counter and watching the church door through the plate glass window to his left. After two cups of coffee he came back outside and began to pace up and down like the sentinel which in fact he was. There was a peanut stand on the corner, locked for Sunday, and last night's hulls crackled under his shoes. From time to time he heard singing from the church, sometimes by the choir alone, in which case he could distinguish the words, sometimes by the congregation too, in which case the words were garbled. Half a dozen pigeons pecked and strutted among the peanut hulls on the sidewalk. They were not only tame and unfrightened, they resented his being there and they let him know it, hardly bothering to swerve aside as he walked up and down. At length he inadvertently stepped on the foot of one of the birds. It gave a low-keyed squawk — and then, instead of flying off, merely backed up a step or two, standing firmly on its coral feet, and looked at him. Head turned sideways to display one perfectly round golden eye dilating and contracting with indignation, the bird began to scold him exactly as a person might have done. Drew stood there, astonished. Then he laughed, looking down at the pigeon, and the singing grew suddenly louder across the street. The doors of the church were open and the minister was marching out, followed first by acolytes bearing flags and the Cross and then by the choir chanting bravely in the sunlight.

They wore vestments and they blinked like people emerging from a cave.

Amanda was among the last to come out, for the Barcroft pew was toward the front and the day was past when those in the rear pews were content to wait, except at such formal affairs as weddings and funerals. Drew watched as she awaited her turn to shake hands with the rector. Today her dress was black, but it appeared to have been cut from the same pattern and there were identical tabs of lace at her wrists and throat. Perhaps they were detachable, interchangeable, he thought. Then she was crossing the street and he saw that she wore a wider hat, with artificial tuberoses at the brim. He stayed carefully out of her line of vision and followed at some distance until the crowd thinned, getting into automobiles parked beside the restaurant and the motion picture theater across the street. When she was quite alone he overtook her. "Miss Barcroft," he said, and surprise was in his voice.

"Good morning, Mr Drew." There was none in hers. She looked at him, then quickly looked away, rather paler than yesterday but not at all surprised, and he realized that she must have seen him from the portico while waiting to compliment the rector on his sermon. So he dropped his pretense of surprise.

"I was late for church," he said. "I thought I'd wait. I hoped you wouldnt mind."

"Oh no" — her voice was tremulous.

But she would not look at him again and he found nothing to say. He was about to say 'Lovely morning' but dropped it as inane. Then suddenly he said it: "Lovely morning . . ." Amanda nodded but still said nothing. They walked in silence. They were halfway down the final block, within sight of the house, and he asked her to let him call that evening.

"I dont think I could do that," she said.

"But I very much want to."

Everything was strange about him, even his syntax. She kept her eyes down, her face turned away, avoiding his smile. He seemed to hover almost above her. She said in a low, choked voice, "I sit with Florence every evening."

Drew had not expected her to mention the sister. He had a sudden vision of the two, the meek figure in black or gray and the mad woman, in an attic room with a low, slanting ceiling and barred windows and a rattly chain on the door. "Oh?" he said, too surprised to think of a reply. Then he tried to think, but it was interrupted; she spoke again.

"Sometimes after supper I take a walk . . ." She drew breath sharply, with almost a gasp of surprise at what she had said.

"What time?" It was a bit too insistent, too quick, and he reproached himself for not remembering that he had determined to be romantically bold but never brash. Then he was reassured; he had not overplayed it. For though she turned her head even farther away and began to walk faster, Amanda answered his question.

"Seven-thirty," she said.

They were at the house now, the big gray dusty-looking structure with its wide veranda and tall windows. Amanda hurried past him and he stood watching her move swiftly up the steps. When she paused at the top and looked back, Drew saw that she was blushing: Like a bride, he thought. As the flush suffused her face, moving from her hairline down her throat and then inside the high neck of her dress, he had another vision: of flaming breasts, quite virginal, the nipples bright like drops of blood.

" — Until then," he said, raising his hat.

From there he went directly to the telegraph office, where he found the telegrapher locking the door, on his way to Sunday dinner. "Caught me," the man said, unlocking and holding the door ajar. "You got here just in time. Step in." He stood aside while Drew drafted and pared the message to St Louis. Then he took it and tapped each word with the metal cap on his pencil: TOUCH OF FLU NOTHING DANGEROUS PROBABLY WEEK DELAY LETTER FOLLOWS. "Ten words," the telegrapher said. "Sixty cents. — Feeling woozy?" he asked as he counted change. Drew just looked at him. "Rock candy and whiskey, and get in bed and stay there. In twenty-four hours youll be good as new; I guarantee it."

"Thank you," Drew said.

He walked to the hotel, had lunch, and went to his room. Taking off his suit to keep from wrinkling it, he lay on the bed all afternoon and looked at the water-marked ceiling. For a while he considered calling for the bellboy to send him a girl. But then he dismissed it; he put it out of his mind. Later the room grew dim. There were reflections from the street four stories below, the whine of traffic, with clashing gears and occasional horns as faint and sad as music in a dream. At six-thirty, when it was quite dark, he got up, switched on the overhead light, and dressed. He had a sandwich in the dining room, eating rapidly in the clattering bustle of families out for Sunday supper. As he left he checked his watch with the clock on the lobby wall. It was seven-fifteen.

At seven-thirty, when Amanda came down the steps, she did not see him. Then something moved in the shadows and she saw him standing beside one of the oaks, his hat in his hands. By daylight the hat had been pearl-gray but now it was silvered with moonlight, like a helmet.

"Miss Barcroft."

"Good evening," she said. Her voice was so low he could barely hear it.

He was there the next night too. As they walked he told her about the war and his work, always with a suggestion of loneliness. He said he had fallen in love with the Deep South. "Elsewhere it's so frantic," he said. "But here a man can *live*. Do you see what I mean?"

She said she did. And Tuesday night, on the third of their nocturnal half-hour walks, he asked her to let him come into the parlor: "For a real visit," he said. But she would not allow it.

"I couldnt," she said. "I'm sorry, I just couldnt."

Drew believed that this was because of the sister, the mad

68

woman; he believed that Amanda did not want him to hear the screaming or gurgling or whatever it was maniacs did in the quiet hours of the night. He wanted to comfort her, to re-assure her, to let her know that nothing in all this world could scare him away. 'As if it mattered,' he thought, alone again in the hotel room. 'For all that goes with it I'd marry the crazy sister.' But this was just talk, bravado: he was goading himself, accusing himself of a greater enormity in order that the lesser would appear that much the lesser, even to himself.

Yet the strain was beginning to tell — the flesh of his face had tightened like a mask; the smile was becoming a grimace. He took up the phone: "Send a bellboy up to 415." The Negro came and stood beside the bed, his face expressionless while Drew told him what he wanted. "Dont send me any crow," he said, lying there in his one-piece summer underwear.

"No *sir*," the Negro said, unsmiling.

Within ten minutes there came a quiet scratching at the door, as if by claws. "It's not locked," he called, and a girl came in — his first since Memphis, almost a week ago. Drew lay with his hands behind his head. She was young, thick-bodied, and wore no makeup. "How much?" he said.

"Three dollars."

"I'll give you two." She looked at him for a moment, then turned to go. "O.K." he said. "Two-fifty."

She began to unhook her placket. "You drive a hard bargain, honey." She sat beside him on the bed, wearing stockings and brassiere. Her flanks were hard as a wrestler's but quite smooth, as if the hair had been sandpapered out. "My name's Alma," she said; "I guess you better pay me now. It's the rule." And soon afterward: "A*ready*? Gee, honey, you were really bad-off, werent you?" She still wore the brassiere; he had asked her to take it off, but when she made no move to comply he had not insisted. It turned out she was from Arkansas, directly across the river, and the nails on her toes were like little oyster shells. That came from going barefoot all through childhood.

On the fifth night, Thursday, Amanda let him walk to the

door with her, but she slipped quickly through the doorway. The following night he took her arm going up the steps and did not release it while they crossed the porch; she was captive and he kissed her. She went rigid with fear of so many things she had never known before — the sudden heady odor of bay rum and tobacco, the harsh, man-smelling tweed as coarse as sackcloth, the thighs against her thighs and the hand at the small of her back, the pliant, nuzzling mustache — then turned with a spasmodic gesture, panting, and hurried into the house, running with her hands behind her, slightly raised, palms outward, as if in flight before fury. The screen door shut with a sharp slap, abrupt against the silence.

For a moment after she had broken away and left him standing alone on the veranda, Drew thought: I overplayed it. But the next night (it was Saturday again, still balmy; the weather had held) she met him as usual, and when they returned from their walk she took his hand and led him up the steps. At first he thought she was going to take him into the house; he was even about to begin rehearsing what he would say to Major Barcroft. Then she stopped beside the door, her back to the wall. This time, when he kissed her, Amanda put her hands on his shoulders and pressed herself against him with a shudder. Drew was surprised at her reaction, too surprised to speak, but he soon recovered himself and told her he loved her; he told her he always would. "I love *you*, Harley," she said, murmuring, and when he asked her to marry him she held him closer and said she would. She said it softly, with her lips against his cheek. "But you must speak to papa," she said.

Bells were tolling when he woke. Sabbath, musical, serene, they called the worshipers churchward. By crossing to the window he would be able to see them, townspeople dressed in Sunday finery, strolling with a deliberate and somewhat pompous sanctity along the Bristol street, clutching their hymnals and mite boxes. But he did not move; he lay in bed, listening. After a while the bells died away, reverberant and forlorn on the final strokes, and he heard a near-by congregation singing *There Is a Fountain* — they were Methodists. The Episcopalians were two blocks farther east, and he imagined Amanda among them, kneeling in the Barcroft pew, thinking of him as she murmured the responses. He remembered that Sunday morning a week ago when he walked up and down among the pigeons on the sidewalk opposite the church, waiting for the service to end so that he could overtake and walk home with her, pretending to admire the artificial roses on her hat and talking romantic nonsense like a scoundrel in a book.

> *There is a fountain filled with blood*
> *Drawn from Immanuel's veins*
> *And sinners plunged beneath that flood*
> *Lose all their guilty stains.*

The organ pealed; the voices rose, gathering strength.

> *Lose all their guilty stains.*
> *Lose all their guilty stains.*
> *And sinners plunged beneath that flood*
> *Lose all their guilty stains.*

Looking back over the past week, he believed he had done well: had moved with proper caution through the early stages of the courtship, never forgetting to be bold, yet always restraining impulses which might have spoiled his chances: had struck hard and swift when the time was ripe, giving an impression of a young man no longer able to contain his feelings. Now that much was done, and well done. There remained only the formality of an interview with the father, the drawing up of the articles of surrender, the scene in which he would offer his hand and pledge his heart and declare himself ready to devote his life to the happiness of the daughter. Amanda had told him to come to the house at four oclock; he would find the major waiting in his study. She had arranged it, with God only knew what fears, what palpitations.

Lying in the transient-grimed hotel room, as he had done the previous Sunday when he came directly from the telegraph office to map his campaign — the wire itself had been an opening gun, committing his forces — Drew began to make plans for the coming interview. Yet the more he tried to concentrate, the more his mind was distracted, crowded with unwanted memories of his boyhood, of the house in the workers' district of Youngstown. When steel was being poured the night sky was a low red dome, like the vault of hell, and workers coming off shift moved in lockstep, their faces slack-jawed, empty, like the faces of the damned. His father's name was Josef Drubashevski. He was short and dark and his head was round as a pot and flat on top. His eyes were a very pale blue, almost colorless, and his arms were long and hairy. Sundays he wore candy-striped shirts with sleeve garters; he played the concertina and sang in Polish, and when he had had enough to drink he would dance the trepak, banging the floor with his heels, "Hi! Hi!" His sons resembled him, all but Charles: Charles was the youngest and he took after his mother's people, who were tall and fair and mostly Scandinavian. Five lunch boxes sat on a shelf in the kitchen, his father's and four brothers', and someday there would be six, including his own.

But one night — he was fourteen and in the seventh grade, which was already one year longer than any of his brothers had stayed in school — he woke and heard his father and mother talking. "Not this one, Joe," his mother was saying. He slept on a cot in their room, in a far corner. "You took the others; that was all right. But not this one, Joe. Not the baby."

"Baby?" his father said. "That boy's a man: almost a man. I tell you, woman, a man ought to do a man's work." He turned over and the bedsprings groaned. It was late; he wanted to sleep.

But the mother persisted. "There's other men beside steel men, hunkies. You think thats all there is in this whole creation? Leave me to do with this one. Just this one, Joe. Youll see."

"Ah, woman," his father said, and he believed that was all; his father had won.

Then it was June, the school year over, and he went to work in the mill as a puddler's boy. That was that, he thought each night when he put his lunch box on the shelf beside the other five. They were made of black tin, all alike, with rounded lids like traveling hutches for lap dogs.

In September, however, he found that he had underestimated his mother. When he came home from work on the Saturday before the Monday school was to start, he found her waiting for him, dressed in her best. She took him to town and they spent his paycheck on clothes and tablets and pencils. He returned to his studies on Monday and continued through high school, working summers in the mill. By commencement he had risen to timekeeper, a white collar job, which caused his father to view him as an apostate. Then he quit. He got himself a job downtown, clerking in a shoe store, and went to night school, intending to become a CPA; that was his goal. He would whisper the words at night in bed: "Charles Drubashevski, Certified Public Accountant."

Finally he took a room in a boarding house — to be near his work, he said. But he did not fool his brothers, who watched him with hostile eyes; it was the Joseph story all over again, though there was no coat of many colors and he was far from being his father's favorite. He didnt even fool his mother, in the end; for he visited home less and less frequently, and at last her eyes were hostile too. Then the war came and he returned — but not to Youngstown — an officer, decorated. He took the three-year 'look round' and the job with the St Louis cotton trust and now he was in Bristol, Mississippi, lying on the hotel bed and looking up at the water-marked ceiling, planning (or trying to plan) what he would say to the major, Amanda's father.

It was momentous — he realized that now. Previously he had not given the interview much thought, beyond considering that parents usually were pleased with an offer that would relieve them of a daughter past her marriageable prime. It was a step he would take when he reached it, he had told himself. But now, with the scene only a few hours away, he began to see it as something more serious. Failure here, he suddenly realized, could be as ruinous as anywhere along the line. He remembered the major as he had been that one time in the office on Cotton Row, his high forehead with its crown of iron-gray hair, his stern manner at once abrupt and courteous, distant and comprehensive, with that glinting pince-nez clamped between his face and the world. Drew wondered if his tactics had been faulty. He began to think he should have gone to work on the major first. Phase Two, perhaps, should have been Phase One.

At two oclock, when he went down to lunch, the dining room was still crowded with Sunday guests. He sat a long time over his food, then ordered a second cup of coffee and sat still longer over that. At three-thirty, the room empty, the waiter standing by with an air of injured but patient martyrdom, a napkin crumpled in his fist — "More water?" he kept saying, chinking the ice in the pitcher — Drew paid the check and left. All this time he grew more and more worried about the coming interview, rehearsing possible checks the major might throw in his direction. His fears were no less present for being formless. By the time he approached the house on Lamar Street he was thoroughly frightened, even demoralized; but he found two consolations. First, like a general deploying for a final battle to conclude a successful campaign, he reminded himself of recent victories, each of them surely more difficult than the engagement now at hand. Second, like a cowardly boxer entering the ring to face a particularly savage opponent, he fixed his mind on the million-dollar purse.

As he went up the steps the door opened suddenly and a man in a belted jacket came out of the house, carrying a small black satchel. This was Dr Clinton; he had paid his monthly visit to Florence and the major. He nodded briskly to Drew at the top of the steps, obviously surprised to see at the Barcrofts' a visitor who brought neither the ministrations of medicine nor of religion. Drew went to the door, where Amanda stood waiting for him. She seemed even paler than usual. Thinking perhaps there had been a scene, he wanted to take time to question her, to discover how much she had told her father and what he had said in reply when she arranged the interview. Perhaps it could be postponed. But she gave him no time for that; she led him straight down the high, dusky hall toward the door of the major's study. Like some general whose Intelligence section has been shot from under him, Drew was going into battle blind, unbriefed. Just short of the door, however, Amanda paused and told him in a low voice that she would meet him at the regular time that evening, in front of the house. Then she turned and left him. It was as if she had vanished suddenly and forever; he was alone.

He rapped lightly. There was no answer. Knuckles poised, he was about to rap again: "Come in," a voice said, and he opened the door.

The small back downstairs room, which the major called his office, was furnished with a walnut rolltop desk duplicating the one on Cotton Row, a squat green steel safe with a scroll design on its door, a button-studded horsehide couch built high at one end, with ball-and-claw legs, and a swivel chair. A leather-spined Plutarch with marbled boards lay open on the desk, an ivory letter opener resting crosswise on it. A fire had been laid but not lighted in the grate, and a scuttle of coal sat beside it; the individual lumps, all of about the size of a fist, had been wrapped in newspaper so as not to soil the hands. The walls were bare except for a space directly above the desk, where two sheathed sabers were crossed below a fading snapshot of a slim young man in wrinkled khaki (Drew recognized the uniform from having seen it reproduced in magazines and motion pictures; it was like the one worn by the Rough Riders) with a dusty bandanna neckerchief, canvas leggings, a wide-brimmed campaign hat, and captain's bars. Another photograph was on the desk. It showed, full length in a silver frame, a young woman dressed in the style of thirty years ago, including a picture hat; both hands were on the knob of a shot-silk parasol, and her head was too large for her shoulders. Major Barcroft sat in the chair, tipped slightly back. His feet, in snub black hightop shoes with creases below the ankles and little hooks instead of eyes for the laces, were planted flat and parallel on the floor, like shoes beneath cots in a barracks when the troops are out for drill.

He did not rise for greeting; he sat with his head held back, looking up at the tall visitor. His pince-nez, opaque with highlight, flashed like a drawn blade. "Have a seat, young man," he said at last. The couch yielded unexpectedly with Drew's weight, and about his thighs there rose a musty, somehow faintly ammoniac odor of straw and horsehide. "My daughter has told me you want to see me. I want you to say what you have come to say."

Drew faltered, perhaps for the first time in his adult life. As the major watched him from behind the glinting nippers, the stiff, iron-gray hair standing above the pale forehead, Drew felt something akin to panic. He had thought that once he began to speak, his confidence would return. But it did not; his dismay grew as he spoke. For one thing, he had trouble with Sir. It came naturally to these people — they used it to punctuate and shape their sentences; it lent their most casual remarks a dignity out of all proportion to what was actually communicated. But when Drew used it he felt that it made him sound subservient, like a man making application for a job he knew he lacked the qualifications to fill. Then, while he was speaking (his mind worked on two levels; he was thinking behind the sound of his words) he remembered that Amanda had said she would meet him that evening in *front* of the house, and it seemed to him, interpreting this, that he had already received her father's answer. Yet he went on with it, hesitating and stammering like a schoolboy caught with a crib or a gambler with six cards, and as he talked the thought occurred to him that perhaps this was best: perhaps it was best to falter, to be at a loss for words at such a time. He remembered such scenes in the theater; the young man had bumbled and gawked and perspired, and the audience had understood and even sympathized. A measure of confidence began to edge into his manner. "I love Amanda very much," he said in conclusion.

The major looked at him, testing the point of the letter opener against the ball of his thumb. The only sign of emotion was a slight expansion and contraction of his nostrils, which caused them to be ringed with white. Suddenly Drew knew he had failed; he knew he was being repulsed. If there had ever been any doubt about the outcome of the interview, that doubt was gone. Then Major Barcroft said softly, watching him: "What color are her eyes?"

"Sir?" Drew said. While the major looked at him without repeating the question, he considered whether to try to bluff his way through. Color? What color were they? A sort of muddy blue, he thought; but he could not say that. He did not know.

Major Barcroft, having waited, rose. He did not say anything; he just stood there, in an obvious pose of dismissal, and did not offer to see the young man to the door.

Amanda was nowhere in sight. As Drew passed down the hall, wondering if he was the first man ever to have his suit rejected — ostensibly, at any rate — because he could not remember the true color of his intended's eyes, he became aware of a sharp hissing sound being repeated insistently, like an intermittent leak of gas: "Sst! Sst!" Then he saw at the end of the hall, to the left of the entrance, a door ajar about three inches and a face peering through the gap. It was a face he had never seen, a woman's face, with flesh the color of putty before it dries and two rigid curves of hair whose points sprang forward toward the corners of her mouth, clamping the upper two-thirds of her face like a pair of parentheses. She made a beckoning gesture with one hand, the forefinger crooked: "Sst! Sst!" and he saw that she wore a cretonne wrapper patterned violently with red and purple flowers. The crazy sister! he thought. She broke out of the attic!

He positively considered making a run for it. However, he controlled his fear and went toward her, holding his hat gingerly like a shield, on guard against a sudden rush — for all he knew, she might be holding a knife or even a hatchet in the hidden hand, waiting for a chance to strike. When she spoke, leaning forward so that only her mouth and nose, half of each eye and her bangs were visible through the aperture, her voice was high and quavery, with a creak like a hinge grown rusty from disuse. But the words were clear enough. "Youre Amanda's young man," she said. Her face was quite close; he could see the pores of her skin. She spoke harshly, hurriedly, as if in fear that someone would discover and interrupt them, perhaps do them harm. "Take her away! Take her out of this terrible house!"

Startled by her violence, Drew recoiled and rushed for the door. He was no coward — the DSC had been earned. But this was outside all his experience or expectation; it was like being in touch with the occult. Besides, he was already unnerved by his encounter with the major. He took the steps two at a time, not bothering to think that Amanda might be watching from an upstairs window.

But on his way to the hotel, recovering from his fright, he thought about what Florence had said. From this distance his fear seemed absurd. The mad woman had not been his enemy; she had been his friend, his adviser. She had given him the one true answer to his problem: elopement, then no doubt a furious scene, a period of estrangement, with perhaps some recrimination — and then forgiveness. After all, Amanda was practically an only child. Faced with the incontrovertible fact of marriage, the old man would come round in time: Drew felt it must be so. He even pictured the scene in which they returned to Lamar Street and stood before the major, not exactly repentant, but anyhow humble. The major would look at them sternly. Then gradually the lines of his face would soften; the glasses would mist over; finally he would spread his arms, and Amanda would hurry to him. Drew himself would stand by, delicately turning his head away from the sight and waiting for the time to step up for the handshake, man to man.

He regretted now that he had not done it that way from the start. And that night, when Amanda came down the steps and met him in the shadow of the oaks, he told her it was their only hope. They walked and the moon was high and pure, like beaten gold, the air still balmy; people were saying there would be no winter this year. "Come out as usual tomorrow night," he told her, pressing her arm and leaning so that his lips were touching her hair. "You neednt bring anything with you; come as you are. We'll be married by the justice of peace and catch the ten oclock train for New Orleans. Say you will." She was doubtful, but she wanted to: Drew could see that. He pressed her arm and breathed into her hair. When they returned to the house she held him close, more tenderly even than she had done the night before, and told him she would go with him.

"I'd go with you anywhere, Harley," she said.

TWO

4. Citizen Bachelor

That night the weather broke. Soon after midnight the wind rose; there were sudden gusts of rain, intermittent and abrupt, like scant handfuls of gravel tossed against the windowpanes. Toward daybreak it stepped up the cadence; all Monday morning it came down with the steady drumming of true autumnal rain, driven in scudding sheets before the wind, stripping the leaves from trees and plastering them on streets and sidewalks and lawns, sodden, viscid, robbed of their gay colors. "Lord God," Drew cried. "Is this the sunny South?" Just after three oclock that afternoon it slacked; within another hour it stopped; the sun emerged, cold and pale and distant, riding a murky haze, bathing the transformed landscape with a sinister yellow glow like the flicker of lightning. The limbs of trees, leafless and black with wet, were gaunt against the sky when Amanda went to meet her father at five.

Drew had told her that she must do nothing to make the major suspicious. But as they walked home together through the leaf-plastered streets, under that eerie refulgence, her father seemed to have divined her plans. This was in his manner, not his words: they were halfway home before he spoke. "Amanda," he said. He paused. "I want you to realize the consequences before you do something youll be sorry for." He did not look at her, and she too kept her eyes to the front.

"You know that when I say a thing I mean it — I mean it to the hilt. So tell your young man this, Amanda. Tell him that the day you marry without my consent I'll cut you off without a dime. Without so much as one thin dime, Amanda. I'll cut you off, disown you, and what is more I'll never regret it. I'll never so much as think your name again." Up to now he had spoken slowly, pausing between phrases. But now the words came fast, like fencing thrusts. "Tell your young man that, Amanda, and see what he says."

Major Barcroft turned his head, looking at her for the first time since they had left the office. She knew that his gaze was fixed on her; she saw the movement out of the side of her eye. However, she kept her face to the front, and after a few more steps on the wet pavement he resumed. No one standing five feet away could have heard what he said.

"But there is something more to it than this, and I wonder that it hasnt occurred to you; I wonder that you havent thought of it." He shook his head. "It isnt like you, Amanda. It isnt like you at all." He leaned toward her and spoke rapidly, still in the quiet tone no bystander could overhear. "*I* hear her in the small hours of the night, and I hear you when you go to her; *I* know what Florence dreams. Will you leave your sister here alone, to wake up screaming and not find you there? Will you leave Florence here for *me* to comfort? For me to be the one who is there, holding her hand when she comes out of that dream?"

Amanda looked and saw her father's face turned toward her, the drawn expression about his mouth, the cobweb strand of golden chain that drooped in a glistening parabola to the button at his lapel, the grizzled, tufted eyebrows, the glazed shirt front with its one pearl stud the color of skimmed milk. Then everything was blurred, for her eyes were filled with tears. They were in front of the house by now, and she ran up the steps and through the hall and up the staircase to her room. She closed the door behind her and turned the key. Then, whirling, she leaned against the panel, arms extended in a pose of crucifixion, her mouth and cheek against the varnished surface, panting. God is awful mean to people, she thought, sobbing against the smell and taste of varnish; God is awful mean to me.

Presently, though, she dried her eyes on her sleeve and crossed the room. She sat sideways on the bed, looking down at her hands in her lap. She sat thus for perhaps ten minutes; she did not move. Then she rose deliberately and went to her writing table, where she took a sheet of paper from the drawer, uncorked the ink, took up the pen, and wrote rapidly. The squeak of the pen was loud in the quiet room. When she had filled a little more than half the page — seven lines, not including the salutation or signature — she laid the pen aside and sat looking down at the paper while the ink dried. Rising, she folded the sheet, sealed it in an envelope, and started for the door. Then, without pausing, she turned in the doorway and returned to the table, where she addressed the envelope. Her hands were shaking; the writing was hardly legible. "*Oh* me," she said, looking down at it. She decided it would do, however, and carried it downstairs without waiting for the ink to dry.

From the veranda she beckoned to a Negro boy who was passing on the sidewalk. He crossed the shallow lawn and accepted the letter which she held out to him. "Take this to the Bristol Hotel," she told him. "Go straight there." She paused, looking down at the writing on the envelope, then said quietly, "It's for Mr Harley Drew."

"Yassum," he said. "At the Bristol *Ho*tel. Yassum."

He did not go, however; he stood there in his scuffed and soggy shoes, his knee-length jeans, his sky-blue denim shirt, looking up at her, showing a good deal of white at the bottoms of his eyeballs. Amanda waited, but still he did not move. So at last she took a change purse from the pocket of her dress, undid the clasp, and selected a piece of money. "Here. This is for you," she said. He took it but for another little while he continued to stand there, watching the dull, not-quite-silver glint of the coin against his pinkish palm.

"Yassum," he said sadly. It was a nickel.

Drew was entering the lobby through the doors that gave on Marshall Avenue — he had just come from the depot, where he had bought tickets and made a drawing-room reservation on the night train for New Orleans — when the desk clerk hailed him. "Mr Drew! Mr Drew, here's a boy with a letter."

The young Negro stood in front of the desk, holding the envelope with both hands hugged to his chest. "You Mr Holly Drew?" he asked, suspicious.

"I am," Drew said gravely.

"Then here," the boy said, even more gravely, and extended the letter, still gripping it with both hands, alert against any sudden attempt to snatch it.

Drew took it, ripped it open. There was a monogram at the upper left of the sheet, a flowery B, and beneath the body of the text the signature *Always Your Amanda* had been written larger than the rest. The stationery was heavy, expensive, and slightly yellowed. It belonged to her mother, Drew thought. He glanced up, still without having read the letter, and seeing the boy still there, took a coin from his pocket and flipped it: a quarter. The boy's dark hand interrupted the spinning arc, and as he passed through the clashing plate glass doors, both rows of teeth showed white against his face.

Drew leaned against one of the columns beside the desk, looking at the note. It required some deciphering, for the tees were mostly uncrossed and the eyes undotted; the ens and yous, the ayes and ohs were indistinguishable. He scanned it first from the bottom up, reading only those portions that caught his eye. *Tonight seven thirty. He will not change. Never regret it. Imposible. Do not buy the tickets.* Startled by this last, he crossed the lobby and sat in one of the leather armchairs where old loafers sat through every morning and early afternoon, spitting into the brass spittoons and talking cotton while they watched the legs of women on the sidewalk. He spread the letter and read it carefully, from beginning to end.

Dear Harley —

I will see you the way we said but do not buy the tickets. What we planned is imposible. Not because Pappa says he will cut me off and said to tell you so, without a dime. I know he would and never regret it, because he said so and when Pappa says a thing he will not change it even if he wants to. It is for another reason, I can not write. I will tell you tonight seven thirty.

Always Your Amanda.

He reread it without pause: *Always Your Amanda, Dear Harley*: not because there was any doubt about its meaning, but because he wanted to delay having to think about it, to delay the realization of defeat. Sitting there with the letter once more folded on his knee, he could have recited it from memory — crowded syntax, misspellings, and all; the hurried, open-looped calligraphy was microfilmed on his brain. The elopement was off. Amanda had said there was another reason, but Drew did not require another reason. Nine one-syllable words of the message had given him all the reason he needed: *He will cut me off. He will not change.* That was enough.

For another hour he sat in the lobby, the letter placed in his inside coat pocket along with the useless railroad tickets, deciding whether to meet her or not. His first inclination was to go away now, to end it without a final scene of parting; he disliked sentimentality, even when there was something to be gained by it. But pride would not let him leave like that. The fact that it was Amanda who was ending it gave him a chance to be remembered with compassion, and he preferred to have her think of him so. Besides — and this had the most weight in his calculations — there might be some way to keep the opportunity at hand. That was when it occurred to him, quite suddenly, that Major Barcroft could not live forever.

As soon as he thought of this he wondered that it had not

occurred to him sooner. He said to himself, Youve been too intense about this thing. But he was wrong. His trouble was he had taken it too easy. Everything had run as smooth as silk, up to the interview with the major. Then he had panicked; he had snatched at straws; he had taken the first advice that was offered him, even from what he called 'the crazy sister,' and merely because that had failed he had despaired. Just settle down, he told himself, like an athlete when the score begins to favor his opponent; Youve been too intense about this thing.

Though it was not really true, it was true in a sense. So much depended on the outcome, and he had thought intensely of the outcome. Drew slumped in the chair, his hands in his pockets, his knees raised almost level with his head. Night had fallen. Beyond the plate glass window, street lamps burned in ordered rows down both curbs of the avenue, the posts like iron trees growing out of concrete, each with a pool of gold about its trunk, and bearing incandescent globes for fruit. He had come far, so far that looking back was like peering down from a height after a climb: all the way from the steelmill years in Youngstown, his father crying "Hi! Hi!" stamping red-heeled boots and squeezing a concertina; the shoe store where he had crouched at the feet of women customers and politely turned his head when they spread their knees; the Army during the war, the nights of screaming metal and concussion, the days of blood, and then the period of occupation when he had formed his tastes and his desires; the three-year 'look round,' including the skimped meals, the luxurious envy; the long days of work at the head office of the cotton trust, studying books and statistics; the season in Texas, glad-handing — and now this. Was it all for nothing? He was asking. Did it all add up to failure when the first real opportunity came his way? He cursed the major. Then suddenly he stopped. It was not much different from the Army, really. There it had been the bullets, and the bullets had stopped; the firing had died to a mutter, then had swelled to crescendo, and had ceased. As for the major — why, the major would die as well. It was merely a question of waiting, now as then, and waiting had been his specialty for years. Meanwhile who could say what might crop up?

On his way out he stopped at the desk and wrote a telegram, addressing it to the head office in St Louis: FLU CURED STOP WILL BE LEAVING TOMORROW FOR VICKSBURG. When he passed through the swinging doors, the clock on the wall marked seven-thirty.

This time it was Amanda who was waiting. She stepped out of the shadows and took his arm, and as they walked down Lamar Street the overhead branches, stark and black against the moon, groaned and clacked in the wind. The dead scurrying leaves of goblin-time, dry now after the rain of the night before, made tiny scraping sounds, like whispers, against the sidewalk. For a while she was quiet, leaning lightly on Drew's arm, but when they had walked a short distance she began to tell him what she had promised in the letter. She said she could not leave Florence. "I dont know how I ever thought I could. Or yes I do: I know. I thought at first we'd be here, you and I — thats what it was. Then later, when I knew we couldnt, I wanted to be with you so much that nothing else made any difference. Thats why. But I know now I was wrong. Florence needs me more than anyone needs anything. We have to wait."

"Wait?" Drew thought he understood, but he wanted to be sure. He wanted to make her say it. "Wait for what?"

"Her heart," Amanda said; she hesitated; "her heart is bad. I know; Ive heard it."

Drew looked at her. "How bad?"

"I dont know. Bad. She's going to die."

That was what he had been waiting for, what he had been edging her toward. And now he said what was in his mind: "Or *he* is."

"Who is?"

"Your . . ."

"Papa?" she said, incredulous. It was clear that no such

thought had ever occurred to her. She thought her father impervious, immortal. "Papa's not going to die."

Drew was silent then, walking with both hands deep in his pockets and thinking of death — thinking of the two of them waiting for it: she waiting for her sister's death, he waiting for her father's: a sort of monstrous horserace, in reverse. We're a fine pair, he thought, and he smiled as he thought it. If Florence died first he simply would not come when Amanda called. But if it turned out that the major was the first to die, he would be there before they got him under ground. It was a race, a gamble — yet not really a gamble, either, for Drew had nothing to lose, no matter who won; but he had a great deal to gain if it worked out his way.

Then he felt a tug at his arm. They were into the second block by now, midway between street lights, and the shadows were deepest here. He stopped and turned and, looking down, saw her face lifted toward him, pale in the moonlight, lips bloodless and drawn, eyes glistening faintly in their sockets. "Oh Harley," she said; it was almost a whimper. He kissed her, nuzzling, murmuring wordlessly, and stroked her backside with one hand. This startled her at first; she hid her face against the tweed at his shoulder. "Ah Harley," she said, and he continued to stroke her, as if gentling a highstrung pony. Soon they turned and came back, and he kissed her again in parting at the steps.

"I'll wait as long as I must," he said. "There will never be anyone else for me, Amanda."

He meant it; he meant it then. And when he got back to the hotel he stopped at the desk. The nightclerk was on. "I left a wire. Has it been sent?"

"A moment, Mr Drew." The clerk turned to the switchboard and began to thumb through some papers; as night man he was also switchboard operator. Drew knew that the search was a pretense, for the nightclerk read the day's accumulation of messages, including even postcards, as soon as he came on duty. "Here we are," the clerk said. He turned, holding the yellow sheet: FLU CURED STOP. "Itll go out first thing in the morning."

"Give me." Drew took it. "Good night."

"Yes sir," the nightclerk said, watching from under the neat fringe of his eyebrows.

Upstairs in his room Drew tore the message across and across, then across and across, again and again, as small as he could tear, and dropped the pieces into the basket beside the desk. Fluttering like yellow snow, some of them fell on the carpet. He took up the phone.

"Yes sir?"

"415. Send the bellboy."

"Right away."

It seemed he had hardly put the receiver back on the hook when there was a knocking, and when he opened the door the Negro stood holding a frosted metal pitcher in front of his chest. "Never mind all that," Drew said. "Just get me Alma. Is that her name?"

"Thats her," the bellboy said.

Drew closed the door. Ice in the pitcher clanked the length of the hall, diminishing. The elevator whined, rattled open, rattled shut; it whined. Then there was silence. It seemed long, for anticipation heightened his perception. The elevator whined again and stopped and rattled open. Footsteps approached. They came abreast, and then went past; a key chattered in a lock at the end of the hall. There was silence again. Drew sat a while longer, not moving. Then suddenly he rose and went to the desk, where he knelt on the carpet and began to gather the scraps of yellow paper, placing them one at a time into the cupped palm of one hand. He dropped them into the wastebasket, then rose, dusted his knees, and returned to his seat on the bed. He lit a cigarette and smoked it fast, sharpening the ash like a pencil point from time to time on the rim of a saucer that sat on the bedside table.

He began to think of Amanda. Why think of that? he said to himself, and went on thinking of her. Should I have taken it further? he thought; Should I have — then grew conscious of the scratching at the door. He had been so absorbed in thinking of Amanda, he had not heard the elevator or the footsteps in the hall. He rose and swung the door ajar. "About time," he said. She was dressed the same as four nights ago.

"I was filling a date," she said. And soon afterward, as they lay in bed, profoundly immobile, looking up at the rectangle of light reflected on the ceiling from the transom, she said: "Gee, honey, I feel just like I'm robbing you. I really do."

"I'll worry about me," Drew said. "You worry about you."

She turned sideways, watching him, her weight on one elbow. "I like you," she said. She put her hand on his shoulder. He did not look at her. "I really do. You remind me of someone." Then she said softly, loverlike, "I'll take off my bra if you want. You want?" Apparently this was a great concession, a more intimate surrender, beyond money. She took it off and hung it, suspended by the straps, on the back of a chair beside the bed. It resembled a badly sprung hammock. "There," she said, "Now. Lets snuggle." They snuggled. "Oh, I *like* you," she murmured. "I really do. I was married once to a boy so much like you. . . . Honey, *whats* your name?"

Somewhat later they were lying there, again watching the rectangle of light from the transom, and Drew heard a whistle blow lonesome and far in the night: a long and a short and a long: a wail and a hoot and a wail. It was five after ten and the New Orleans train was approaching open country. He lay thinking of the empty drawing room, the berths turned down, the vibration, the faint and not unpleasant smell of cinders, and suddenly it occurred to him that Amanda must be hearing

92

it too, alone in her bedroom or sitting with her sister in the big house on Lamar Street; she had stopped whatever she was doing and was sitting perfectly still, hearing the wail of the whistle. "I should have canceled the reservation," he thought.

"What?"

"Nothing," he said, realizing he must have thought aloud.

He got up, naked, and crossed the room to where his suitcase sat in front of the dresser; it had sat there, packed and strapped, since early afternoon. He knelt. "What is it?" the girl said, sitting up in bed. Drew did not answer. He unlocked the suitcase and without having to fumble — for he knew just where it was, in just which corner; he had been prepared to do this in the dark — took out a parcel wrapped in tissue.

"Here," he said, coming back to the bed where Alma sat with the edge of the sheet held under her chin despite the darkness. "This is for you."

"What is?" she said; "What . . ." and then she had it. The tissue made whispering sounds, being unwrapped. "Golly," she said in a tone she might otherwise have reserved for prayer; "a nightgown. It's a nightgown."

Drew had bought it that morning, going from store to store on Marshall Avenue until he found what he wanted, at a price he was willing to pay. It was Amanda's bride-bed gown, and it had cost eight dollars. "Go on; see if it fits," he said. He reached for the lamp.

"Not yet." She caught his arm. "I'll tell you when." Her feet padded on the carpet. The gown rustled and whispered, much as the tissue had done, but softer, muffled. Drew could see her in silhouette against the window, with a few faint stars beyond. She made some final adjustments. "Now," she said. He clicked the switch and she stood there with a froth of lace at her throat. "Aint that something?" she said; "I'm trembling like a bride." She turned this way and that for his admiration. The gown was long and fell in pleats below the waist, its hem resting on the insteps of her broad thick feet so that only her toes peeped out, showing their crusted nails. She said again, "Aint that something?"

"Well," Drew said — he paused. "Anyhow you fill it better than she would."

"Who would?"

"She would. Come on back to bed."

"Wait till I get the gown off — "

Next morning he woke late. He lay for perhaps five minutes, taking stock. Then, in accordance with a resolution he had formed last night on the way back to the hotel (and which he had already begun to act on when he reclaimed and destroyed the telegram to St Louis) he took up the phone, cleared his throat, and gave a number. "Mr Tilden, please. Yes. Hello, Til? Yes: Harley Drew. Fine. Say, Ive been thinking . . ." He laughed, or anyhow he imitated laughter. "That offer: I'd like to talk it over. No, seriously. Sure, anytime you — All right. Sure. Twelve-thirty. That will be fine." He lay thinking; then he took up the phone again; "Toast and coffee. Right away," and put it back. He mused, lying naked in the soiled bedclothes, the wrinkled sheets and tumbled spread, looking up at the water-stained ceiling where the rectangle of light had been reflected. "The things a man will do," he said aloud.

At twelve-thirty, bathed and shaved and breakfasted, he was climbing the steps of the Planters Bank & Trust Company when a man came out of the double doors and cried his name; apparently he had been watching from a window. They stood together in the sunlight, shaking hands. The man was in his early forties, already with a low tight round little paunch. He had to tilt his head far back, looking up at Drew, for he was only just over five feet tall. His face was baby pink, round without being fat; it had a well scrubbed look, and though the morning shave was four or five hours old by now, he appeared never to have needed to shave at all. Except for the paunch and the baldness, which was exposed when they entered the restaurant and removed their hats, he had changed very little since the war. That was where Drew had known him.

94

His name was Lawrence Tilden; he had been adjutant of Drew's regiment — Aunt Tilly, they had called him because of his fussy, excitable manner with documents and the way he took off for the rear whenever the first warning order came. He had shown a great fancy for Drew; it amounted to hero worship, in fact, though Drew was ten years younger. Anything he could do for him he did, everything from arranging a few days' extra leave to sharing his boxes from home, and this had resulted in even more jeers from the other officers and sidelong, knowing glances from the men.

Drew had seen him early the previous week, soon after coming to Bristol. "Drew! Lieutenant Drew!" he heard a voice cry; he was on the street, and he turned and it was Tilden. He took Drew into a restaurant for coffee. They stayed an hour, talking about the war and what had happened since. Tilden did most of the talking. He had taken over his father's bank, the leading one of three in Bristol. He was married, had been married more than eight years now, but there had been no children; "Not yet," he said in the tone of a man repeating a hope he has long since ceased to believe in. Then he began to talk business and his voice rose to a wail. "Ive got plans," he said; "such plans. But no one to work with." That was when the notion first came to him, apparently. "Why dont you come in? A few months learning the ropes and youd be set." He leaned over his cup of cooling coffee and his voice dropped to a whisper. "Youve got what I need, what the bank needs. Salesmanship, personality — someone to jar them out of their rut. My God, Harley, you ought to see the deadwood I have to work with." He was leaning half across the table, gripping its edge so hard that his dimpled knuckles were white with the strain.

It was really a little absurd, Drew thought, looking into the round smooth baby-pink face, the eyes showing a bit of white between the irises and the lower lids because of Tilden's need to look up at whomever he talked to, even when seated. Now the eyes held urgency, desire — it was really absurd. Drew laughed, but more from nervousness than amusement; he laughed as a young girl might have done in a comparable situation. Then he regretted the laugh, also as the young girl might have done, and explained that he was committed to Anson-Grimm, the cotton trust. He made it as kindly as he could, and he did not exactly decline the offer (he never exactly declined any offer): he merely said he was tied up. And Tilden listened with his eyes averted, looking down into the cup of quite cold coffee as if it had been perhaps as deep as a well. Then they parted. He had called the hotel three or four times since, inviting Drew out to his house for dinner; once he had even had his wife do the calling. But Drew had always declined; he was tied up, he said.

That was last week and he had not seen him since. Then Monday night, returning from the parting scene with Amanda — the one in which he told her, "There will never be anyone else for me" — he began to worry; he began to imagine fears. He had told himself at the outset he was lucky no one else had thought Amanda worth the gambit, and now he could not believe his luck would hold. Someone else ('local talent' he said to himself) would see it, would move right in. He had been the first and it had been easy; perhaps it would be that much easier for the second, now that he had shown the way — the right as well as the wrong way, for he knew now that he should have worked on the major first. It would be necessary to stay, to protect his investment. Then he remembered Tilden and he halted in his tracks, halfway between the house and the hotel: "Thats it!" he cried; he actually snapped his fingers. He hurried on, stopped at the desk, and reclaimed the telegram.

And now he and Tilden were sitting in the restaurant, the same one they had gone into that first time; they had given their order and were sitting there. So far nothing had been said about the object of their meeting. "What made you change your mind?" Tilden asked suddenly. He kept his eyes down, rearranging the silverware with hands as pink and hairless as his face. He was more businesslike today, not exactly distant but anyhow cautious. Drew regretted those declined invitations.

"I got to thinking," he said. He sat well back in his chair, watching Tilden, who still would not look at him. "A man, a traveling man — I never was meant for that kind of life in the first place. Ive seen them and they go to seed at fifty. A man wants to settle down, call someplace home, and I decided if I didnt quit now I never would. Tell you the truth, thats why I waited to see you: I wanted to think it through for myself, on my own. Because I dont mind telling you it's a mighty good job I'd be leaving." Drew paused to let this point sink in; then he continued. "Well, Ive been thinking. Ive decided. And I dont mind telling you something else, though it might sound foolish to some. Part of the reason is Bristol. The river, the trees, all this — " he gestured vaguely; "Ive been walking around and talking to people. Ive fallen in love with this sleepy little town."

"Not foolish at all," the other said, and the waitress put plates on the table.

"Will that be all, Mr Tilden?"

"Thank you, Flora," Tilden said. She went away.

Drew looked down at his plate. It held a slice of roast beef oozing blood as if it had just been cut from the living cow, mashed potatoes, canned asparagus, and green peas; the salad was a leaf of lettuce under a cube of Jell-O, ruby red, with a dab of mayonnaise and a sprinkling of grated cheese — the two-color ice cream would come later. This was the business-man's lunch. He wondered how many years he would be eating it before he moved on to home-cooking in the house on Lamar Street. Major Barcroft had a tough and stringy look: that kind sometimes lived on past a hundred.

Tilden thawed in the course of the meal, recovering from his peevishness at the declined invitations. They went from the restaurant to his office at the bank, and by that time he was as enthusiastic as he had been a week ago, over the cooling coffee. "Here's how it will be," he said, sitting behind the polished expanse of a desk about the size of a billiard table. He explained the hierarchy of banking. Normally a man started out as a runner, but they would skip that; Drew would begin as a teller. "Youll handle money: get the feel of it. Thats important." After six months of this he would move back to the general bookkeeping department, where he would get 'the big picture' and an outline of bank policy as to its loans and its relations with other banks.

"With other banks?"

"Yes. Thats important."

"I see," Drew said. He did not see at all.

There would be a year of this, more or less, depending on how well he did. "Youll do all right," Tilden said. "Youll do fine. I'm sure."

"Hm," Drew said.

Then would come the big jump: Assistant Cashier. An assistant cashier was an officer; he had a desk out front, where he sat and heard requests for small personal loans. More important, though, he handled the accounts of cotton buyers, such loans being covered by cotton receipts. Here was where Drew's experience with Anson-Grimm would be invaluable. "This is cotton country, and of course like everyone else down here, we make our money out of cotton, one way or another."

"I see," Drew said. He had resolved to ask no more questions at this time, and he was having trouble resisting a desire to squirm.

The next step was Cashier, but they would skip that; "It's just technical," Tilden said with a deprecatory gesture. Drew's next step would be Assistant Vice President. As such he would be one of the policy makers. "Thats where I'm counting on you," Tilden told him. "Youve no idea the deadwood a bank accumulates over the years."

Drew thought it best not even to say Hm to this, but he nodded as if he understood — or anyhow sympathized. Two things were bothering him: 1) Salary, and 2) Tilden had men-

98

tioned no time-span that would apply to the intermediary position of assistant cashier.

"Now — salary," Tilden said; it was as if he had read Drew's mind. He looked down at his hands, which rested pink against the polished surface of the desk. "Banks are notoriously low on salary. The usual beginner draws a hundred a month; when he moves up to teller he gets one twelve fifty. We'll start you at that, with a raise to one twenty-five as soon as you go back to the books, in say six months. Within a year (after that, I mean) youll be making one fifty-seven fifty. How does that sound?"

"Well . . ." Drew was making a hundred and thirty now, plus expenses. It amounted to quite a come-down. He had thought it would be more.

"But dont just think of the salary," Tilden told him, hurrying on. "There will be bonuses, chances for investment — think of those things, Harley."

Drew, however, was thinking of Amanda. He really had no decision to make; he had made it last night, walking down Lamar Street. He rose. Tilden rose too. Suddenly, as if by signal, they leaned across the desk-top and shook hands. "Fine then," Tilden said, smiling. "That will be fine."

Back in his room two hours later, Drew sat looking down at a sheet of hotel stationery and nibbling at the penstaff. For a long time he wrote nothing; he looked and nibbled and thought. Then he began to write, phrase by phrase at first, then rapidly, and the pen made a steady scraping sound like mice in a wainscot. When he had finished he set the sheet aside to dry while he addressed the envelope:

> *Hon. Leo G. Anson*
> *Anson-Grimm Bldg.*
> *St. Louis, Mo.*

Then he set the envelope aside and read the letter. As he read he nodded appreciation of its tone and style, then folded the sheet and put it into the envelope. He mailed it, air mail, special delivery, when he went downstairs for supper.

12/5/28

Dear Mr. Leo:—

This is hard to write — hard to make clear, for you know how much all you have helped me means, & I would not if I could help. I can not help it, laid up here with Flu & convalescing, I have fallen in love with this sleepy little Southern town, & a position having been tendered me in the leading Bank by their board of Directors, I could not feel justified in turning down. I express myself poorly from my Emotion, thinking of your Many kindnesses on so many occasions & our many long talks & all, but the position I could not feel justified declining, as I said. I herewith tender my Resignation as of this inst., hoping your understanding will see with me on this. I want a home like any other man & all that goes with it.

Sincerely, your friend,
Harley Drew.

P.S. *Mr. Leo, regarding severance pay I do not feel justified asking for it on such short notification. However if you feel I would be, send it c/o Planters Bank & Trust Co. here in Bristol. That is the name of the bank.*

So he stood in his cage, the brass bars matching the brassy gleam of his mustache in the tiled, marble-slabbed, cavernous, high-windowed gloom. MR DREW was printed in small capitals on a metal shingle over the arch, so that even strangers could call him by name: which they did. Already in this first week, while he was yet a trifle slow in counting money and still none too familiar with the forms, his window was the most popular with the ladies; they asked him to explain again how to fill out deposit slips and indorse checks, while the teller in the adjoining cage stood idle looking daggers. His name was Sanderson; he had patent-leather hair and was said to resemble Rudolph Valentino (of blessed memory) or anyhow Ramon Novarro. He had done two years as a runner and was into his second year in the teller's cage, yet Drew had come to work at an equal salary and obviously was being groomed for higher things. No wonder Sanderson looked daggers, like Valentino in *The Sheik* or anyhow Novarro in *Ben-Hur*; he had been shoved aside, like so much extra baggage for a better load to ride. So he thought. It was months before he realized that he had nothing to fear from Drew, that there was no more a question of competition between them than there had been, say, between Dempsey and Kid Chocolate.

Though this was Drew's first week in the cage, it was really his second week in the bank. He had spent what was left of the first week getting acquainted, getting settled. Tilden (who was Mister Tilden now, during business hours at least) took him around and introduced him to the others. "Howd you do," they said, or just "How do" — without any tone of interrogation; they merely recited the words. The handshakes were quick and cool and distant, perfunctory. This was true of them all, from Mr Cilley the old bookkeeper who wore detachable collars and cuffs and had been there in Tilden's grandfather's time — the founder — down to Sanderson with his dark good looks and glossy hair; he was the youngest, five years younger than Drew, who was the next youngest. All their eyes were mistrustful, just short of enmity — though that was there too, veiled — and each handshake was like the one that precedes fisticuffs; Drew kept reverting to these comparisons with boxing. There was one exception: the Negro porter, Rufus, who was almost as old as Mr Cilley. "How do?" he said. It was really a question but he lost no dignity asking it, as the others had seemed to fear they would do.

"Fine," Drew said. For the first time he smiled. He knew

that Rufus knew he had nothing to fear from him, yet it was pleasant to find friendliness in the midst of constraint, wherever. Besides, he was not worrying; he knew it would come out all right. He had been through this before, when he entered the head office in St Louis.

That night he waited outside the Barcroft house from a little after seven till almost eight, long enough to smoke four cigarettes, with even some interval between them; but Amanda did not come. She's grieving, he thought. She hasnt got over hearing that ten oclock train last night and thinking I was on it. He ground out the fourth cigarette, and turning up his coat collar — for it was really cold now, down around forty; December had come with a vengeance — walked back to the hotel. Maybe she just comes out in mild weather, he thought: "Like the primroses," he said aloud.

But the next night he was there again, and he had no more than lighted the first cigarette when the door opened and someone came out. The moon had not risen. Drew cupped the cigarette and stayed behind the tree, thinking it might be Major Barcroft. Then whoever it was came down the steps and he could see, not well but almost; he was almost sure. So he stepped out — he took a chance. "Amanda?" he said.

She turned and it was not surprise; she did not gasp or cry his name; she did none of the things he had expected, but merely stood and watched him take her arm. It was as if she had lost all capacity for surprise, being involved already in events so far outside her experience or hope: as if, after the initial shock of finding herself loved — or, at any rate, loving — all other surprises were bound to be anticlimax. Drew took her arm and they walked, and it was as if they had not missed a meeting the night before; it was even as if their meeting two nights ago had not been one of parting; the lonesome wail of the whistle two hours later might have been something heard in a dream, a sort of languid nightmare whose horror consisted of just that languidness, and now was false.

"I couldnt go," he said. "I couldnt leave you."

They walked, and at first his voice was only a murmur as he told her how he had missed her, how he had tried to steel himself to catch the train, and then how he had lain in bed and heard the whistle. Such a lonesome sound, he said, and he had lain there, alone and lonesome, hearing it.

"I heard it too," she said.

"And thought I was on it?"

"Yes."

"I meant to be; I really did. But I couldnt."

He was settled in Bristol for good, he said, to be near her. And then his voice stopped being a murmur: he spoke carefully, giving instructions. "We must not see each other often. I stayed here to be near you; I didnt stay to make life miserable for you. I know how he feels about me, Amanda, and in a way I dont blame him — on such short acquaintance. If you were my daughter I guess I'd feel the same." They walked and he appeared to think. He said, "We'll be together in the end, whatever. We know that, dont we? Dont we?" He squeezed her arm.

"Yes," she said.

"And as long as we know it, nothing else can matter. Not really, I mean. Can it?" He squeezed her arm.

"No," she said.

"The thing is, I'll always be here if you need me. All you need do is call and I'll be with you, Amanda. Otherwise it's better not to give him grounds for anger. The main thing is, we know we'll be together in the end." He kept saying that, returning to it like the refrain in a ballad, like Theme A of some rondo he was humming in her ears.

They parted at the foot of the steps, but tonight he did not return to the hotel. He had moved that morning, into the Pentecost house out on Marshall Extended. Tilden had recommended him; Mrs Pentecost, whom Tilden called Aunt, was a second cousin, niece of the grandfather founder's. The house was in the best residential section; Drew had two rooms and bath on the ground floor, with a private entrance under the porte-cochere. Mrs Pentecost was highborn — what was called highborn; she was old Judge Hellman's only child. But she had married beneath her station, as she frequently reminded her husband after marriage began to pale, and he had turned to whiskey in his early middle-age. He was dead now. His death had managed to be at once scandalous and tragic, for he died one night ten years ago in a cell at the city jail. The police had put him there for his own good, intending to take him home later, as they had done so many times before, always being careful to get him into the house before dawn so the neighbors would not see. They had thought the apoplexy was drunkenness — he had had DTs before, right there in the same cell — so that by the time they saw it was serious he was dead. Public sentiment was with the widow in the suit that followed. Though they knew that they would have to pay the judgment in taxes (and though they knew too, in varying degrees, depending on their various perceptions, that it was she and not the police who had killed her husband) almost none of them begrudged her the fifteen thousand dollars the jury awarded. And yet to look at her youd never know it, never imagine the nights she had waited for the husband she herself had driven to drink because of her inveterate pretension and because marriage had not measured up to the dreams her people had taught her in her youth: 'Poor Edward' she called him now, demure and put-upon and so soft-spoken you had to lean close to distinguish what she said. Drew heard her story soon after moving in, yet he was not surprised. By then he had heard many such stories; Bristol was full of such people. Maybe every town was, he thought, but in Bristol everyone knew about everyone else — as if God, an enormous Eye in the sky, were telling secrets.

He had said at the outset that he had fallen in love with "this sleepy little Southern town"; he had said so twice before he so much as knew its population, first to Tilden and then, since it seemed to make such an impression, to Leo Anson in the letter to St Louis. It was not true, either when he said it or when he wrote it. The truth was he had hardly noticed. Besides, the statement needed some translating: for when he said 'Bristol' he meant Amanda, and when he said 'love' he meant something else as well. Yet now he did — notice, at any rate. He was plumped into the middle of it; all he needed to do was look around.

Soon he knew Bristol's history, from back in the days when it had been a nameless river landing where steamboats took on cotton and firewood without staying long enough to affect the pressure in their boilers. In time, however, though it still was scorned by the floating palaces, the landing became a stopping-off place for flatboat men; they had slept and worked off their excesses by then (Memphis was a hundred and fifty miles up-river) and by the time they reached Bristol they were primed for another bender — "carrying a load of steam," they said, that would not wait for Vicksburg, another hundred miles downriver. So the landing became a settlement, though its 'stores' were mostly grog shops. Then it grew and was a town. The war in the Sixties provided a sort of pause, a breathing space. Gradually during the era that followed and rapidly during the postReconstruction building boom, which was in full swing in the Eighties, after the fever deaths of '78, the town thickened within its boundaries. But the Barcroft house was the last big private residence to be built within the old limits, for then the town began expanding eastward, beyond the silver sweep of the railroad tracks, where old Mrs Sturgis, 'the Mother of Bristol,' was subdividing her father's plantation. Soon townspeople were pointing out more or less far-flung areas for visitors and telling them, "This used to be country, out here. That was a brier patch where we hunted rabbits; I used to sit under that big elm and wait for doves to come in of an evening. See how Bristol has grown." Then one morning they woke to find the Chamber of Commerce calling it a city: 'The Queen City of the Delta.' Two years after Drew got there, the census showed a population of more than fifteen thousand.

Two weeks after entering the bank he joined the Kiwanis

Club. This was at Tilden's suggestion — for business reasons. "Later we'll move you up," he said. "Youll come into the Rotary with me." So every Tuesday at high noon Drew made one among the Kiwanians, singing group songs and serving on committees. They took him in; they gave him a sense of belonging. Sometimes he almost liked it. Then he would pause; he would look at the others down the length of the table, with their ready-made suits, their not-quite-country haircuts, bending forward over the melting remnants of ice cream as they listened to some speaker who told them of business trends, and Drew would remember the New York years and the years among the rich. At such moments time seemed to stand still; all down the table they would be frozen in motion. And he would ask himself, Is this me? Is this really me? What have I to do with these people? — knowing well enough what he had come to and what compromises he had made. But that was bad for him: it made him unhappy, made him even regret. So he tried to think only of the future, when he might well be proud of all he had endured, just as he already had begun to be proud, in retrospect, of the skimped lunches and long walks of the New York phase. Yet sometimes he could not help himself; the past would rise up into the present, and all down the long table his fellow Kiwanians in their store-bought suits and Mississippi haircuts would be frozen in motion. He would find himself thinking, Is this me? Is this really me?

By the time he left the teller's cage to move back to the general bookkeeping department — where he familiarized himself with what Tilden had called 'the big picture' (and found that it was not so big after all. The mystery of banking lay in incidentals that could be grasped within a month; the essentials were as simple as a child's game. If a measure of awe still attended each transaction, that was merely because of the fact that money changed hands) — he was also a member of the Elks, a big three-story stucco building on Marshall Avenue, four blocks from the levee. Like Dante's Hereafter it was in three parts, one part to a story. The top floor was a ballroom; the second contained reading and billiard rooms; the bottom floor was honeycombed with card rooms — Paradiso, Purgatorio, and Inferno. In this last, men sat at white-clothed tables under cones of diamond-blue light. Hugging cards to their chests and hunching their shoulders, their faces expressionless, they resembled corpses propped in their chairs. Cigars and cigarettes raised steely plumes, forgotten, and the only sounds were the whispering slither of cards being dealt, the clicking of chips when they ante'd or bet, and the dispassionate, monosyllabic language of poker: "Raise. Call. See you. Pass. I'm out."

Here in this sterile, clicking hades, Drew learned something else about the people he had moved among. Just as his contempt was reaching its highest, based on seeing them in the congenial, somehow false, Kiwanis atmosphere, he discovered that they were the best poker players in the world. They took him quick, who had cleaned out a whole boatload of officers intent on getting nest-eggs at a time when poker was the one interest, the one occupation, even, of the westbound AEF. So he gave it up; he moved on to the hearts game always in progress in one of the corner cells of the honeycomb. He found a new respect for his new associates. From now on, even at the Tuesday noontime gatherings, he was not so quick to look at them askance.

Then it was October, nearing the anniversary of his arrival. The days were getting shorter. And suddenly the bottom fell out of the market. Everyone knew it was serious, everyone said so; but no one really believed it. They saw it merely as a culmination of the long Republican rule, and they told themselves they had expected it. Now that the big-time money men had learned a lesson, the market would stiffen and climb again on a firmer basis. So they said, incurably optimistic. Yet there was a scrap of doggerel they were repeating, grinning while they recited:

> *Hoover blew the whistle.*
> *Mellon rang the bell.*
> *Wall Street gave the signal*
> *And the country went to hell.*

In the middle of all this, Tilden advised Drew that it was time for him to join the country club. "It's your next move," he said. He spoke in a conspirator's undertone, adopting the manner he reserved for these discussions with Drew about his progress at the bank. Sometimes he actually spoke behind his hand, like a boy engaged in a game of Cops and Robbers.

"I cant afford to," Drew said.

"You cant afford not to," Tilden told him. They were in the restaurant; they came here once a week for what Tilden called a Progress conference. Soon now Drew would be leaving the bookkeeping department. He had done well there, as well as in the teller's cage; even Mr Cilley had grown fond of him. Now that he was about to move up again, Tilden told him, he would have to assume various — a — social obligations that went with having a desk out front and talking with customers on a more or less equal basis. Membership in the country club would be a good beginning.

Drew's objection that he could not afford it was based on an exaggerated respect for the clubs he had visited over the country during the three-year 'look round'; anything so desirable was sure to be expensive, so much so that he had never been able to bring himself to the point of asking the cost. When Tilden explained the requirements for membership — possession of a two-hundred-dollar share of stock (which he would sign over to Drew, and which Drew would sign back over to him as soon as he was a member) and agreement to pay monthly dues of five dollars and fifty cents — Drew at first was amazed and then delighted. Then a reaction set in: he was somewhat disappointed too, as a result of finding that one of his great desires was cheap after all.

While Tilden talked, continuing to explain, Drew noticed a new hand-lettered sign behind the counter.

COFFEE 5¢
NO WARM UPS

If the bankers and brokers, the money men North and South, believed this market collapse was something 'temporary' — "A readjustment. Now watch it go up again" — the restaurant owner at any rate thought otherwise; he was retrenching, digging in for a siege. A year from now it would be: *Coffee 5¢. Free warm ups. Tell your friends.* Tilden had paused and was looking at him expectantly, waiting for him to reply. Drew started. "I'll be glad to join," he said.

"I'll arrange it this week then," Tilden told him.

As a member of the club he took up golf. Soon he became quite good at it, being seeded number three on the Bristol team within a year of the day he played his first nine holes. There was nothing really unusual about this, not from his point of view. He simply would never have taken it up in the first place if he had not intended being serious. He approached golf with the same intentness he brought to everything, including the courtship of Amanda Barcroft. No diversion remained merely a diversion in his hands, and thus he never really had one. Which was all right too; he never would have been happy otherwise, knowing he could not afford it — not because of the cost in money, but because of the cost in time. He had come a long way, still with far to go, and Time's chariot always rumbled at his back.

He also attended the Saturday night dances, the get-togethers held nominally in the ballroom though actually they spread wider, onto nearby greens and tees and into the back seats of automobiles parked hub to hub along the gravel driveway, where husbands huddled with other husbands' wives, relaxing from a six-day stretch at the office. Up East the jazz age was over. Down here it had started late and it lasted longer, into the early Thirties. Middle-aged men, with rumpled shirt-fronts and hair broken over their foreheads and eyes, still borrowed the orchestra leader's baton, and women in last year's knee-length dresses still did the shimmy.

Drew moved among them, affable, urbane, drinking his share of the bootleg corn which he soon learned not to gag on. They knew of his courtship and surmised what it was based on; they knew that the major had routed him and they suspected why he had taken up residence here. It gave him a certain romantic air which the women found attractive. They wanted to comfort him. But he did not stroll with them on the links or sit with them in cars; he kept strictly to the ballroom, careful to dance at least twice each night with the wives of the bank's best clients. That was where he first saw the rich young blind man, Jeff Carruthers. That was where he first saw Amy, the blind man's wife.

5. Another Courtship

However, it was almost six years before he knew them by more than name. This was not so much because they were 'exclusive' (though they were — as much, at least, as anyone in the Delta ever could be) as it was that they were gone: first to Carolina for Jeff's father's funeral in the spring of 1930, soon after Drew joined the country club, and then to Europe. Josh Carruthers died at the breakfast table; he was sitting bolt upright, his jowls oozing over the sharp edge of his collar; "Pass the sugar," he was saying, angry at having to ask for it, when suddenly, like a jointed doll whose spinal string has snapped, he slumped forward, upsetting his coffee, cup and all, into his wife's lap. It was as if he had thrown it and at first she thought he had, for he had been subject to such fits of temper since his prostatectomy three years before; her presence was an affront, an unanswerable challenge. But just as she was about to run, she saw his hand jerk toward the pocket where he kept the little nitroglycerin capsules and he was dead before she reached the telephone.

Jeff and Amy got there in time for Amy to take one look at him before the casket lid was closed. She remembered her uncle as being above the average size, seeing him in her mind as he had seemed to her in childhood, replacing her father. But now he looked cramped and small in the satin-lined box, as if in death he had gathered into himself; the aura was gone and the cockatoo crest had wilted and thinned, not white but a dirty yellow. The undertaker, patting rouge on the strangely pointed cheekbones and arranging the mouth in a frown — he felt that a frown was more dignified than a smile: he always buried his moneyed clients frowning — had transformed what was left into a caricature of what had moved and breathed and worn the aura.

"Whats he like?" Jeff said beside her, one hand on the rim of the box, crowding close as if for a better look.

"Like always," Amy said, and they turned away.

From time to time, while they waited for the minister to begin, the widow would rise from her chair and cross the room to the casket. Looking down through a mist of tears, she would put out her hand, wrist stiff, and pat the corpse's forehead, stirring the little wilted plume of hair. "Poor you," she kept saying; "poor you." Then the eldest of her three stepsons by the dead man's first marriage (two of whom were older than she) would come forward and take her arm and lead her back to her chair. Soon, though, she would be up again, at the casket, her face wrung with grief. "Poor you; poor you."

"I wish she wouldnt *do* that," a voice said, loud against the silence. Turning, Amy saw that it was the youngest of the three stepsons. Past forty, he had an infantile, indeed a stupid face. He was the brains of the business now. "Tell her to leave him lone," he said, like a spoiled child when a visitor plays with his toys.

Then the minister rose and began to pray. At first the drone was punctuated by strangled sobs, but soon the widow controlled herself or perhaps was merely exhausted; there was only the murmurous monotony of words all run together, rising and falling. Above the mantel the portrait of the grandfather, the patriarch, looked down in his middle-aged prime, the mouth not so much cruel as sardonic, the eyes clear blue, one hand grasping the carved knob of the chair-arm like a claw; this was his son they were gathered to bury. A fine strong man, the minister was saying. By such was the nation built, made powerful. "Amen," he said, and Amy believed for an instant that she saw the portrait smile.

The family filed out and the pallbearers took position by the door. Coming down the sidewalk toward the hearse, two of them to each of the six silver handles, they staggered with their burden; lines of strain appeared at the corners of their mouths and the cords of their necks stood out, as if the old man had all his gold with him in the box. At the cemetery, when the patented rollers slacked the straps and the coffin began to sink, the widow suddenly pitched from her chair, her knees on the bright green artificial grass at the lip of the grave. The two older stepsons, flanking her, leaned forward and caught her arms. "A fine display," the youngest said from down the line. "She thinks she's back on Broadway where he found her."

Afterwards, at the conference when the family lawyer read the will, she was quite different. She had her own lawyer there — a young Jew, though her husband had been violently anti-Semitic in his old age. Her grief was over, apparently consumed by its own violence, like some highly inflammable, highly volatile substance that leaves not even ash or smoke. At forty-two, strapped and corseted, she was still Venus-shaped, with breasts a little smaller than (but quite as hard as, and curiously even shaped like) footballs; the paraffin injections had been continued and increased. Her hair had not changed either; it had the same hard bright metallic glint, as if each strand had been burnished individually with brass polish — you could smell it, or you believed you could, oily and acid. But her eyes were no longer dewy. Having watched her husband die, she was afraid she too would die like that some day. Meanwhile she was determined to enjoy her inheritance: her *earned* inheritance, she said, intending the emphasized word as a reproach to the stepsons, who had done nothing to get the money but be born. She wanted more than was left her in the will.

Her lawyer did the talking, apologetic and deferential. "We

dont want litigation," he kept saying. This was his trump card and he played it periodically. "Who can say, gentlemen, how long the estate would be tied up once we let it get into the courts?"

Jeff and Amy did not much care what settlement was made. Nor did the two older brothers, one of whom was a model-railroad enthusiast and the other an alcoholic, both to the exclusion of other interests. The youngest did the arguing, the holding out: he spoke with the authority of comparative virtue and outrage. Yet finally he gave in, as he must have known at the start he would have to do. The widow — Mama — won all she had asked at the outset, and something in addition for her lawyer, who had earned it. This was six months later. Jeff and Amy got a million dollars; anyhow Jeff did. They came home to Briartree on a hurried packing trip, and one week later took the train back East and sailed for Europe.

They sailed in August and were gone five years. Now there was no more waiting for dividends or quarterly payments, which usually had been spent by the time they arrived. In a perverse application of *noblesse oblige* — which they translated as an obligation inherited by the rich to behave as the poor expected, if only for the sake of giving the poor an opportunity to envy the rich by reading of their doings in the highlife magazines — it seemed wrong not to spend at least a part of it flamboyantly. Mississippi gave scant opportunity for such spending, Carolina not much more. So they sailed for the old world, after the honored custom, and it was flamboyant enough for the most avid reader of the slick-stock magazines whose photographs gave an impression that their subjects' wardrobes were limited to riding clothes, evening wear, and abbreviated swimsuits.

It was a strange interlude in a strange marriage. Some of their experiences got back even to Jordan County, in one garbled form or another. In Paris (though he had just come four thousand miles from the river where it was born, though Bessie Smith herself had sung at a Negro dance ten miles from Briartree while they were packing for their trip abroad, and though Duff Conway, the greatest horn man of his time — for whose scratched and worn recordings Jeff was to pay as high as fifty and sixty dollars apiece — had been born and raised in Bristol, son of the cook in the Barcroft house on Lamar Street) Jeff discovered jazz. He fell among the cultists, the essayists on the 'new' American rhythms, including the one of whom Eddie Condon, when asked for an opinion, later said, "Would I go over there and tell him how to jump on a grape?" From Paris on, wherever Jeff and Amy went their record collection went too, packed in hundred-and-fifty-pound cowhide boxes that made the bellboys earn their tips. The phonograph would be set up, the boxes opened — Jeff had the contents cataloged in his mind — and from then on, as long as they stayed, their wing of the hotel would pulse with the thump and throb of drums, the wail of clarinets, the moan of saxophones, the scream of trumpets, all building up to a climax known as 'ride out.'

In Vienna they both underwent psychoanalysis, but it was a failure: the doctor was a small, squeak-voiced, almost hairless man, and since neither could effect a transference they moved on. In Brussels Jeff broke a leg in a taxi collision and lay for a month on a hotel sunporch, playing records, his leg suspended in a traction device. When it had almost knit he broke it again, stumbling and crawling the length of the suite because he thought he heard Amy in the bedroom with a man who was undressing her and calling out the name of each article of clothing as it came off. Jeff might at least have wondered how she came to be wearing six pairs of stockings, for when he managed to push the door ajar the 'man' turned out to be a deep-voiced chambermaid helping Amy get up the laundry list, and Jeff spent another month with his leg in traction. In Italy there was trouble with the carabinieri — something to do with disrespect to the State; they never understood just what, except that Amy had got into some sort of argument with a customs official about the jazz collection and called him a goddam spick. Back home the election was over; the country had a new president: 'Mr Roosevelt' he was called at first, then 'Roosevelt,' then 'that Roosevelt,' and finally just '*he*' or '*him*' by mouths that twisted bitterly on the pronoun, for the westering boats were crowded with expatriates — "A traitor to his class," they said. By then the new inheritance tax laws had been enacted; Jeff and Amy heard what they had escaped and, looking back, saw that old Carruthers had been a businessman to the last: he had even died on schedule, financially speaking. They were in Berlin when Hindenburg appointed a chancellor; Amy had seen him in Munich the year before, on a café terrace drinking beer with a group of men wearing trenchcoats in clear weather; "He looks like Charlie Chaplin," she had said, and the waiter had smiled as if he knew a secret. In the Swiss Alps there was trouble about a ski instructor, a tall wide-shouldered Austrian browned by snowglare. This time it was no deep-voiced chambermaid heard in the night and Jeff had wanted to fight him. "A blind man?" the instructor said. "Fight a blind man? Excuse me, Sir — and Madam," he said, standing beside the bed; he made a shallow bow, quite dignified, and sidestepped Jeff and went out, walking naked down the hall with his clothes in his arms, including ski boots. Jeff sat on the bed and began to weep. For a while Amy watched him over the edge of the sheet, her face solemn, her head cocked sideways, speculative, bemused. Then she tried to comfort him, stroking the furry cap of hair through which the windshield scars showed.

"Seeing Europe — " Jeff said bitterly, wagging his head. "All I'm doing is collecting a bunch of stinks. I want to go home."

"Youre just wrought-up," Amy told him. Her arm was across his shoulders now. "It's been too long. Dont you want me to get you a girl somewhere? Or a boy? I will."

Jeff raised his head with a quick motion like a skittish horse. For a moment it was as if he were looking at her, except that his eyes had lost the habit of focusing. "Youre evil, Amy." He hid his face in his hands. "Youre wicked; youre all the way evil."

But they did not go home quite yet. They went to the South
of France; summer had arrived down there and they could
catch up on their sunbathing. Here was the scene of the final
European incident. Their hotel was near Cannes, toward Juan-
les-Pins. They had been there a month, both well toasted by
then, and one day they were crossing the terrace when they
heard a voice cry *"Baby!"* — "It's *Mama*," Jeff said, and Amy
turned and saw her coming toward them, bearing her high hard
bosom like arms to the fray.

She had changed very little, you thought at first, until you
looked closer and saw that she had changed indeed. Her skin
had a hard high polish as if it had been glazed by some ceramic
process in the oven of fast living. Powder lay lightly upon it,
ready to be blown or flicked away as from a porcelain surface.
"And Amy! Child!" she cried, closing in. She moved within a
circumference of scent — Chanel Number Whatever, Amy
thought: it struck them across their faces in a gust, while the
widow was still ten feet away. "How wonderful! I want you
to meet . . ." She looked around. "Where are you? There. — I
want you to meet Crispin." She had him in tow; he was being
sucked along in her rearward vacuum, like a leaf behind a
speeding truck.

He was slight and olive-skinned, with a face as smooth as an
egg, small blue-white teeth like a child's, and a tiny mustache
— a señorito, a refugee from Spain. His sideburns ran down
almost to his jawbone. He wore thin-soled gunmetal pumps so
tight on his feet that the knuckles of his toes showed through.
Jeff heard about him from the widow while they were alone
together on the beach, she under two umbrellas, wearing an
ankle-length wrapper pinned close at the throat and a pair of
enormous smoked glasses that gave her a rather startling aspect
under a flop-brim hat — hardly an inch of flesh was exposed
to the sun, even by radiation — and Jeff out on the dazzling
sand, generally face-down to keep from sunburning his eyeballs. Amy and Crispin would be off somewhere shopping; the
widow had recommended him as an adviser in the selecting of

women's clothes. She made no pretense as to their relationship. "I'm supporting his whole family and it's worth it. You mightnt think so at first glance (— *I* didnt) but I tell you, baby, there never was a man like that before. European to the fingertips. You know what I mean?"

Jeff thought he did know what she meant: so much so, in fact, that he was not surprised at what developed. He was not even much outraged — certainly not to the extent his actions seemed to indicate. He merely did what he had promised himself he would do, back at the time of the incident involving the ski instructor. That was when he bought the pistol he had carried in his phonograph ever since.

He waited until he was sure, or almost sure. Then one afternoon he and the widow were down at the beach and when a waiter came soliciting orders for drinks: "Here," Jeff said, speaking with the strained voice of a man who turns at last to face a crisis he has steeled himself to meet. He rose, brushing sand from his knees and chest. He put on a terrycloth robe that resembled a burnoose. "Back directly," he told the widow (but she was asleep behind her glasses) and laid his hand on the arm of the waiter, who guided him up the beach and across the stone terrace where a dozen women sat at backgammon and mah-jongg, chattering like so many birds against the more or less constant rattle and clatter of dice and tiles. Jeff and the waiter crossed the lobby to the elevator entrance, where the waiter left him. "Three," Jeff said, stepping into the cage.

"Three," the operator said. The elevator glided to a stop. "Help you to your room, sir?"

"No," Jeff said. He stood alone in the corridor while the elevator sank, a diminishing whine. After a short period during which he stood with his head cocked, hearing nothing, he turned to the right, walked thirty confident steps, then raised both hands like a sleepwalker and proceeded cautiously for six more steps until his hands touched the door at the end of the hall. The key was in the pocket of his robe.

This time there was no voice from an adjoining room to lead

or mislead him. He went straight to the phonograph, lifted the used-needles tray, and reaching into the nest of wires beneath, took out the pistol — a small nickel-plated automatic, one of those models designed to be carried in a woman's handbag. He paused, feeling for the arm of the chair to get his bearings, then stepped forward with his left arm raised, and halted with his hand on the knob of the bedroom door. There was no sound beyond the panel; he did not even know if the door was locked. Yet he threw it ajar as though there could be no doubt on either count, paused for two rapid ticks of Amy's pigskin traveling clock on the bedside table, and stepped across the threshold. He stood barefoot, wearing swimtrunks and the Arab-looking robe, the pistol pointed generally toward the bed. "*Got* you," he said gruffly, like an actor. Still there was no sound. Then suddenly there was: the faint, tentative creak of a bedspring, no sooner begun than stopped. If he had had time to think, he might have doubted that he had heard it. But Amy said:

"Jeff — "

It was a six-shot weapon and he fired six times, as fast as he could squeeze and release the trigger — first at the sound of the little Spaniard's voice: "Mr Crutters . . . Mr Crutters . . . Por Díos, Mr Crutters!" and then at the hurrying patter of thin-soled pumps, thinking: Dear God, he didnt even take his shoes off. Then the room was quiet as before, maybe quieter; the ticking of the bedside clock came through. He stood with the pistol hot and empty in his hand, smelling the burnt powder that swirled and banked around him, a thin, acrid smoke. "Amy?" he said. There was no answer. And suddenly a terrible suspicion came to him. "Was he doing anything unnatural with you?"

Recovered from her fright by now, and knowing the pistol was empty, Amy rose from the floor on the far side of the bed. "Unnatural hell," she said: whereupon, with relief and anger, but mostly from amusement, she began to giggle nervously. Jeff was left wondering; the laughter might have been sobs.

What she said next resolved it, however. The laughter was plainly laughter. "You should have, should have, seen him!" she cried between giggles and gasps. "Running in those dancing pumps with bullets zinging round him!"

Soon there was a knocking at the door: three knocks deliberately spaced, one! two! three! The house detective, Jeff thought. But the shots had not been much louder than handclaps, really, and when Amy drew on her kimono and went to the door it was the widow. She stood there for a moment in her long-sleeved Mother Hubbard, saying nothing, then marched past Amy into the room and began to gather Crispin's clothes from the chair on which he had arranged them so neatly half an hour ago, folding them so that the creases would not be disturbed. Jacket, trousers, shirt, hand-painted tie: they made an absurdly small bundle, like doll clothes, when she turned in the doorway, holding them under her bosom as beneath a protective shelf of rock. She seemed about to speak, but gave them instead a single baleful glare, the smoked glasses like dead black target centers under the flop-brim hat, and then was gone, heels thudding on the carpet down the hall. They never saw her again.

Amy laughed. Pitched on a rising note it reached a certain climax and stopped abruptly, curiously mechanical, incomplete. In the silence that followed they heard the rattle of dice and the clatter of tiles from the terrace four stories below and a buzz of voices all run together, indiscriminate save for an Englishwoman who shrieked at more or less regular intervals: "Two bam! Four crack! East wind!" Jeff, sitting at the low end of a chaise-longue with the pistol still in his hands, listened gravely. He seemed to be trying to find some meaning, some clue. But there was nothing. This was all Europe was to him: a rattle, a clatter, a buzz. "I want to go home," he said.

"Mah-jongg!" the Englishwoman cried below.

She had had enough by then herself; this time they did come home. They landed in New York the last week in August, within a couple of days of the fifth anniversary of their departure. All during the crossing she had kept to her stateroom, indifferent to everything except her seasickness, but landfall morning, suddenly cured, she came on deck. Jeff was with her; they stood gripping the rail. His cap bill dropped a shadow whose rounded edge fell across his upper lip. "Whats it like?" he said, his mouth pink in the sunshine. Ambrose Light was a disappointing bell buoy. Then off to the right lay Coney Island, its ferris wheels and scenic railway distributed in spidery silhouette. The ship's wake described a milky curve, pale on the limitless green, and leaving the no-man's land of sea they entered the harbor where Liberty, gigantic and bland, held up her torch. Ahead the city waited, shining white and vertical, with dissolving and renewing plumes of steam announcing noon; a long gray smear fed by stacks was banked above it like an error on a student's watercolor; this was America, clean as slabs of marble newly quarried and set on end. The ship mooed and the tugs came out and suckled.

Descending the gangplank, then clicking her heels on the concrete quay that passed for the soil of her native land, Amy felt at once an almost mystical elation. After five years of the old world she had returned to the new, where sin was mostly unintentional, or anyhow artless, and covered by a sort of invincible ignorance like that which protected some of the saints when they were wild young men. Mouths were filled with magnificent teeth; the very sidewalks glittered; the taxi seemed to run on silk. When the driver turned his hard, high-blooded American face, speaking out of the side of his mouth with the harsh accent of Brooklyn, Amy shrieked with pleasure: "Jeff!

We're home!" And without waiting for his usual 'Whats it like?' she began to describe all she saw, turning from side to side on the seat and leaning across his knees to peer through the opposite window.

Home, she said. It was a word she seldom used in even its vaguest sense. But the following night, at one of the brassy nightclubs off Times Square, a quartet of young Negroes, in white tuxedos whose satin facings shimmered under the spotlight, sang *Walking in Jerusalem (Just like John)* and halfway through it Amy suddenly reached across the table; she gripped Jeff's wrist, her nails like drops of blood against his cuff. "Let's go home," she said. Jeff thought she meant the hotel, but there was a quality of urgency in her voice. It was not yet midnight. Back at the room she called Pennsylvania Station and made the reservation; she even got most of the packing done that night, though they had all day tomorrow before traintime. That made twice she had said 'home'; but now she meant the Delta, she meant Briartree.

By the first of September, which fell on a Sunday that year, they were there. The trip south had been like traveling backward through time: they left the flare and haze of early fall and rode into late summer, the hottest week of the Mississippi year. All the servants had been kept on; the house was little changed. Amy was somewhat disappointed, though. In her first taste of homesickness she had remembered it as being even grander. Consequently they had no sooner arrived than she was ready to resume her search, her casting about for excitement, and the following Sunday evening they rode up to Bristol, to the country club.

A change had come. They had missed technocracy and the apple sellers, the terrible ten-inch snow of '33, the foreclosures and the rather desperate laughter at poverty jokes. That was all over now, or almost over; at least it was in the process of being over — there was not even a crap game on the terrace. What remained was not so much a true sobriety, however, as it was a lack of franticness; people had the apparent calm that sometimes comes with fright. This was reflected in the dancing Amy saw when she came out of the powder room and took Jeff's arm again. Five years ago the ballroom would have been crowded to the walls—or would have appeared so, at any rate, due to the ubiquity of the dancers prancing tangle-footed, lifting their knees and shaking their shoulders, performing sudden sidelong rushes and unpredictable retreats. But now they made only a handful on the floor. Dancing with an almost comical concentration, stiff-backed like automatons, as if everything depended on precision and economy of motion, they had what Gogol calls a hemorrhoidal aspect.

Whatever else it was, it was certainly dull. Toward the climax of the evening, about eleven, Amy had had enough. She went looking for Jeff. Knowing that he would be in either the locker room or the taproom, she decided to try the latter first, since that would not involve a messenger. Meantime something had happened; people were collecting in scattered groups and talking excitedly. She heard scraps of conversation.

"*Shot* him."

"Shot who?"

"Huey Long."

"*No!*"

It had come over the radio. Then she was past and there was another group, further along with the news and less excited.

"What kind of doctor?"

"Medical doctor."

"Named Wise, you say?"

"No: *Weiss*."

The name was hissed and she went on; Huey Long meant very little to her. For a moment she stood in the taproom doorway, looking over heads and through the smoke. Then she saw Jeff. Smiling, he sat with a tall blond man at a table in front of an electrical music machine equipped with what at first appeared to be some fantastic kind of cow-catcher or radiator grille consisting mostly of glass tubes filled with bubbles in slow motion and neon in all the colors of the spectrum:

juke boxes, people were learning to call them, though Amy had not been back long enough to know this. Dorsey's *Marie* throbbed from it; dawn was breaking and theyd be waking to find their hearts were *aaa*ching, Marie. Jeff had about two dollars' worth of nickels in front of him on the table, and from time to time he would turn in his chair and punch one into the machine, between whiles shuffling them with one hand — he had learned it from a Monte Carlo croupier on vacation at one of their hotels near the Italian border — making two stacks, then one stack, then two stacks, over and over.

Then she was nearer and she saw why he was smiling. The tall blond man was telling a story, something that had happened at the bank. *The* bank, he said: which meant that he either worked in one or owned one. Looking at him it was hard to say which, for though his clothes were good, they were not all that good. Well, anyhow, this lady came for a new checkbook ("She's lost a dozen already this year") but when he reproached her for carelessness (—"Not seriously, you understand: I was only joshing") she told him there was no cause for alarm; she had prepared for such a mishap by signing all the blank checks in advance, so that no unscrupulous person could use them, she said. Jeff laughed. Up to then he had only smiled but now he laughed. It had an odd, wild sound; he laughed so seldom.

"Want to go now?" Amy said. She was beside him and she put her hand on his shoulder, which shook with laughter. Across the table the other man was rising.

"This is Mr Who," she thought Jeff said. "Mr Who: my wife." He turned his blind face from one to the other as he spoke. The tall man was still rising. Then he was up. He bowed and his hair was golden in the smoke.

"Hel-lo," he said.

Mr Personality, Amy thought. She made a sound of acknowledgment — somewhere between Hi and Hm, closer to Huh; it expressed her disapproval clearly enough — and turned to Jeff. "I'm tired. I want to go."

"Ah, sit down. Have a drink."

"Yes — do," the other said.

"No, Jeff. Really."

"Now damn it, Amy —"

But she had turned away. She spoke over her shoulder, carelessly. "I'll get my coat and meet you at the door."

She took her time in the powder room, wondering if Jeff would defy her, perhaps with the other's encouragement. But when at length she came out into the vestibule she found them waiting for her, Jeff with his hand still on the man's arm, though they must have been here some minutes already. Now he was doing the talking, and the other the listening. Amy came past them, reaching for Jeff's wrist. "Thank you, Mr —"

"Drew," the man said, smiling. "Harley Drew."

There was an awkward pause, almost a scene, for Jeff stood with his hand on Drew's arm, reluctant, tugging a bit at the wrist that Amy held. Thus he made a link of flesh between them, and they looked past him at each other. In the taproom she had no more than glanced at Drew, though she had been aware that he was staring, but now they looked directly at one another for perhaps ten seconds. She observed that he wore a light tweed jacket in spite of the heat, one of those new tab collars, and a small-figured foulard tie with the knot pulled tight. His sideburns were a trifle long, as was the hair at the back of his head and on the nape of his neck, which usually here in the Delta men kept shaven. There was something outlandish about him — not uncouth, far from it: but foreign — at least in a relative sense: English or Scandinavian, she guessed. Then she looked down at his hand, extended almost rigid from the arm that Jeff still grasped. The nails were flat and pale, filed close, the cuticle pushed well back; the fingers were rather snub, with a few gold hairs just forward of the knuckles. Without being splayed or callous, it somehow resembled the hand of a workingman. She could imagine it cupping a woman's breast or stroking her rump, administering what was called a going-over.

For once, however, she was angry at such thoughts. She jerked Jeff's wrist. Tipped off balance, he let go of the other's arm, calling over his shoulder as they went out, "Good night"; "Good night," Drew said from inside the door. Not looking back, Amy walked fast and still kept hold of her husband's wrist. He stumbled, finding the gravel treacherous under his shoes. "Take it easy," he said. "For God sake, whats the hurry? Whats the matter?"

He would be thirty in November; Amy was already thirty-two. They had been married for more than eight years, but this was her first taste of jealousy. Beginning that night — though her recognition of it was delayed, as pain may be delayed for a person shot or cut without a warning — her life entered a new phase. At first it moved slow, then fast, like a sped-up film.

Drew was Assistant Vice President of their bank in Bristol, recently promoted from assistant cashier. She saw him sitting at his desk when she went in next day to cash a check, but he was busy with a farmer and did not see her. Or perhaps he did, she thought; perhaps he only pretended not to see her. She turned and did not look again in his direction until she was almost to the door, tucking a sheaf of bills into her purse. When she glanced back she saw that he was looking at her; his face was completely solemn. He smiled and it was as sudden as if he had tripped a switch to make his teeth shine. She went out.

In the course of the next few weeks, without inquiring, she heard a good deal about him. He was forty and unmarried; he was waiting for a girl whose parents had other plans. There was some such romantic situation to explain his bachelorhood and lend him glamor; she never heard the straight of that, for people assumed that you knew all about it; they made only passing references, having long since tired of it themselves. Amanda was the girl's name; "Amanda's waiting," they said. Amy knew that much. But she let it pass; she would not inquire. Whenever she was near him she felt a sharp dislike. He was too smooth, too urban. If she had wanted his kind around she would have stayed in Europe or up East, she told herself.

The slow part lasted better than two years, during which time they were thrown more and more together. Drew was the Carruthers financial adviser, appointed by the bank. He and Jeff had one or two conferences a week: either Jeff would ride into town or Drew would come down to Briartree, his briefcase under his arm. When Amy's shopping days coincided with her husband's in-town conference days, they would go together in the station wagon. (It was the first such car in Jordan County. People would look at it and smile or frown and shake their heads, depending on the extent of their envy or indignation. Quoting Bob Burns, they said the Carruthers were the sort of gentlemen farmers who would put on riding breeches to plant horseradish.) On the way to town Amy would watch the blind man's impatience mount until finally he would be sitting on the edge of the seat, leaning forward with the heels of his hands on the dashboard, perhaps from a desire that his body arrive a split second sooner, perhaps in an illogical attempt to add to the speed of the car by shoving at it. Though this had its comical aspect, it was mainly disgusting, she thought. Then they would arrive and she would escort him to the door of the bank. Later when she came back she would find him calmer, though his cheeks would still be flushed.

The displeasure she felt on those days was nothing, however, compared to what she felt on the days when Drew came down to Lake Jordan. He got there after banking hours and if the conference lasted till dark (which it usually did: Jeff saw to that) he would stay for dinner. At table Amy would watch her husband. Disgusting, she thought as she observed the way his hands trembled with excitement; he could barely hold his fork. If she glanced across at Drew he would smile at her — a conspirator's smile. Then she would leave them and they would retire to Jeff's study, continuing their conference. So they said: but presently she would hear the phonograph blaring jazz and she wondered what went on in there. Granting it was what she rather supposed, she wondered just how far it went. Not far, she guessed. But she wondered.

Drew came to the Briartree parties too, where even Amy had to admit he added to the 'tone' if only in contrast to the planters and the planter imitators. But the parties were different from the ones of six and seven years ago; the guests were fewer — at least they gave the impression of being fewer, for they had that same false sedateness Amy had seen at the club when she first got back. There was beginning to be a sense of history, made immediate by the fact that an English king had given up his throne for a woman: "the woman I love," the king said and they thrilled to hear him say it, huddled about their radios as for warmth. *Romance wasnt dead*, they told themselves. Even in their time such things could happen — and they were on hand, almost a part of it, leaning toward the loudspeakers. Yet there was something weak and sordid about the affair: they could not help but feel this and they were vaguely dissatisfied, knowing it would not have been so in their fathers' and grandfathers' time.

Amy was aware of this, since it went on around her and colored all she saw. Then too there was this situation in her home, this invasion, this alienation not of affection (for there had been no affection from the start) but anyhow of attention: that was it, an alienation of attention. But her reaction was merely a vague dissatisfaction which took the form of increased languidness, which in turn — though there was no one to read it, not even herself — signaled a coming disturbance as plainly as a falling barometer warns of stormy weather. This, then, was the low-pressure lull, the vacuum that invites the wind, and she was at dead center.

Past thirty she was approaching her very prime, the period of smoothest articulation when the flesh of the belly and arms and thighs has softened but has not begun to sag — that was a good five years away, with care. The bobbed hair of the Twenties had grown shoulder length, worn 'page boy' now, with the ends curled under and bangs clipped low on the forehead. Her eyes were darker, as with ripeness, and she had this peculiarity, that when she smiled the corners of her mouth turned down, giving her face that suggestion of 'craft,' of latent cruelty — or anyhow meanness — which men find so attractive on short acquaintance, looking at them across a ballroom, say, or from the pages of a magazine or off the motion picture screen, but which on further intimacy (especially the dreadful, bone-deep intimacy of marriage) they learn to regret and hate and blame for all their woes: the immemorial face, that is, of Lilith or Helen or, in our time, Joan Crawford.

Observe her, then, as she sat on an evening in late February beside a log fire in the living room at Briartree, wearing a turtle-neck cashmere sweater, a tweed skirt, silk stockings, and gillie ties, her chair between two stacks of magazines, one with the top and binding edges neatly squared, the other not so much a stack as a pile, the magazines looking as if they had been dropped all at once from a height, spread-eagle and crumpled. She wet her thumb to turn the pages, going rapidly, hardly pausing for even the illustrations, and when she came to the end of one she tossed it to the right, reaching simultaneously with her left hand for a fresh one from the stack on that side of the chair. From time to time she did pause, but this was not for anything in a magazine. She would raise her eyes and look at the closed door on the far side of the entrance hall — Jeff's study — from behind which, faint and faraway, with an almost subterranean murmur, came the wail and throb of jazz; then she would return to her thumbing. Finally, though, she lifted her chin abruptly, at once alert; the music had stopped — she did not know how long ago. For almost a minute she sat listening to the silence, her mouth drawn in a lipless line. Then suddenly she rose, tossing the unfinished magazine aside. "I'll break it up," she said, and moved to do so, thus demonstrating that what sometimes passes for a deep feminine wisdom, 'intuition,' even forthrightness — the absence of conflicting thought which so often clouds the interval

between conception and execution — may be nothing more
than (as in Amy's case) a lack of mental equipment.

But she had taken no more than half a dozen steps toward
the study door when it came slowly open; Drew stood holding
it ajar. She stopped. For a moment he was looking gravely at
her. Then, smiling, he moved aside and she saw Jeff in the
armchair beside the phonograph, his chin on his chest, both
arms dangling limp outside the chair arms. Fingers curled half
into fists, his hands were just clear of the carpet, one of them
still holding the little complexion brush that he used to dust
his records before and after each playing. He was snoring
faintly and the phonograph lid was raised. "He fell asleep,"
Drew said in a low voice, almost a whisper.

"How long ago?" She said it for lack of anything else, and
when she had spoken she was surprised at the words. They had
the sound of encouraging conversation, which was not at all
what she had intended. Also she had whispered, which added
to the air of conspiracy she believed Drew had been trying for
more than two years to establish between them. What was
worse, she had smiled: was smiling still, returning his smile.
But as soon as she discovered this she stopped.

"I thought I'd leave without waking him," Drew said, ignor-
ing her question.

Then she came forward again, walking slowly, still with her
'I'll break it up' in mind: so that what followed was based not
on desire (though it certainly reached that shortly) but on
something quite the opposite. Drew had turned to take his coat
and hat from the table beside the study door. When he turned
back, surprised to find her standing almost at his elbow, she
smiled at his surprise and they moved together toward the
outer door.

Though she could see that he was intensely conscious of her
beside him down the length of the hall, past the long refectory
table with the two brass lamps eight feet apart on a strip of
velvet the color of dried blood and stitched with gold, it was
only after they reached the door, after Drew's hand was on the

knob and the door was even a bit ajar, clear anyhow of the resistance of weather-stripping, that he turned and looked at her. She stood her ground, quite close; her face had the open-eyed seriousness of a child's. That was when he made his move. With the suppressed despair of a gambler deep in a losing streak, he took hold of her upper arm, feeling beneath the softness of cashmere the resilience of flesh. Amy looked down at the hand, and remembering all she had thought of it the night of the Long assassination, she smiled her slow down-tending smile. When she looked up again she saw that, though he kept his grip, he expected her to strike him; his face was even set for it, jaw muscles bunched, lips tense.

Instead she pivoted on her hips and swayed toward him. Her head thrown back as if in an effort to recover her lost balance, she kept her arms at her sides and would have slid past him and fallen if he had not caught her. They paused, joined from the knees up, she with her head still thrown back, her hair swinging free of her neck and shoulders, and he with a look not of ardor but alarm, made awkward by the burden of his overcoat and hat. Thus they were poised and then she struck; her head darted suddenly forward and her hair, seeking to re-gain contact with her shoulders, flared in a curved spread like the hood of a cobra. Drew was not at all prepared for this. The gleam of wide open eyes came toward him, enlarging, already tilting for the contact — they bumped teeth. It was painful; it was somehow ridiculous too. But then he forgot the pain, the ridicule, for she had raised her hands beneath his coat and was stroking the silk panel of his vest; she was feeding on his mouth.

Afterwards she was to tell herself that she had known from the start, that something had flowed between them at their first meeting. For a moment she thought he was going to take her there in the hall, perhaps on the long refectory table, be-tween the two brass lamps. She was willing, wherever — and the quicker the better, too. Then: 'Not there,' she thought she heard him say, as if he had read her mind. But this was unreasonable, she realized in the same instant, considering the extent to which his mouth was occupied; Drew could not have spoken. The voice returned, louder, and this time she heard the words as they were spoken.

"Who's there?"

They started apart, both heads turning at once, and it was Jeff. Standing in the lamplight just outside the study door, one hand on the jamb, he seemed to be looking directly at them, eyes focused. "Who's there?"

The outer door had swung open of its own accord while Drew and Amy kissed. With one hand she pushed him through; with the other she closed it behind him. Then, turning and glancing down at her feet, she saw his hat lying upside-down on the carpet. "Who's there?" Jeff said again. That made four times.

"It's me." She raised her hand to her throat as she spoke, for she was panting a bit. "I took a walk."

"Where's Harley?"

"*I* didnt see him," she said. She took up the hat and smoothed out the dent where it had hit the floor. "Did you fall asleep or something? And did he run off and leave you?" She came toward him down the hall, placing the hat on the table as she passed. "Dont fret, Jeff boy; he'll be back. I see he left his hat."

$$\triangle$$

It was not so simple for Drew, shoved as he was into the night without even his hat, his overcoat clutched in his arms: a cold night, too, though just as a hand removed from a basin of hot water and plunged without delay into a basin of ice water will not register the change until after a certain lapse, he did not realize this until his blood began to cool. Also there was the problem of starting the car: Jeff would hear it. But that was all right; Briartree's drive sloped down to the lakeside road and his car was already headed in that direction. Careful not to slam the door, he got in, turned the ignition on, pulled the choke half out, and disengaged the clutch. Near the gate he let the clutch in and the engine sputtered and caught. Then it died. "I'm damned," he said. But that was all right, too; he was out on the road by then and it might have been any passing vehicle with an engine failure.

After such delays and problems he settled down for the thirty-mile ride to Bristol, hatless with his overcoat collar turned high about his ears, remembering the taste and texture of her kiss, the scratch of her nails against the silk at his back, the small whimpering sound she made after the shock of contact: Man, she was *ready*, he told himself with elation. It was in his memory now and always would be, that first clench; he drew a certain satisfaction from knowing it was available to him, waiting to be summoned up for warmth the rest of his life on cold and lonely stretches such as this. He even grew philosophical about it, drawing on the experience to deduce broad laws of behavior, attractive because they were at once paradoxical and optimistic. For he had plotted and planned for this from the outset, from the first day he saw her on the links, scuffing about in forty-dollar shoes with the same loose-jointed indolence as the teen age waitresses and shopgirls (whom he also found attractive) in two-dollar 'loafers' with pennies in the flaps. He stopped in his tracks at that first sight of her: Man, thats for me, he had thought. And now she was.

Yet the strange thing was — and here was where he waxed philosophical, striking a paradox — it had come after he had despaired, had given up. Immediately after that first sight of her, now almost eight years ago, she and her husband had gone to Carolina for their inheritance, then to Europe for the five-year celebration. He had met them when they returned, the night Huey Long got his, and at first he had been dismayed at her reaction; he was not accustomed to being disliked. But then, though without much satisfaction, he had told himself it was better than indifference — he could wait; waiting was one of his specialties. Meanwhile he had cultivated the husband, at

the cost of no little displeasure and some distaste, being exposed
not only to long hours of nigger music, which merely bored
him, but also to the risk of being the object of advances the
threat of which really frightened him; he had been that way
about homosexuals all his life, having early formed the notion
that such practices involved a loss of manhood for both parties,
and the fact that he was willing to risk even that (though with
a shudder) was a proof of the extent of his desire. Yet in this
case, apparently his diagnosis had been wrong, for much as the
blind man schemed to get him alone, and often as he succeeded, nothing ever came of it, nothing really fearsome anyhow. Drew gradually relaxed, at least as far as Jeff was
concerned.

When Amy was concerned he never relaxed. He chose what
he thought was the proper approach and followed it. She had
been right in thinking he was trying to establish an air of conspiracy between them, under the blind man's nose so to speak.
That was the approach he chose, and he could not understand
why she refused to cooperate, for the situation was perfect on
both sides. Wives were faithful for one of two reasons: either
they were in love with their husbands ('satisfied' he called it)
or they were 'frigid' — a category with many subtypes, from
lesbians to nuns — and since Amy was obviously neither 'satisfied' nor 'frigid,' it was inconceivable that she did not desire
him; it was a refutation of all he had learned and lived by. Yet
at the end of two years he was obliged to admit this must be
so; he gave her another six months and then, just as he was
about to abandon the whole campaign, it happened. Thus he
returned to the memory of that first embrace, savoring again
the warmth and elation of it. He took one hand from the steering wheel and slipped it inside his coat, over the breast pocket
of his jacket, above his heart, where apparently the warmth
was generated. This time he spoke aloud, his breath fogging
the windshield: "Man, you cant tell about women, no way in
the world."

The lights of Bristol came in sight. As he slowed to enter

the speed zone the traffic signal ceased its lidless, peremptory, alternately ruby and emerald glare, and winked a topaz eye for caution. That meant it was midnight. He turned down Marshall Avenue, then into the Pentecost drive, and parked his car in the converted carriage house which still had the faintly ammoniac smell of old Judge Hellman's matched bays, dead fifteen years. Drew walked back under the porte-cochere, up the steps to his private entrance, and unlocked it with a key on the end of his watch chain. The sitting room was cozy; the grate still held a base of faint red coals. In the adjoining room the bed had been turned down and his pyjamas were under the pillow. He put them on in the sitting room, hanging his clothes on a rack beside the fireplace. The moon had risen late; now as he lay smoking a final cigarette it was framed in the window he had raised at the foot of the bed. Cold air invaded the room and he put out the cigarette and lay warm beneath the covers, his eyes shining in the moonlight. Just before he went to sleep he imitated deep in his throat the little whimper Amy had made, but it was not a very successful imitation and he broke off with a laugh. At the end of two and one-half years his prayers were about to be answered after the flesh. The thing was to waste no time, he thought; strike now. Tomorrow would tell, he said to himself as he sank into sleep.

But when he woke up that was not what he remembered first. Habit, the alarm clock of emotion, caused him to remember it was Thursday — the first Thursday of the month. This evening he would walk on Lamar Street with Amanda after supper. That was the arrangement: the first Thursday of each month. Then he remembered the other; she had come to him in his sleep, big luminous eyes with jazz being played in the background. Strike now, he remembered thinking as he fell asleep. He thought again of Amanda and his first inclination was to forego the meeting; he could say he was out of town or sick or something. But he rejected this. Amanda was still his first concern, his reason for being here, 'protecting his investment': he was not going to be panicked into taking any

risk in that direction. Let Amy wait. She probably was expecting him, but let her wait — most likely it was even better
that way. And having made his decision he felt a sort of pride
in his loyalty to Amanda.

At eight-thirty, brushed and shaved, he entered the dining
room where Mrs Pentecost was seated at the head of the table.
"Mr Drew," she said; "Mrs Pentecost," he replied, both formal;
this scene was repeated every morning. "Sleep well?" "Yes
maam. And you?" "Oh yes," and the cook brought in eggs as
crisp as lace around the edges. Such politeness was repaid not
only in good cooking and lodging (at forty dollars a month,
including maid service); he knew that from the start his land-
lady had gone from friend to friend, singing his praises: "Such
a nice young man, for a Yankee. So genteel." She still did,
though now she even left out 'for a Yankee.' "I feel certain he
must have been well born," she added. "And mind you, I can
tell."

She had in fact a reputation for such insight (in spite of her
unfortunate marriage) and Drew credited her with much of
his success in getting established. Not that he actually needed
her help: he had his position at the bank, once he moved to a
desk up front, to bring him into contact with people, which
was all he ever needed — he who had supplied the handshakes
for a cotton trust — in any situation such as this. And it was
not only charm that won them; it was ability too. The year
spent in the teller's cage and back in the bookkeeping department with Mr Cilley had given him a knowledge of what went
on behind the façade of a bank that was comparable to a
watchmaker's knowledge of what goes on behind the face of
a clock. Tilden frequently had cause to bless the day he hired
him; for not only the women liked him now, the men too preferred to do business with him. No one ever refused a loan
with such graceful regret; no one ever brushed aside small diffi-
culties with such a flattering air of confidence. It was no time
at all before Drew had more than made up for the loss of the
Barcroft account.

Socially his position, though of the highest, was somewhat

anomalous. This was because the whole town knew of his arrangement with Amanda. It had been the subject of much conjecture all that first winter and into the following spring. Then it faded as a topic of conversation, and he had their sympathy. But it kept him off the list of 'eligibles' compiled by the parents of daughters, even when those daughters were in the frantic stage of passing their marriageable prime. He was the extra man at dinner parties, though occasionally he was recruited as an escort for a visitor. In such cases his conduct was exceedingly proper; he gave them no more than a goodnight kiss when he left them at the door, and only then if the girl seemed specially willing and discreet. If, as sometimes happened, one of these discreet, willing visitors returned to Bristol and asked her hostess to arrange another evening with Harley Drew, the hostess would find him confined to bed with 'a touch of flu' or 'just leaving town on business.' He had made it clear from the start that he could not afford to get involved, and this added to the town's respect for him. They admired an existence which, if not monastic, was anyhow faithfully chaste.

What they did not know of was an arrangement he had with one of the waiters in the hotel dining room where he frequently went for the midday meal, usually with business friends and always sitting at the same table, served by the same waiter. "Charming weather," the Negro sometimes would say as he held Drew's chair — in spite of the rain or sleet outside or the press of heat. The friends supposed that this was merely a long-standing pleasantry between them, meaning nothing. But it was a signal, a code: it signified that a new 'girl' had arrived, and Drew could judge the impression she had made by the breadth of the waiter's smile as he said "Charming weather." He averaged a visit a week, whether there was a new girl or not, going up by the service stair at the rear. By now there had been better than three dozen of them, starting with that first Alma eight years ago. They were nearly always fond of him, especially the young ones, the beginners.

Mostly his days were like the one he faced when he rose from the breakfast table on the morning after that first clench

with Amy. At nine oclock he wished Mrs Pentecost good day;
by ten minutes after, he was at his desk. During interviews or
while he sat thumbing through papers he found himself glancing from time to time at the door. He had done this several
times before he realized that he was expecting Amy. Then he
stopped; he did not let himself glance away from his work
again. He told himself he was glad he was not seeing her tonight. Anticipation would have lengthened the day, and much
as he enjoyed his work, he did not like a day that dragged. The
appointment with Amanda, on the other hand, neither added
to nor subtracted from its length.

At eleven oclock there was a National Guard meeting in
Tilden's office, attended by Drew and two other officers on
Tilden's staff. The regiment had been activated two years ago
and Tilden was its colonel; he had been spending more time at
this than at banking, now that Drew had taken hold so well
at the bank. Assistant Vice President really meant Assistant
President; Vice President was merely something that went on
the letterheads. Drew was a captain in the Guard (S-3: 'plans
and training') with a promotion 'in the mill' — a mill, however, that ground exceeding slow. At the meeting the men
addressed each other by rank: Tilden had insisted on this from
the beginning. "None of this Joe and Harley stuff," he said.
"When we're military, lets be *military*." To everyone's surprise — perhaps most of all to his own — he was making an
excellent regimental commander, and he was celebrating his
success by growing a mustache: no mean feat for a man with
as scanty a beard as Tilden had.

The clock on his desk was crowding noon by the time the
meeting broke up (it had had to do with the supply of shoes —
"If nothing else, I want them shod right," Tilden said decisively; he might have been speaking of cattle) so they ad-
journed to the hotel dining room for lunch. By then Drew was
thinking of Amy again. "*Charming* weather," the Negro said
as he held Drew's chair (this was a further refinement of the
code; emphasis on the first word meant a blonde, on the second

a brunette. Red heads, having no coded designation, were kept
for a surprise) but Drew was so absorbed in thinking of Amy
that he did not even look for the breadth of the waiter's
smile — who, as a matter of fact, was beaming his brightest.

Back at the bank Drew caught himself glancing again at the
door. But this time he did not stop; he kept it up till closing
time, expecting her every minute. He got very little work
done. Then, as he watched Rufus lock the door, he had to
admit that Amy was not coming. His reaction was anger: she
had done this on purpose, knowing full well what his reaction
would be. He took what satisfaction he could from the knowledge that tonight, at Briartree, it would be she who would be
watching the door, her anger mounting, and he who would
not arrive.

He cleared his desk, putting the unfinished work in a drawer,
and drove out to the club. Nobody was there but the pro, who
sat in the taproom drinking beer and playing canfield. After
some taunting Drew got him out on the links, which were a
wasteland, sear and deserted, like photographs of the surface
of the moon. They were the only players out in this weather,
and even so they had to share a caddie. Playing for a dollar a
hole, Drew topped a couple of his drives and spent three
strokes in a sand trap. They came down number nine in a chill
blue dusk. Drew's tee shot had gone into the rough. After ten
minutes of searching — by which time night had almost come
and the caddie was mumbling, mutinous and cold — they gave
it up and came back into the taproom. Drew paid the five dollars he had lost with a disgruntled air which the pro interpreted
as anger at losing money, and was at least partly right.

What a day, Drew thought, back again in his sitting room
and looking into the fire. All because of one foxy bitch; "I'll
make her pay," he said aloud. And liking the sound of this he
said it again: "I'll make her pay." There was still half an hour
before six oclock dinner, time enough to bathe and dress, but
he sat looking into the fire. He was still there when the cook
rapped on the door for him to come to dinner. At table Mrs

Pentecost found her lodger less congenial than usual. But then we all have our off days, she thought, darting timid, sidelong glances at the young man as he ate.

There was still time for a bath if he hurried, but he rejected the notion almost savagely, as if that too were some kind of affront, and contented himself with changing his shirt and tie. Then he set out for Lamar Street, on the other side of town. In the beginning these meetings had been once-a-week affairs; later they were reduced to alternate weeks, and at last to once a month. "We must be more and more careful," he had told her, and Amanda had sighed and agreed. Parking his car around the corner he took his accustomed first-Thursday station in front of the Barcroft house. Where the four large oaks had stood, only two remained. One was lost in the big wind of '32, during the bank holiday, the other in the ice storm of the following winter; it came crashing down like a cutglass chandelier, cracking the brittle armor of ice that incased each twig and branch and scattering the pieces up and down the street, where they lay reflecting the early morning sunlight like so many points of fire. The depression years had been as hard on trees as they had on people.

Waiting, Drew became more and more restless, standing with his hands thrust deep in his overcoat pockets and shifting his weight from foot to foot. His breath, which came faster as his impatience grew, made little rapidly vanishing clouds of steam. It seemed to him he had never been so cold, not even up in Canada on the goose hunt that had ended the golden look-round. She might at least have some consideration, he thought with resentment. Just then a tall, narrow rectangle of light flicked on and off; the door had been partly opened and then closed, and he could hear her crossing the veranda. Despite the cold he removed his hat (a lightweight felt too summery for the season, but the other was down at Briartree) and stood holding it in both hands, like a basin. "Evening, Amanda," he said. There was no moon, nor even stars; the night was black. She paused and then came on.

"Good evening, Harley."

6. A Renouncement

They walked and it was as always; he was attentive, cupping
her elbow in his palm when they stepped down or up the
curbs, and handsome — he really got more handsome all the
time. If tonight he seemed a bit distracted, why that was all
right; she understood that men had business worries from time
to time. She had taken to reading the agony column in Florence's paper and there the advice was always the same. Be understanding but not prying; a husband or suitor had a right to
occasional moods after a hard day at the office; that was when
you showed your mettle as a sweetheart or a wife, and dont
think this would go unappreciated when the fair weather days
returned. Then too Drew must be thinking that with another
girl (— and he of course could have his choice) he would be
sitting in a nice warm parlor or at least at the picture show,
not out in the weather like this. The truth was, theirs was so
exclusively an out-of-doors courtship, she never saw him without his hat either on his head or in his hands. It was up to her
to make up for all this with 'understanding.' She understood
that. But it was strange.

"Youve been well, Amanda?"

"Oh yes." The pause that followed seemed longer than it
was. "And you?"

"Oh yes."

They walked and his air of distraction was heavy upon him. Not knowing what to say, she said nothing. At last, however, midway down the second block, he appeared to shrug it off, to pluck up heart, and began to tell of his experiences during the past month at the bank. It was a strange world, mostly humorous by his account. People said and did such funny things in their anxiety for money, and others were so incompetent, so much beyond their depth in the world of finance — like the lady who signed all the checks in case she lost them: he had told her that story twice, saying both times that it happened 'yesterday.' But that was all right; she understood; his life was so dull otherwise, he had to double his jokes. She had her home and family, her sister to feel close to, but he had no one, nothing but his work and these few secret meetings, always with the danger of being discovered.

During all their years of waiting, these walks were what sustained her, and though they had become more and more widely spaced because of the dictates of prudence — first once a week, then every other week, and finally once a month — Drew was no less attentive, no less affectionate, and he always said he was waiting. That was enough. It was not only enough: it seemed to Amanda that he was the one who had the harder time, carrying the anguish of his love through the outside world, among strangers with prying eyes. She had learned that particular form of torment during the first year of their secret engagement. Wherever she went there were the turning heads, the following glances, and the hand-cupped whispers. They had begun to gossip before Drew was in town a week: "Amanda Barcroft's got herself a beau. She slips out to meet him. Yes. They walk together every night, by the dark of the moon." Sometimes she heard them call her poor Amanda and she knew they made conjectures and said they were sorry for her, for most of their talk was based on their dislike for Major Barcroft, his ruthlessly honest business methods and what they called his high-and-mighty ways. However, she heard very little of it. Her marketing trips and her weekly attendance at church were the only times she was actually thrown with the watchers: during the five oclock walks from Cotton Row she and her father were apart from them, she in her identical gray dresses with the pale swatches of lace at her wrists and throat. There was hardly any change in her beyond a certain fixity of expression which the watchers were hard put to identify as either hope or despair. She kept her head up, her eyes to the front, her shoulders drawn well back, and watching her they were reminded that she was her father's daughter. It was as if she were defying them, flaunting what they called her scandal in their faces. Her own face at these times was blank, like an empty page inviting them to read into it whatever they chose, and they were quick to do so; there were almost as many versions of the affair as there were tellers. When it became known around town that the courtship had been thwarted, there was a good deal of talk about that too. But presently they grew weary of it — it was too vague, too long-drawn-out; it palled, much as a popular song will pall with too much playing. She became merely an attraction for strangers being shown the secret, somewhat seamy side of Bristol: "Look yonder. Thats Amanda Barcroft. A young man tried to marry her, but her papa interfered: old Major Barcroft. Now theyre waiting. Maybe youve met him — Harley Drew. He works in a bank."

She had had all that to face, to live with. Also there was her father. But Major Barcroft showed no change at all, neither to the searching eyes of the townsmen nor to Amanda herself. He certainly never spoke of Harley Drew, though it was known that soon after the newcomer went to work at the Planters Bank the major withdrew his account and did no more business there — doubtless on the theory that anyone who would attempt to steal a man's daughter from under his nose would not be likely to hesitate before stealing his money too. Amanda knew nothing of this transaction, but sometimes at the dinner table she would glance up from her plate to find her father looking at her with a coldly speculative expression, and she knew that he was wondering, though he was too proud to question her or mention the suitor's name.

Tonight in parting Drew kissed her at the steps, and that made twice. Usually there were three: once halfway out, once halfway back, and once goodnight at the steps: but tonight he had been so preoccupied with whatever worry was on his mind, he had neglected the first. He made up for it, however. For when he kissed her that second time he whispered with his jaw pressed to her cheekbone and his mouth beside her ear, "These are the hardest years: I know. But never mind. Our time is coming, and we'll make up for them. Just you wait; youll see." With that he turned and left her and Amanda crossed the veranda completely happy, to await the passing of another of those months which, accumulating thus, had amounted to years: 'the hardest years' he called them, though in truth to her they were anything but hard, for she had Drew — if only once a month — and she had the future, and she could imagine what life would be without either.

She had Florence, too —her Albatross, her Old Man of the Sea: though of course she never thought of her as either. Even though she knew that Florence's death was the one event that would make the future Drew painted become the present, she never allowed herself to hope for it, not even in her secret heart. Tonight, returning from her walk with Drew, she shut the outer door and turned at once to the door on the right, entering the room where Florence waited, eager and anticipant as she always was on these first-Thursdays, hands clasped under her chin.

"How is he?" she cried before her sister had time to close the door. Amanda turned with one forefinger on her lips, the other pointed toward the back of the house where Major Barcroft was reading in his study. Florence put her hands over her mouth and drew up her shoulders. "I forgot; I really did. How *is* he?"

"He's fine," Amanda said. "It was just like always."

"Oh Amanda, I'm so happy for you. He does love you, dont

he." This was not a question; it was a congratulatory whisper, and Amanda smiled and nodded, removing her coat. Florence looked forward to these first-Thursday nights as much as Amanda did, for having seen Drew that one time in the hall, she felt that she was engaged in a love affair too, if only by proxy.

Her feet, in shapeless green felt carpet slippers, were propped on the pull-out, and her legs — in contrast to the rest of her body, which had thickened on inactivity — had grown so thin that the lisle stockings hung on them in wrinkled folds. Except for these Thursday evenings, she had retired into herself more than ever. She kept to her sewing and her newspaper, her monthly solace of medicine and religion; the last time she had looked out of her door was when she asked the young man to take Amanda away. Her greatest excitement of the past nine years had been the career of Dillinger, which she followed in her tabloid. He was for her a bright particular star, from the first photo of him handcuffed between two deputies and grinning at the camera, just before he made his wooden-pistol break. Florence had shared all his exploits, cheering him on. But alas, that too had reached an end (on a midsummer day in a theater lobby, betrayed by a woman in red and shot down by what amounted to practically a whole brigade of G-men; "Oh the cowards!" she cried when she read it) and all that was left was a picture of him stretched out dead on a slab in the morgue with a police tag wired to his toe. She had clipped the picture and now she kept it folded in her Bible along with the others, Bonnie Parker, Machine Gun Kelly, and Pretty Boy Floyd — the Billy the Kids and Johnny Ringos of our time.

Her greatest adventure was still in front of her, though. Perhaps she knew it; for from time to time, and more frequently of late, Amanda would see her pause in her work with a sudden, startled expression. Her hand would rise to her breast, lingering there with a slight pressure; she would remain motionless, her head bent in profound and breathless auscultation. Then it would pass and she would return to her needlework or her tabloid. And when Amanda would question her, "What *is* it, Florence?" she would not explain; she would shake her head:

"Oh Amanda — it's the *strangest* thing."

That was the way the years passed in the big gray house on Lamar Street, the three of them circumscribed within a narrowing circle of pride and fear and guarded hope, breathing the close atmosphere of death — a family group, father and daughters, set in an oval frame, reflected in the huge fuliginous pupil of the enormous Bristol eye — until a night in late September, eight months after the one when Drew was kept waiting out in the cold in a summery hat. Florence sat in her chair. Under the yellow, down-funneled glare of her reading lamp the newspaper headlines stood out harsh and bold, shouting the imminence of war along with the reassurances of the diplomats. "I declare," she said, petulant because Munich had disturbed her accustomed reading: "I declare this old Hitler meeting is crowding all the *news* out of the paper."

On the back page, however, she found an interesting item. When she had read it she cried happily, "Oh Amanda, Amanda, here's the most dreadful thing! It happened in Los Angeles; everything seems to happen in Los Angeles. An old man killed a little boy in a rooming house. Then he tried to smuggle the body out in a rolled-up carpet. Imagine. He was walking along the street with it over his shoulder — like this — when somebody bumped him and the carpet slipped off and the little boy's body came rolling out, right there in the busy part of town." She paused, glancing down at the paper in her lap. "He's pleading insanity, it says."

Amanda left her at ten oclock and went upstairs to bed. There were no screams in the night, no cries for protection from the terrible dream-shapes; next morning when she came down she found her sister sitting bolt upright in the Morris chair, her hands folded on the newspaper in her lap and her feet on the cushioned pull-out. In the early morning light the carpet slippers were a bronzy green, like that which gilds the heads of flies in summer. At first Amanda moved cautiously to keep from waking her, but as she backed through the doorway she saw that one of Florence's eyes was open in the steady glare of a sunbeam lanced through a chink in the window blinds. And as she stood there, one hand on the door knob, looking at her sister's face — the jaundiced skin and the deep sooty sockets of the eyes, the arched nose with its dark nostrils lined as if with fur — she thought almost immediately of Harley Drew, wondering whether she should notify him now, by telephone, or wait until after the funeral.

That afternoon the undertaker brought Florence back in a gray steel casket lined with satin — like Malcolm's, only larger — and set her in the parlor where her brother had lain when she and her sister were girls, which she had called her bedroom though it had no bed, and which still smelled of her fumigations though the newspaper calking had been removed from the doors and windows and the room itself had been swept and dusted and aired since early morning when Mr Barnes came and took her away. He had crossed her hands on her breast and combed her hair so that the spiked ends lay against her throat, giving her a softer, more girlish look, far under her actual years. Wearing Amanda's Sunday dress, with touches of rouge at her cheekbones and a hesitant smile that he had stitched in skilfully, she denied by her appearance the lies Bristol had told about her raving behind bars in an attic room.

They were there to witness the denial. They came by avid twos and threes, elbowing each other a bit as they craned about the coffin. "She looks so natural," they said. "My. Youd think she was sleeping, wouldnt you? Wouldnt you?" They were all women. Bearing plates of warm food — a custom held over from the days when no cooking was done in a house where a corpse was on display — they would stand in the high dim hall, examining the furnishings and the cutglass chandelier with the feverish eyes of archeologists breaking into an Egyptian tomb, until Amanda came and received the food and invited them in to view the body. There was a steady procession of them, first a trickle, then a stream, beginning a little after five oclock and continuing into the night. Since the women arriving always outnumbered those departing (some did not leave at all), by dark there was quite a group of them in the parlor. They spoke in low tones out of respect for the dead, their heads leaned toward each other, at once compassionate and prying, officious and perverse, while their husbands returned to supperless homes. Here human cruelty was displayed at its worst, youd say, until you considered the reverse of the medal and saw the possibility of a worse cruelty still: an absence of concern, that is, or even curiosity.

Amanda was kept busy, moving between the front hall where she met the callers and relieved them of their plates — like tickets of admission — and the kitchen where she set the plates in increasing numbers on tables, on the stove, and finally on the drainboard of the sink. In the parlor the visitors were waiting for Major Barcroft to make an appearance, but he disappointed them; he kept to his study. It was a long time — after eight, and the women were still arriving — before Amanda could step out on the veranda and look for Drew beside the oaks. He was not there; she would have seen him if he had been, for moonlight flooded everything. She went back into the house, telling herself that he had waited and then had left in the belief that she would stay indoors tonight.

He was not there the next night either, though she could not have missed him; she came home from the funeral and sat with the major until a quarter to seven, when she took her station beside the oaks. At eight, when he still had not arrived, she came back in and sat again with her father. He was watching her with the coldly speculative expression so intensified that she could almost hear him thinking the words: 'What will she do? What will she do now, without Florence to hold her?' However, this did not give her much concern; she thought mainly of Florence, out there under her raw mound, and of Harley Drew — wondering over and over again why he had failed to come for her now that she was free.

"Good night, papa," she said at last. The major looked up from his book.

"Amanda," he said. The pince-nez flashed once, like a heliograph, and he returned to his reading.

Then, as she was undressing for bed — after a last peep through the window at the oaks standing their lonely vigil in front of the house — she believed she knew why Drew had not come, and it was so simple, so obvious, that she could not understand why it had not occurred to her before; it was just another instance of his delicacy, his consideration for her. He was giving her a grieving time. She fell asleep at last, believing that.

But the third night, when he still did not appear, it was too much; it was more than she could bear. She lay in bed, moonlight shrouding the room with cloth-of-gold, and though she was weary to the verge of nervous exhaustion, she could not sleep. Each time she was about to drop off she was brought wide awake by the sound of his voice calling her from in front of the house: 'Amanda! Amanda!' Twice she got out of bed and went to see, but there was nothing, only the oaks shining in the moonlight. She wanted him now. So next morning she wrote a letter telling him so, and mailed it that afternoon on the way to meet her father on Cotton Row.

Dear Harley —

I know why you have not come and I suppose you are right, you know best. But I don't care what people say, I don't need a greiving time. Come now, I am waiting — seven tonight [deleted] tomorrow night, Tuesday in front of the house. I will go with you anywhere, either here in town or any where.

Amanda

It was on his desk next morning at ten after nine when he entered the bank; Rufus always picked up the mail on his way to work and sorted and distributed it as soon as he had swept and dusted. Drew stood beside the desk with his hat still in his hands, looking down at the stack of mail centered neatly on the blotter. Though Amanda's letter was not on top, he recognized it almost immediately. This was partly because of the old square envelope, duplicate of the one handed him nine years ago in the hotel lobby, canceling the elopement; he even anticipated the heavy, expensive feel of the paper, the way the flap would spring unglued at a touch. Mainly, however, he recognized it because he had been expecting it for four days now — ever since the Friday when he opened the afternoon paper, reading above the fold of Chamberlain's report on the Munich conference ("Peace with honor . . . in our time") and then glanced down at a small one-column headline buried at the lower right: MISS BARCROFT/DIES IN SLEEP. *Florence Barcroft, daughter of Major Malcolm Barcroft, 214 South Lamar Street, died in her sleep of a heart failure some time last night. Miss Barcroft, who was forty-one and a life long resident of Bristol, had been confined . . .* But he did not go on with whatever facts the reporter had been able to gather. She was dead: that one fact was enough. He put the paper down and turned his head, bemused. Major Barcroft had won the monstrous horse-race.

Four days later he was in no hurry to read the letter either, for he had anticipated its contents as well as its arrival: 'Why havent you come for me? Why are we waiting, Harley?' or some such words. He pushed the stack of mail aside and it toppled, spreading fanwise off the blotter, the thick, square envelope left uppermost, displaying his name like a cry of distress: *Mr Harley Drew, Planters Bank, City.* He sighed. His original plan had been to leave if this happened, to catch the next train out if Florence died first; he had told himself he would go without explanation or farewell. But now two things had come to pass that he had not figured on when he made those early calculations. First, he had done so well at the bank that he could not afford to leave, especially considering the fact that Tilden had no child, no proper heir and successor.

And second — chronologically, but first in importance, in its bearing on this — a terrible thing had happened to him. He had fallen in love.

It had begun with that clench eight months ago and the hatless cold drive home, had continued with the following long day's wait at the bank, the first Thursday in February, and next morning — Friday — he was at his desk, in conference with an applicant for a loan. "Mr Drew: telephone," someone called from down the line.

"Excuse me." He took up the phone. "Hello," he said crisply, businesslike, straightening the crease of his upper trouser leg as he crossed his knees. He even had time to uncross his legs and polish the already gleaming tip of one shoe against his calf.

" — Why didnt you come last night?"

"Maam?" Having said it, he winced; he felt like a fool. This was the first time he had heard Amy's voice over the phone, disembodied, and he had been so engrossed with the applicant that he had neither recognized it nor understood the words. But now he did.

" — You heard me."

"Yes. Well . . ." The man across the desk was watching, big and thickset in a mackinaw, with two days' gray stubble of beard, and it seemed to Drew that he was smiling at his discomfort. "I'll call you back. Where are you?"

" — Where would I be? I'm home. But you dont need to call; just come to supper. Seven-thirty." Amy said this not as if she were asking him, but rather as if she were acceding to a request or answering a general advertisement in the newspaper, under the Personals: *Gentleman available as dinner guest, with possible further services in addition. Call H. Drew, Planters Bank, this city.*

"That will be fine," he said coldly, and just as he was about to relent and thank her, the line clicked and then went dead; she had hung up in his face. Drew replaced the receiver, looking blankly at the man in the mackinaw. "I'm damned," he said.

"How was that?" the man said. Drew's eyes came into focus. "Excuse me," he said, all business again. "Now then, as to collateral —"

This turned out to be merely a prolog to the first act of a comedy of errors, one of those farces of mistaken identity and cross-purposes which sometimes are funny to the observer but which at the same time are invariably painful to the persons involved, the actors. Drew was at Briartree shortly after seven oclock, bathed and shaved, brushed and groomed, but still wearing the summery hat he had worn last night on Lamar Street. The houseboy answered the bell and Drew came past him into the hall. "Who's there?" he heard Jeff say from the study. Amy was nowhere in sight.

"Harley," he said, and Jeff appeared in the doorway. He seemed pleasantly surprised.

"Hello hello. Youre just in time for dinner. Come on in. Amy — " No answer. "*Amy!*"

"Yes?" Her voice came from the living room, but Drew looked around the door and did not see her.

"Tell them to lay another place for Harley."

"Youre up: you tell them," she said, and then he saw her. Only her legs and one arm were visible past the side of a fan-back chair drawn up to the fireplace at the far end of the room; she was hunched deep in the cushions, turning the pages of a magazine. He noticed, however, that she had put on high-heeled pumps and black silk stockings, and she wore a diamond bracelet on the wrist of the arm he could see. Jeff laid his hand on Drew's sleeve and they went into the study. Presently the houseboy returned, announcing dinner, and as they entered the hall and Amy got up from her chair and came toward them, Drew saw that she was wearing a black taffeta dinner dress. He took all this — the pumps, the bracelet, the dress — as a sign that he had been expected, though she continued to make him play the role of an unbidden guest.

Except for an occasional sidelong glance, interrupted as soon as Drew returned it, this was no different from all those other evenings the three of them had spent down here at Briartree. He might almost have doubted the phone call that morning and even the kiss exchanged here in the hall two nights ago. The biggest difference was that when he left, saying good night to Jeff at the door soon after eleven — Amy had gone to her room an hour ago — he took two hats. Back in Bristol, preparing for bed before midnight, he shook his head and muttered to himself. Was this some kind of game she was playing, some kind of cat-and-mouse affair? Whatever it was, he did not like it; he didnt like it at all.

But next morning — Saturday — Amy was on the phone again, and this time he was not in conference; he could talk. She said, "It didnt go so good, did it?"

"It certainly didnt."

After a pause they both began to speak at once:

"If you — "
"Wellp — "

There was another pause. This is pure crazy, Drew thought. But she spoke first: "Come Monday night. Same time. We'll try again."

"Now *wait* a minute . . ."

"You want to come or dont you?"

"Yes, but — "

"Well then, come. All right?"

"All right . . ." And again he was holding a dead phone. He put it back on its cradle, shaking his head and thinking of the hotel girls, forty-odd of them over the past nine years, who asked only a little money and whatever signs of affection he felt he could spare.

Monday was even less different, up to a point. She had not even dressed; she was wearing the low-heeled shoes, the tweed skirt, and the cashmere sweater of all those other nights. Drew came early, bringing his briefcase, and Jeff urged him to stay for dinner — so at least this time he was there as one invited. Soon after nine they were sitting in the living room and Jeff excused himself, going into the study where his ground-floor bathroom was. As soon as he had closed the door behind him, Drew turned to Amy. But she had already begun to speak. "This is no good, is it?"

"No," he said promptly. "It isnt."

What followed was not really a pause. It just seemed so because of his surprise at what she said next; it took him a while to assimilate the words. "Are you free weekends?"

"I can be," he said.

"This weekend?"

"Yes."

"I'll come by the bank. What time?"

"What time what?"

"Do you get off."

"Four oclock, about." He had a feeling of being led by the hand and he did not like it; he would have preferred to be doing the leading himself.

"All right. I'll pick you up."

"Friday?"

"Saturday."

"Friday," he said.

"All right, Friday: at four."

Then suddenly she looked doubtful, as if she had just remembered something. She was about to protest and he was prepared to counter it (having snatched the lead he was determined not to yield the smallest point) but Jeff returned and the three of them sat together about the fire. It was as always; it was even as if he had fallen asleep and dreamed the conversation, for Amy gave him not even a sidelong glance. Presently she yawned and went upstairs. Drew rose and watched her go, the two-way swing of her skirt. 'Look back!' he told her in his mind, attempting telepathy; but she passed up the stairs, eyes front, and out of sight. Not long afterwards Drew rose again, saying he had a hard day at the bank tomorrow. Jeff helped him into his coat.

He made arrangements to be gone for the weekend: "A duck hunt over in Arkansas," he told Tilden. The days limped by

and at last it was Friday; he came back early from lunch and
had his desk cleared by three. At a quarter to four he put on
his hat and coat and took his post at the top of the concrete
steps in front of the bank. At four she had not come; he was
pacing up and down the portico, thinking again of those hotel
girls whom he saw at *his* convenience, not theirs, and whom
he had not visited for more than a week now, saving himself —
for what? for pacing up and down past the fluted pillars like
an actor depicting rage, back and forth across the proscenium,
muttering imprecations. The sky was lowering, livid, like the
whorled surface of molten lead when it cools. At a quarter past
four Rufus put his head around the door. "Mr Drew. It's somebody wants you on the foam."

Inside he said, "Yes?" gripping the phone with both hands.
He was trembling.

"It's me . . ."

"All right. What now? *Now* what?"

"I cant come."

"Why? Why not?"

"It's Friday," she said.

He waited for her to explain, but she stopped as if this were
all the explanation needed. He took a deep breath. "*I* know it's
Friday. I ought to: Ive been counting the days. Whats Friday
got to do with it? — except of course it's when we said we'd
meet."

"Friday was your idea. . . . I thought maybe I could, this
once, but I cant. I never go *any*where on a Friday; I had a
friend was killed once in a car wreck on a Friday."

"So?" he said coldly, glaring down at the mouthpiece as if
he could see her in the Bakelite cup. "I had a friend was killed
once on a Thursday, but it doesnt keep me home." He paused
and a heavy hum came over the wire. "Hey!"

"Yes?"

"I thought youd hung up."

"No: I'm here." There was another pause. This time he
thought he heard chuckling. Was she laughing at him? Was

this some more of her cat-and-mouse carryings on? She said, "Anyhow . . ."

"Yes?"

"Anyhow, I cant go." She wasnt laughing.

"How about tomorrow, then?"

"Tomorrow?"

"Yes. At ten oclock."

"In the *morn*ing?"

"Yes."

"Oo, that sounds kind of immoral," she said. A pause. "Anyhow, I always sleep till ten."

"All right: eleven."

"Well . . ."

"Yes?"

"All right. In front of the bank."

"Promise," he said.

"Promise what?"

"Youll be here."

"I'll be there."

"Promise — "

"I promise," she said.

This tells the tale, he said to himself that night as he undressed for bed. If she's not there tomorrow I'm through trying.

He did not mean it; he knew he did not mean it — he was just snatching at straws of self-respect. But he was not called upon to put it to the test, for to his considerable surprise she was waiting in the station wagon in front of the bank when he came out next morning at eleven. "You drive," she said. She slid over, wearing another in her sequence of cashmere sweaters and tweed skirts, and he got in beside her. The door closed with a thick, expensive *cluck*, not at all like the sound of his Ford, and the steering wheel had a well-greased, ponderous feel, like the wheel on the door of the big vault at the bank.

"Where are we going?" she said. She watched him but he was busy threading traffic. The car drove like a boat.

"Where did you *say* you were going?" he said at last. They were on the highway now, entering open country where last year's cotton stalks stood bare in a mizzling winter rain. All the cabin doors were closed; each chimney let fall a feathering of smoke.

"Shopping. In Memphis."

"Lets go there, then."

"All right." She settled back and closed her eyes. "Wherever you say. *I* dont care. I'm not due home till tomorrow."

They did not make it all the way to Memphis. Just short of the Tennessee line, Amy cried "Look there!" — she was pointing and he saw neon glowing rosy through the mist. CABINS. BIDE-A-WEE; then he was past it. He turned around and came back. *Beauty Rest Beds. $2. No ups* was printed in smaller letters at the bottom.

Inside, the cabin had that clammy, penetrating, almost liquid cold peculiar to houses uninhabited in winter. Following the attendant, they breathed steam. He tripped a switch and an overhead bulb, screwed unshaded into the center of the ceiling, came on with a sudden yellow glare that made them wince and shield their eyes. Presently, when their pupils had shrunk to pinpoints, they saw that the room contained a dresser of birch veneer, one split-bottom chair, and a bed already turned down, with dank gray rough-dried sheets, two cotton blankets, and a tufted spread of a shade called nigger pink. The attendant knelt and lit a butane heater; it hissed on a single note which, after continued hearing, seemed to mount to a scream — you kept waiting for it to pause for breath. Their only luggage was Amy's overnight bag. Though the attendant apparently saw nothing unusual in this, he paused beside the door. "It's in advance," he said mournfully, gray-haired, wearing steel-rim spectacles. Drew gave him the two dollars and he left them alone in the cabin. It was not at all as Drew had imagined it so often this past week.

Attempting to hide his anxiousness, he moved about the room: first to the dresser, then to the bed, testing the mattress — the sign had not lied; the mattress was one of those

patented inner-spring models called 'a fast-feeding work bench'
by Negroes — and at last to the door of the bathroom, a
cubicle partitioned into one corner. "You want to go in here?"
he said. These were the first words he had spoken since they
were alone. Amy looked. The seat on the commode was split
and a coffin-shaped stall was lined with galvanized metal; the
shower head dripped steadily, like the tick of some enormous
clock.

"Good God *no*." She said it fervently, with a sort of determined revulsion, standing on the other side of the room and
watching him. This made him nervous. Now he had what he
had been wanting: he was in charge. Yet he felt awkward.
Nothing was going at all the way he wanted. It was like the
fumbling honeymoon of runaway adolescents.

"Then I will," he said. "You go on, get in bed; I'll be right
out." This was said bravely enough, but as he entered he
stumbled over the raised sill, more conscious than ever of
seeming ridiculous, and closed the door behind him. Undressing in the dark, he gave her plenty of time — too much in
fact; "Hi!" she called and he opened the door, barefoot in
pale blue drawers and a sleeveless undershirt, his toes curled
away from contact with the icy linoleum. The light was still
on and again he had to wait for his pupils to shrink. At first
he thought the bed was empty. Then he saw that she was
drawn up in a ball, knees under her chin; only the top of her
head showed from under the covers. Her clothes, thrown at
the dresser, had landed mostly on the floor beside it. "Hurry!"
she cried, teeth chattering, voice muffled under two blankets
and the spread. "Hurry! Come on in! Come on; I'm freezing!"

They returned to Bristol the next afternoon and Amy let
him out in front of the bank; his car was parked in back. He
stood watching her go, then drove home through the quiet
Sunday streets. Thus his prayers had been answered after the
flesh, after the week-long comedy of errors. He feared it might
be an end as well as a beginning, for as he stood watching her
go she had not looked back and they had made no definite

arrangements for another meeting. He feared it was probable that he had failed the test, for time after time — while, eyes rolling, she moaned "Not yet! Not yet!" writhing and panting like a swimmer in high surf — he had been unable to restrain himself. Accustomed to the docility of the hotel girls, who were as circumspect in their pleasures as they were in their displeasures — the customer was always right — he had been infected with Amy's frenzy: except that whereas in her case it had meant a prolongation, with him it had precipitated matters. Before long the butane heater had increased the temperature of the room to somewhere up near blood heat; he groaned like a wrestler, slick with sweat, spread-eagle on the mat, and each time he had risen he had risen to be thrown. His performance had been sophomoric at best, and he feared that he had been admitted to a single intimacy — for after all, Amy had been all over; she had lived up East and even in Europe, where he understood men worked like dogs to acquire the very proficiency he lacked. As the days went by and she made no attempt to get in touch with him, Drew became more and more convinced that he had failed, that he would never be readmitted, that he had lost his chance.

However, he might have spared himself these fears. On the fourth day, Thursday, she was on the phone again: "You doing anything tonight?" He breathed a sigh of pure relief. They were together that night and it was all right, or nearly all right; he had recovered from his initial excitement, or rather he had it under control, at least to some extent. And over the span of the following months — as winter merged into green and leafy rain-washed spring, with a few raw days thrown in to mock their pleasure, and as spring gave way to summer, dusty and hot and waxing hotter, until finally in early August the nights were as hot as the days — they met often; there was hardly a tourist court within a hundred miles that could not claim their patronage; they had been on three trips to Memphis and two to New Orleans. Drew kept score on a calendar, a tick for every meeting, and they had averaged better than a meeting a week since that first one back in February, up near the State line.

Meanwhile his position began to rankle, touching his pride. For it was always Amy who called to make their assignations; it was she who determined what nights they were together and what nights he spent alone on his bachelor bed. "I'll call you," she would say each time he broached the subject of another meeting. She even addressed him by his last name, like a servant. It was as if that original advertisement he had imagined in the newspaper, under the Personals — *Gentleman available as dinner guest* and so forth — had been much simpler, shorter, in bolder type: AT STUD: H. DREW.

That was the state of affairs, the pass he had reached when Florence Barcroft died in late September, and that was what was on his mind when four days later, in early October, he found Amanda's letter on his desk. He waited until he returned from lunch to open it, for though he knew already what the letter would say, he knew himself to be so tender-hearted that, faced with the actual words of her appeal, he would lose his appetite. Not that he had a decision to make: he had made it long ago, back at the very start when he told himself he would catch the next train out if Florence died before the major did, thus avoiding a painful explanation and farewell. The truth was — like many men who have reason to suspect (without believing) that they are scoundrels — his nature was essentially so kind and considerate, he could never bear to inflict an injury face to face, not even when he stood to profit by it. He could be ruthless at a distance, either in space or time, for then, not having seen it, he could manage somehow not to believe in the resultant suffering; thus he was able to lay all sorts of plans for exploitation and even carry them through, up to a point — he had come far. But then, brought face to face with his victim in the moment of final action, he closed his eyes or turned his head or, womanish, merely ran. It is unlikely that any man was ever a pure scoundrel, despite the evidence of history and fiction.

He came back early from lunch, the bank quiet with the lull preceding the rush that always followed the noon hour, and took up the envelope. Except for the address below his name, it might have been a facsimile of the one nine years ago. For a moment he felt the weight of all those years piled on his back, like a ruined millionaire looking at old stocks and bonds issued by corporations long defunct; this too was an investment that had failed. The death of Florence had made no difference, really: it had merely forced a showdown. That original intention to call off the engagement if this happened had been confirmed and reinforced, but altered. Now he would not leave: he could not leave. This time he would have to stay and see. As the Carruthers financial adviser he knew the estate to a penny. It was at least twice the size of Major Barcroft's holdings, which were vague at best, especially since the major had stopped banking in Bristol; and what was worse, there had been rumors of reverses on the cotton market, as well as an old story (heard by chance) concerning the purchase of German Reichmarks after the war. And that was only the financial side of the picture. There was also the comparison, the choice to be made between Amy and Amanda, which requires as little comment as Drew required time to make it. So the need for a decision lay not in that direction; he had already made it, even before the death of Florence abrogated the possibility of choosing. What he had to decide was whether to meet Amanda at all, whether to stage a final scene and make some sort of explanation.

As he had predicted, the envelope flap sprang open at a touch. He read the letter rapidly: *I dont need a greiving time. Come now*, then put it back in the envelope; it was just as he had expected and there was no change of expression on his face. Sitting in the vaulted, cavernous gloom, looking down at the rectangle of stationery, slightly yellowed with age but pale against the dark green of the blotter: "A tryst," he said, stroking the under side of his mustache and the corners of his mouth, first left then right, with the knuckle of one forefinger. This was an accustomed gesture with him lately, almost a tic — though it would have been difficult to identify as troubled or exalted, decisive or indecisive: Laocoön without the snakes, as Browning said, might appear to be yawning.

Then the postnoon rush was on; Drew plunged into work. He pushed the letter aside. It was as if he had forgotten it — as in a sense he had. For he had decided; he had made up his mind, and therefore he could forget it for a time. He would meet her at seven as she asked. This seemed to him the lesser of two cruelties, and he prided himself for basing his choice on this. He said to himself it had been thus all along: her feelings, her probable reactions had been his consideration from the outset, and anything that concerned just the two of them (which ruled out anything concerning him and anyone else — Amy for instance) had been planned with Amanda's best interests in view. That her best interests were also his was incidental, or at least nonabrogating. He told himself that, and at least in a sense it was true. He told himself something else as well: 'If I hadnt come along, probably no one would.' And that was also true, or probably true. It gave him a good deal of comfort anyhow.

Toward four oclock, remembering a golf date, he called and broke it. "Sorry, George, I'm all tied up. How's about tomorrow? All right: fine. Tell Pete and Snooky I'm sorry, will you? Fine." He stayed on past quitting-time, clearing up some back work; he kept a supply of this on hand for days of tension and excess energy. It was after five when he left and the sun was going down beyond the levee. He parked and watched it flare rose-and-crimson, like blood on the water, with Arkansas black as a burnt-over forest beyond. He still had time to bathe

before supper, and did. Dressing, he felt a strange elation —
provoked no doubt by a sense of cleanliness, well-being, and
appetite; this was his favorite time of the day — and as he
knotted his tie before the mirror he whistled, off-key, Larry
Clinton's version of *M'Appari*. Then, making Grand Opera
faces at himself, he broke into song, improvising the lyric from
a few remembered scraps:

> *Martha-Martha, I adore you*
> *And implore you to be mine.*
> *I adore you and implore you,*
> *Martha-Martha, to be mine.*

He leaned closer, grinning at his reflection as he gave the knot
a final touch. "Boo! you good-looking devil," he said, and then
instinctively glanced past his shoulder in fear of having been
overheard. He was practicing golf swings with the fire tongs
when the cook rapped on the door, announcing supper.

Mrs Pentecost had never known him when he was more
congenial, more charming. He kept up a rapid-fire series of
anecdotes and comments all through the meal, lingering when
it was over, and she smiled and blinked and bobbed her head,
laughing behind her napkin. At last, however, the grandfather
clock in the living room made a sound as if it were clearing
its throat and then began to chime. Drew paused in the middle
of a story, listening with his head bent sideways while the
clock pealed six forty-five. When it was over he folded his
napkin hurriedly and laid it beside his plate. Unsmiling, he rose,
bowed once abruptly: "Excuse me," and was gone.

"I'm afraid Mr Drew is becoming a man of moods," Mrs
Pentecost said when the cook came in to clear the table.

"Yessum. He is that," the cook said. She took up the plates.
"Dont seem like it affect his appetite, though. That man's a
eater. He sho go make some nice little white lady a problem
one these days."

Meanwhile Drew, whose spirits had taken so sudden a drop
when the clock tolled the passing of the third quarter of this

final hour, was driving across town. He had not wanted this at all. Even now, almost there, his expression becoming increasingly morose as he approached Lamar Street, he considered turning back; it seemed to him that tonight of all nights he would most enjoy a hearts game at the Elks. The high spirits all afternoon, and up until five minutes ago, had been assumed to occupy his mind, keep it from considering the interview that lay ahead. Yet he went on, cursing the tenderness, the lack of moral courage, that would not let him leave Amanda waiting. He had no more than begun to convince himself that perhaps it would be kinder that way, in the long run, when he arrived. It was too late; he had to face his own cruelty, make it clear.

He parked around the corner, the same as always, and set out walking as if this were another of those regular first-Thursdays: which in fact it would have been if she had waited two more days. Summer was over — there was a breath of coolness in the air. At the end of the avenue, somewhere out beyond the country club, the great rose-golden ball of moon was coming up, not yet clear of the C&B railroad ramp: a little more and it would appear to be rolling along the tracks. He passed a group of children out after dark, mostly little girls, dragging at strings attached to shoeboxes with windows cut in the walls, crepe paper pasted over the windows, blue and orange and pink, and candles twinkling inside; they called them show-boats and their voices came shrill through the darkness. Then he was there, beside one of the oaks in front of the Barcroft house — the only one left undamaged now, for the other had been struck by lightning in the early spring; its top was dead and the sickness was moving down, the leaves curled tight, like little pale brown mummy fists, fragile as the ashes of burnt paper.

Amanda came out exactly at seven, and it occurred to Drew that she must have been standing with her hand on the knob, waiting for the clock to strike. The door came open wider than usual — for a moment he saw her in silhouette against the lighted hall, struggling with something large and square and apparently quite heavy. He realized with a pang that it was a suitcase. The door shut; the veranda was dark. She was already at the steps with her burden by the time he recovered from the shock (which, after all, he might have expected) and moved forward to help her. Their hands touched, but she did not jerk away as she had done that first time with the market basket. "Oh Harley," she said, as she had said so many times, but this time she was panting from exertion.

"Come on," he told her, more harshly than he intended. He had the suitcase by then and it was heavier than he had imagined; the sudden weight of it made his voice sound gruff. He would never have thought she owned so much. Staggering a bit as he came down the steps, he told himself the suitcase must contain every stitch she had worn since childhood: or else, he thought, a gross of those identical gray dresses with snaps at the throat and wrists for the collar and cuffs and a dozen of the Sunday ones thrown in for good measure. Then they were clear of the shadows; the moon was above the landline, round and full now like a disk of beaten gold, and Drew saw that what he had thought was a suitcase was in fact a sort of undersized trunk, a portmanteau they called them, mostly of wood, with metal corners and straps: obviously her mother's, for it still held a few faded stickers from the interrupted honeymoon of more than forty years ago; Amanda must have brought it down from the attic. He set it on the ground beside the dying oak. For a moment he remained bent over, panting; I'm not in shape, he thought. Then he rose and turned to her, taking her arm. "Come on," he said, more gently than before.

They walked a few steps and he wondered if she suspected. But no: she probably thought they were going to get the car and come back to pick up the trunk in front of the house. "Amanda . . ."

"Yes, Harley?"

He looked at her in the moonlight. Her eyebrows were

straight and rather heavy, at a time when other women's were plucked and arched like segments lightly struck by a twirl of compasses. Her eyes, whose color he had forgotten at that critical time, seemed black now in the shadow of her hat. Her mouth was pale, barely defined in this rich light, but ready to lend itself to any voluptuousness a lipstick offered. A virgin: he had never had a virgin, and if at times he prided himself on this, there were also times when he regretted it — especially now, when it seemed likely that he never would have one. He thought of Amy, then put the thought aside and got back to the business now at hand.

"Amanda, do you know how much I make at the bank?" He waited but she did not answer. "One hundred and seventy dollars a month," he said. He waited for her reaction, and when it came — if indeed it could be said to come at all — it was not at all what he had expected or wanted. She obviously thought this a large amount. He continued. "All my life Ive told myself my wife would be free from all care. She'd have silver and servants, a fine big house, all the things all women want so much . . ." They were passing the place where the children had been playing, but the little girls had gone in for their bedtime baths; all that remained was the wreckage of one of the show-boats, which had burned. "A hundred and seventy dollars may sound like a great deal to you, Amanda, but it's not. It's very little." Then they were at the usual turn-around point of their Thursday evenings and he stopped as if from habit. She stopped two steps beyond; she turned, looking up at him, watching the flicker of his lips as he spoke. "I couldnt ask you to live on that, Amanda."

Now that he had said it he felt relief — the sort of relief a man may experience who, having decided on suicide, finally draws the razor across his throat and discovers to his surprise that he feels no pain, but rather a sudden relaxation of tension. He had looked away in midsentence, avoiding her eyes, but when he looked back he saw to his horror that she had not understood; she thought it was just one of those 'budget conferences' she had read of in the agony column. She smiled.

"I'm really a good manager, Harley," she said. "I ran papa's house on much less, including six dollars a week for the cook. Thats twenty-four dollars we'll save right there, on that. Just wait; youll see."

Thus these last four words returned to plague him, who had said them so often himself to reassure her. Everything was going all wrong — Drew looked at her and shook his head. She had trusted him so completely for so many years that her trust was carried forward by a sort of secondary inertia, irresistible and blind. Nothing he had said could make her confidence falter. She did not even wonder, much less question, why he took her arm and led her back the way they had come, following the routine of all those first-Thursdays — over two hundred of them — except that tonight he did not stop to kiss her. Returning they walked faster. He spoke of taxes, clothing, gasoline, the rising cost of living, of all the things that were not included in her present household expenses, but none of them made any impression at all. "I'm a good manager, Harley," she kept saying; "youll see. Others seem to get along — young couples. I guess we will too. Ive even been taking cooking lessons from Nora. She says I'm doing better all the time."

He was getting nowhere and he knew it. Faced with the necessity for a cruelty beyond anything he had foreseen, he panicked: he threw caution and even consideration to the winds. They were almost back to the house by now. Drew hurried forward, crouched beside the oak, and rising with the portmanteau in his arms, staggered across the sidewalk, up the steps, and crossed the veranda at a stumbling run. He put it down beside the door, not caring how much noise disturbed the major.

"What is it, Harley? Whats the matter?" Amanda was coming up the steps. The moon was higher, silver now through the blasted limbs of the oak. He went past her, then turned, halfway down the steps; she stood above him and he flung his last words at her just before he turned again and ran.

"I wont marry you!" he cried.

THREE

7. Death of a Soldier

She got the trunk in somehow, as far as the foot of the stairs at least, though it seemed twice as heavy now — as if to its original weight had been added all the grief that was to flower from those four words, "I wont marry you," flung at her from scarcely three feet away but in a voice as faint and distant as if he were already halfway down the block: which soon he was, walking fast, heels clicking, then out of sight, gone perhaps forever, and she was left alone on the veranda, the sidewalk pale and empty in the moonlight, pointing straight as any arrow: *He went that way*. But this was as far as she got, the foot of the stairs; she sat on the bottom step and looked at the trunk, like Sisyphus and his rock. Thus far her eyes were dry, her motions curiously lethargic, like a boxer dealt a knockout blow or a soldier shot through the heart, who staggers before his mind realizes the damage. "I wont marry you," she said, sitting on the bottom step and looking at the trunk; the words sounded as faint and faraway as when Drew said them. Then for the first time she began to weep, leaning her forehead against her knees.

"Amanda — "

She did not hear it; she had her hands to her face and the sobs, though soundless, racked her. It came again, sharper. "Amanda!"

This time she heard it. For a moment she froze: this might be Drew, come back with a speech of apology. But when she looked up she saw her father standing in the doorway of the hall that led back to his study, and she realized that he must have heard the clump of the trunk when Drew set it down outside the door; he had come to see what was the matter, had been standing there all this time, watching her, and had even heard her repeat Drew's words, "I wont marry you," corroborating the packed trunk and the tears.

His face seemed kinder, softer — she had an impulse to hurry to him, to throw herself into his arms for comfort. But then he spoke again and she saw that what she had taken for softness in his expression was due to the fact that she saw through a haze of tears. She blinked and the major's face was as stern as ever, or sterner. 'I *told* you so,' he seemed to be saying: whereas in fact what he really said was "Never mind that," not bothering to indicate the trunk; "Nora will tend to it tomorrow morning. Go to your room. Dont sit there crying like that."

She went, not looking back. The staircase seemed as steep as a ladder, each step requiring an exertion out of all proportion to the gain involved; for though she had left the trunk, as her father instructed, she had not left the heavier burden of those four words, "I wont marry you," containing her grief packed tight like petals in a bud — Drew was the only one who could relieve her of that, and he was gone. Then she was at the top. She looked down and saw that the major had come out into the hall: he was standing there, foreshortened, watching, angry because a Barcroft had been humbled. She went quickly into her room and locked the door.

This despair was immediate, unrelieved; this was what came before her mind, receiving the message 'I cant bear this,' went to work inventing reasons, extenuations. She told herself it was only a quarrel, provoked by something she said; perhaps he hadnt been able to face the prospect of her cooking. (That was guilt: she had said that Nora had complimented her on her progress, and though it was true it was only relatively true, for she was a very bad cook and always would be.) So she thought of writing another letter: *It's true, Harley, I cant cook. Come back; we'll hire a cook, we'll save the money some other way. Come back.* She did not write it, however. Next morning, rising from a daze that only resembled sleep between fits and starts, she realized that tomorrow would be Thursday, the first in October, and she grasped at that. The present difficulty was only a quarrel, a lovers' quarrel; he would be waiting for her at seven oclock, as he had been waiting so many first-Thursdays before. Not that she really believed it: she knew well enough that Drew was gone for good. This was her mind at work. Having received the message 'I cant bear this,' it was trying to blunt the sharp immediacy of despair.

That day passed, and then the next; it was Thursday, seven oclock. But she did not wait in front of the house. She stood at her bedroom window, holding the curtain aside, and watched and waited. The moon through the oaks, brighter through the dying one, was barely on the wane, flooding lawn and side-walk with a light almost as rich, as brilliant as two nights ago. She did not try to put all doubt from her mind. Rather, she nurtured it; "He wont come," she said aloud from time to time — so that at eight oclock, when she let the curtain swing back over the window, her disappointment was tempered by fore-knowledge. That was also why she had waited up here instead of down there: the disappointment was easier up here. Thus Amanda was learning to live with despair.

Then the November first-Thursday came, nearing the an-niversary of their meeting. She did not stay the full hour at the window, but rose from time to time, drew the curtain aside, and peered down into the darkness as into a well, not allowing herself to believe for a moment that she would see him. Fall became winter; Christmas went past and New Year's, the earth frozen iron-hard. Amanda was learning. Then spring came on, with summer fast on its heels; the year burned toward a climax, cotton beginning to split its bolls, pickers moving in ragged skirmish lines across the fields, dragging nine-foot sacks like windless flags, and the gins whined soprano round the clock. It was September: war had come to Europe. Newsboys cried Hitler, cried Poland, and it all meant less than nothing to Amanda, widowed before she had even been a bride.

Early that week she was on her way to market and she stopped at a curb, waiting for the traffic light to change. Just as it did, a long low car pulled up. Mostly varnished wood and bright blue fenders, considerably wider than tall, it eased to a purring stop and Amanda saw that the driver was Harley Drew. He did not see her; he was busy talking to a coral-lipped young woman with smooth brown hair. "What I dont like is all this waiting. Damn it, Amy — " The young woman appeared not to hear him; she was gazing straight ahead. Then she turned languidly, her eyes moving past Amanda without pause. "Damn it, Amy — " He had on a brand new pearly hat. The traffic signal changed; they moved on, the engine purring like a dynamo, and Amanda had to wait again for the light. But when it went green she did not move; she stood there another moment, her face drained of everything, even despair. Then suddenly she turned and hurried home, holding the empty basket with both hands and restraining her tears until she reached her room.

But this was only a temporary relapse. Within an hour she was back downstairs and she set out again with her market basket. Now that Thursday was no different from any other day of a month's first week, her life was built more than ever around her father's schedule. His day began with eight oclock breakfast, after which he was gone until half past twelve, when he came home for lunch and a nap before returning to the office. He never varied his regimen; people along the way could set their watches by the times he passed their doors. At five oclock, as always, Amanda would meet him on Cotton Row and walk home with him through the gathering dusk of winter or the fierce high sunlight of late spring and summer. The big gray house, its cupolas soaring grim and pristine among filling stations and neighborhood grocery stores, was more remote than ever — a reminder, like the major, of an era that was gone. Workers' houses were just beyond it and a new cotton-seed oil mill took up half of the second block; it made a constant crunching sound through the long autumnal nights, like a beast grinding its teeth in pain, and filled the air with a smell of frying ham. Radios and phonographs belonging to the workers' wives shattered the quiet of other seasons with dance music, the blues, dramas consisting mostly of shots and screams, the bland commercial voices of young men selling soap and breakfast foods, and the shrill, desperate laughter of sponsored comedians. Against this background Amanda followed her daily rounds, leading a sort of posthumous existence in a world reduced to a population of two.

She was no longer on the public tongue save in rare instances when strangers, seeing her pass, would ask about her: "Who was that? Whats the matter with her?" for her face was not only vacant now; it was dazed, distrait, like that of a person just recovering from an unexpected blow. The new versions were more prosaic than the old, without the eager surmises, the improbable conjectures. "Who? That? Thats Amanda Barcroft, old Major Barcroft's daughter; she got jilted. Remind me to tell you about her some time." It was as if a shadow were moving across the family portrait reflected in the enormous Bristol eye. Already one of the figures had been obliterated, and the shadow continued to move, reaching now for the shoulder of the central figure. Major Barcroft's heart, which had murmured through the years after denying him a final chance at glory, gave warning that it was about to make its final claim.

In late September — the anniversary of Florence's death (and consequently within a week of the anniversary of Amanda's last meeting with Drew) — father and daughter were walking home through the lingering heat, the sun just clear of the levee and the moon already up in the daylight sky.

Major Barcroft walked fast, wanting to be in his study, where he kept a large-scale map of western Europe on the wall beside his desk, marking the positions of the armies with drafting pins. Warsaw, with its swarm of black- and red-headed pins, had fallen that afternoon, and he was anxious to get back and make the changes.

Halfway home Amanda was surprised to see him stop suddenly and lean against a tree beside the walk. He was frowning, his face contorted; she had never seen him look like this before. She turned, one hand extended: "What *is* it, papa?" but he motioned her away with an angry gesture.

"Let me lone," he said, speaking through clenched teeth, hardly moving his lips. He stood there, pale and breathless. Indigestion, Amanda thought. That was what it seemed to be, for presently he pushed himself clear of the tree and resumed his walk, wanting to get to the house where he could sit down, look at his map in peace, and wait for the flicker of pain to go away.

He did not make it to the house. As they entered the last block, within fifty yards of the front steps, he knew he was not going to make it and he halted for the second time, looking for something to lean against, to clutch. There was not a tree at hand, so with panic in his eyes he tottered across the strip of grass to a telephone pole at the curb. He was paler now, for pain was like an iron hoop drawn tight around his chest. Nostrils dilated with the effort of holding himself erect, he gripped the metal rungs of the pole; big drops of perspiration stood on his face and neck and the backs of his hands, where the liver spots were black against the paleness. Amanda moved to help him but an inexorable pressure buckled his knees. He slid down the pole, breaking his pince-nez and barking his face against the scars left by linemen's spikes, and lay in the dusty gutter, his breathing labored, his eyes bulged with terror.

Amanda knelt at the curb, bending above him, crying "Papa. Papa. Papa" over and over; "What *is* it, papa?" until a Greek fruitstand proprietor, who had watched the scene with an air of unbelief like that assumed by sophisticates at the theater when they wish to show that they disapprove of the play or the performance, came out wiping his hands on his apron, lifted the major in his arms, and followed Amanda down the block and up the steps, then into the house and through the hall to the study, where he laid him on the horsehide couch. The major had not lost consciousness. His clothes grimed with dust from the gutter, he lay with that awful terror in his eyes, looking up at his daughter, and the uproar of his breathing filled the room. Amanda could not take her eyes from the straining face, the left cheek and temple of which had been raked raw against the spike scars on the pole. She stayed on her knees beside the couch, holding his hand and watching his face until the doctor came.

They thought he would die that night, and the major apparently thought so too; they could see it in his eyes. But he was alive next morning, lying on the button-studded couch and breathing with the harsh, stertorous groans that had continued through the night. Amanda and the fruitstand proprietor had removed his coat and tie before Dr Clinton arrived, but he still wore the soiled trousers and shirt, for the doctor would not risk exposing him to the exertion that would be involved even in cutting them off. An oxygen cylinder stood at the head of the couch; it resembled an artillery projectile designed for use in super-deadly futuristic warfare and it made a treble hissing, sweet and clear, mounting toward some unattainable climax. A thin red tube drooped from it, the end inserted in one of the major's nostrils and held in place by a strip of adhesive across his upper lip like a stage mustache put on in a hurry and awry. From time to time, looking up at his daughter, he would blink his eyes and twitch one corner of his mouth. It was some kind of signal; it had some meaning she could not understand. She hardly recognized him anyhow, lying in the dusty, rumpled clothes. Without the pince-nez his eyes looked out-of-focus, blurred and vague — not like Major Barcroft's eyes at all — and the two little red marks left by the nippers, one on each side of his nose, were beginning to fade. Amanda was standing beside the couch, holding his hand, and suddenly he spoke. His voice was hoarse and low but surprisingly clear. "Lean down," he said.

She knelt and his face was even more unfamiliar at close range. The nurse had salved his lips to prevent the oxygen from chapping them, and somehow this seemed terribly pathetic, this thought of a dying man, a man in mortal combat with a thrombus, being protected from the slight discomfort and disfiguration of chap. "Papa?" she said. Their eyes were less than a foot apart; she had not been this close to him since childhood.

"Amanda — I . . . have a thing to ask you. I havent — havent spoken of that person, that unhappiness. I wouldnt speak of it now, except . . . " He paused, watching her, the corners of his mouth drawn down, and she saw that this was costing him a terrific exertion, entirely apart from his physical condition.

"I understand, papa," she said quietly.

"I want you to tell me that you . . . realize — that you realize I was right. *I* know I did right but now I want to know that *you* know I did right. Do you, Amanda? Do you know it?"

Amanda kept her head down, feeling his eyes upon her. She did not nod or shake her head; she knelt there, motionless. Major Barcroft glared at her for half a minute, as if he were timing her silence with a clock. Then, when he was quite certain that she was not going to answer him, he turned his head away. She remained beside the couch for a while, still holding his hand. Finally, however, she rose and went into the hall.

It was the first time she had left the room since her father had been brought into it yesterday. Soon she returned; she stayed near him constantly. She would have spent all her time hovering over the couch but it angered him to see her always there, so she slept the second night in Florence's patented chair, which had never been removed from the front parlor. By the third day the thrombus had begun to canalize; he was past immediate danger. "You cant tell about these things," the doctor said. He frowned, after the manner of medical men when developments, whether good or bad, surprise them. "Sometimes that one clot is all; the attack clears up the condition. He may live to see a hundred."

By the end of the following week Major Barcroft was sitting up, reading the war news and directing Amanda where to place the pins in the map on the opposite wall. He was furious when she could not locate the French and Belgian border hamlets whose names he mispronounced. In mid-October, three weeks after the attack, he was back at his office and they resumed their old familiar schedule. He was as well as ever, apparently, but there was a certain deliberateness about his movements, like those of a man obliged to carry a time bomb set to detonate at an hour unknown to him.

Sometimes Amanda looked at him, remembering his face the way it had been when he asked her to admit he had done right about Harley Drew; she had bowed her head and refused to answer (which in itself was an answer) and now they were like strangers in the house. Formerly he had spoken to her but seldom: now he never spoke to her at all, beyond signifying incidental desires with grunts and gestures. Instead of saying 'Pass the sugar,' for instance, he would point to it and grunt. He kept more and more to his study, following the war news in the paper and shifting the pins on the map. Walking together, home from Cotton Row, they were as uncommunicative as soldiers on parade.

This continued. Then one morning toward the end of December they were at breakfast and the major folded and rolled his napkin and put it in its ring. He rose and went to the door; it was as always. But there he paused, standing with his back to her, and made a clucking sound to clear his throat. "Amanda," he said. He turned in the doorway and looked at her, after all these months of studied indifference. She had time to wonder what was coming. "Have you and Nora made plans for Christmas dinner?" He said it as if reciting something committed to memory, and she knew that he must have been phrasing it all through breakfast.

"Dinner?" Startled, she said it to gain time; but he just stood there, watching her. "Not yet, papa. But it will be the same as always. Turkey and dressing and . . . everything. Like always."

He turned to go, then turned back; he made the little clucking sound again. "Very good. But when you plan it, plan for three. We'll have a guest." This time he went. She heard him pause in the hall for his hat and stick (he carried a stick now, remembering the heart attack when he stood looking desperately left and right for something to clutch, to hold to); then she heard the front door close behind him.

Henry Stubblefield was the guest, and that was how she met him. Or rather that was how she learned his name, for she had been seeing him every week-day afternoon for two months now. When she walked to her father's office at five oclock he would be there, and after the first few afternoons he began to nod to her and mumble "How do" and she would nod back, but that was all. He had been working in the office since October, learning the cotton business, and people up and down the Row were saying that he was Major Barcroft's protégé. Anyhow, the major and his daughter were sitting in the parlor late Christmas morning, Amanda excusing herself from time to time to see how the turkey was coming; it was almost noon and there was a knock at the door. She looked at her father but he just sat there, giving no sign that he had heard. The knocking came again. So she got up and went to the door and it was the cotton clerk. "How do," he said.

Amanda stood aside for him to enter, then closed the door and turned and he was waiting; he stood with his hat in both hands, holding it gingerly in fear of roughing the nap. She came past him, leading the way to the parlor. Major Barcroft had already risen to greet them: they might have been returning from a stroll or even a trip. That was her first real inkling of what was to come, for he was smiling. "Amanda, help Mr Stubblefield with his hat. No: wait." He put out one arm, the hand making a gesture that was strangely like a blessing, thumb and fingertips joined. "Henry, this is my daughter; this is Amanda. And, Amanda, this is Henry Stubblefield." He was cavalier, Old South — she had never seen him like this before: *galant*. The smile looked forced, however, as is always the case with people who smile but seldom. This embarrassed her; it was like having to sit and listen to lying, wearing a look of belief and corroboration. It also seemed to embarrass the young man.

"How do," he said.

She took his hat and was on the way to the hall with it before the name meant anything to her. Then she remembered. Henry Stubblefield: he had lost his wife ten years ago in a freak accident, one of those occurrences we are apt to pronounce 'outrageous' in fiction and 'absorbing' in real life. It was one of the few local events that Florence, for instance, had shown an interest in. He was twenty-five then, six months married, and one fine day of early spring he put the lawn mower on the back seat of his car, a Chevrolet convertible with the top down. He was taking the mower to be sharpened, and just as he was about to drive off, his wife came running out of the house, wearing a light print wash dress. "Yoohoo! wait," she cried, "I'll go with you," and she ran around and got in. She was a pretty thing by all report, just turned nineteen. So they pulled off, and that was when it happened; she was waving to someone on a porch across the way and they were approaching the corner when a car came blurting out of the cross street; he had to jam on brakes, and then it happened. The handle of the mower sprang forward, then down: crack! and broke her skull; she lived two hours, and the only comfort the doctor could give was an opinion that she never knew what hit her — small comfort indeed. Yet the general belief was that the young husband's mourning was exaggerated, perhaps abnormal — even when it began to be told around town that the wife died three months pregnant (which incidentally was not true, though perhaps it made a better story that way) — for he went into seclusion; they only saw him once a day, when he took his midafternoon walk to the cemetery with a newspaper cornucopia of flowers. He lived with his mother; his father had died twelve years ago, leaving them a half interest in a downtown office building. There was a flurry of talk when someone reported seeing him drop the lawn mower into the river one dark night (— 'the death weapon' they called it, and added behind their hands: "Maybe this was that 'perfect crime' youre always hearing about") but it soon died down; probably not even those who told it believed it. Still, as they watched him going to and coming from the cemetery, carrying the cornucopia of flowers on the way there, empty-handed coming back, they shook their heads: "Thats a strange one, that." Ten years after the death of his wife his mother died too (— of cancer of the liver; he had that to watch, to live through: three months of it) and then he was alone. Major Barcroft, who owned the other half of the office building, was appointed executor, and when the estate was settled it amounted to enough for him to live on but no more. The major said, "Henry: how would you like to learn the cotton business?" "Business?" "Yes. You can come in with me. Do you want to?" "Well — all right. Yes sir." Thus he ended ten years of seclusion, and that was how it came about that Amanda had been seeing him at her father's office for the past two months.

He rose when she returned from hanging his hat on the rack in the hall, and then when she sat down he sat down too, fists clenched loosely on his knees. The major watched with approval. However, all this was done with a certain hesitancy, like that of a foreigner anxious to be polite but made awkward by his fear of committing a gaffe because of his unfamiliarity with the customs of the country. The ten years of seclusion had left their mark on his manner as well as on his face, which Amanda thought was the saddest she had ever seen. He was talking with the major and she looked at him. Seated he seemed tall, though when she had seen him standing on the porch and in the hall he had appeared to be of average height. Now she saw that this was because his legs were very short and his trunk was long. His hair was blond, his skin rather pallid: from lack of sunlight, she supposed — And then she stopped, amazed; she could not understand how she could have failed to notice it before. The resemblance was unmistakable. Add a mustache, lengthen and smooth the hair, liven the features, stretch the legs and shorten the trunk (all of which she did in her mind's eye) and he was the very image of Harley Drew.

She did not look at him again, but sat with her hands in her lap, staring straight ahead — much as Florence had done when the major sketched her haircut for Sam Marino — until Nora announced that dinner was on the table. The men rose. For a moment they stood watching her. "Amanda," the major said. She looked up, startled. "After you," he said. He made a flipper gesture with one hand, indicating the door, still with that false gallantry, and she got up and hurried into the dining room. Henry followed to hold her chair but she was already seated before he reached it. Major Barcroft gave his head a slight but rapid shake of disapproval which made his pince-nez glitter; his eyes behind the lenses were hard as agates. This soon passed, however, for he became absorbed in carving the turkey. Another ten years and carving would be one of the lost arts, he said, watching the slices of white meat as they sheared back over the knife. He took great pride in his carving.

All through the meal he maintained a running fire of comment on the war, the cotton market, and the weather, drawing his daughter into the discussion from time to time with brief but direct questions fired point-blank: "Wasnt that so, Amanda?" or "Did it, Amanda?" or "Wouldnt they, Amanda?" and she would reply, more or less according to whichever applied: "Yes, papa" or "No, papa," looking at him out of the corners of her eyes, then down at the food on her plate. The young man glanced uneasily at her from time to time, then quickly back at his host. It was obvious from his expression — like that of a captive among savages, not quite certain whether he is to be fed or to be eaten — that the major never talked this way on Cotton Row.

Henry put in a word from time to time, much as Amanda did, but whenever Major Barcroft paused for chewing, a heavy silence fell and the three of them sat motionless save for the up-and-down and slightly sidewise thrust of the major's jaw — as if, chewing, he were still talking, incurably garrulous though no words came. When they had finished the dessert the major laid his napkin unfolded on the table (a concession to the guest) and said, smiling, "I congratulate you, Amanda. An excellent meal."

"Yes indeed," Henry said. "I too: I do too."

Aware (as her father was also) that her contribution to the preparing of the meal had been limited to occasional peeks into the kitchen to see how it was 'coming,' Amanda said nothing. They returned to the parlor, where she and the young man sat merely silent, whereas the major, dejected and glum in contrast to his former volubility, seemed doubly silent, like a run-down talking machine. Yet she could see that he was about to begin again — he raised his chin and cleared his throat, and she knew that she could not bear it. She rose, excused herself, and left the room without waiting for permission or noting Henry's astonishment and the major's disapproval. Upstairs, she heard the drone of her father's voice downstairs, punctuated from time to time by the brief murmur of the young man's assents and acknowledgments. Not for long, however. Soon she heard them in the hall and the sound of the front door closing. The silence that followed was like the interval that falls between a drawn breath and a scream. Then it came: "Amanda!"

When she was halfway to the door it came again: "Amanda!" and from the head of the stairs she saw her father standing in the hall below, foreshortened, looking up at her as on the night of the renouncement.

"Yes, papa?"

"You werent very hospitable to your guest."

"Yes, papa." *Your* guest, he said: not 'my' or 'our,' but *your*. Waiting for what was coming next, she gripped the banister rail and looked down at her hands. But he turned away, exasperated by her combination of docility and resistance, and Amanda went back to her room.

Henry was there the following Sunday, however, and the next, and the one after that; he was a regular Sunday dinner guest. His resemblance to Drew was nothing like as striking as Amanda continued to suppose. It was remarked by no one but herself — certainly not by the major, who (in contrast to what she originally imagined when she thought that he had brought the young man into the house to taunt her, as with a wretched reproduction of the lost original) would rather have gotten rid of him merely on the grounds of resembling a scoundrel — for in fact he resembled Drew but grossly, like an unfinished bust, or vaguely, like a watercolor left out in the rain. Yet to her they not only resembled each other, she came to believe that if they were placed side by side before her she would have trouble telling them apart. This was because she was seeing Henry every Sunday, whereas (though she never suspected this, and would certainly have rejected the notion if it had been suggested to her) she was already beginning to forget the shape of Drew's face, the play of his mannerisms, and even the inflection of his voice; that one time she had seen him since their separation, in the station wagon with the smooth-haired woman, she had been surprised at how much he had 'changed,' though the truth was he had not changed at all; the actual image had merely failed to match the image in her memory. Nevertheless it seemed to her, one following thus hard upon the other — and rhythmically too: once a week, where formerly it had been once a month — that she was being placed in double jeopardy.

All this time, encouraging the young man, Major Barcroft

wore the obsequious, false joviality of a procurer, a pander, an attendant even — lacking only the basin and towels, a jar of petroleum jelly and a box of coffin-shaped bichloride tablets — and Amanda, though she did not (could not) push the analogy this far, saw clearly enough what he was leading them to, her and the backward young man. Soon it came. On a rainy Sunday in late April they were sitting in the parlor after dinner, the major looking from one to the other from time to time, covert and speculative behind his glasses. Suddenly he rose; "Excuse me," he said decisively, and went toward the back of the house. Amanda and Henry sat silent, the fine rain coming faint as whispers against the windowpanes. The major returned, buttoning his raincoat. "I just remembered," he said. He held out a book wrapped in last night's paper to protect it from the rain. "It's due today." As he turned to go, Amanda saw that he gave Henry a meaningful look, and she knew what was coming.

The front door closed; they were alone, and again the rain whispered on the windows. She would not look at him. After what seemed a very long time she heard him clear his throat. He paused, then said in a desperate, choked voice: "Miss Barcroft — Amanda . . ."

"Dont," she said. She kept her eyes down. "Dont."

"All right." He said it quite calmly; she was not at all prepared for what she saw when she raised her eyes. He was halfway across the room, then into the hall, and she realized that he had not only sounded calm, he had sounded relieved. Then he was gone; the front door closed behind him. She could hardly believe it was over so quick — a proposal and a refusal, both in less than twenty seconds.

The rain continued, steady, sibilant, and presently the door came open again. She heard her father stop beside the rack in the hall, the rustle of his raincoat coming off. He entered speaking: "Well — " Then he stopped, seeing Amanda alone. The brightly polished caps of his shoes were speckled with tiny raindrops. "Where's Henry?" he asked, taken aback. He looked at her and she looked at him, and now that he understood he seemed to swell; rage purpled his face; he drew himself up, looming, prepared to launch a flood of hot reproaches. She raised one hand before her eyes, palm outward in a gesture of defense. But then he stopped; he shook his head as if that were part of a deflation process, for now he seemed to shrink. He said, "I give you up, Amanda. Ive tried: God knows Ive tried. Ive done my best and now I give you up."

He left and she was alone again. The rain hissed steadily. Yet the dazed expression on her face was not in reaction to Henry's proposal (which had been expected) nor even to her father's announcement that he was abandoning all concern about her (which for that matter would have been far more likely to produce relief, apart from the fact that she had scarcely heard it, or at any rate, having heard it, had put it out of her mind); no. The trouble was interior. She had inherited Florence's malady: bad recurrent dreams: except that in her sister's case they had been confined to sleep, whereas in Amanda's they were carried over into the daylight world as fantasies. This was her original dream — the others were merely variations on it:

She is walking on smooth turf, apparently in some kind of park for there is a cast-iron fence around it, each picket ending in a spear point, like the one around the courthouse (the one the City Council was debating whether to donate to the rearmament program for scrap; and two years later did) — yet the courthouse is not there, nor the marble Confederate soldier on his shaft; this is not the courthouse lawn. This is an asylum. But where are the people, the inmates? She herself is a visitor, not a patient, but whether she is here by permission of the authorities she does not know, and this is a source of some uneasiness. 'After all,' she tells herself, 'I didnt sneak in; I just found myself here, the way it nearly always is in dreams. Surely they wouldnt persecute — prosecute me for something in a dream.' Somewhat reassured she looks around, shading her eyes with the flat of her hand — an unnecessary gesture, like certain stylized movements in ballet, for the light is pearly and sourceless — until she sees in a far corner of the grounds a clump of stunted cedars with the end of a park bench showing around one side. 'Ah,' she thinks, relieved (for everything up to now, though charged with a sort of nervous deliberation like the opening pages of a Balzac novel, was merely preparatory. In later repetitions of the dream, when she already knew what was to follow, this prelude seemed interminable; yet even the first time, seeing the bench, she felt relief, knowing it marked a turning-point in the dream, like the tap that alters the snowflake pattern in a kaleidoscope), and moves toward the clump of cedars. There she stops, for directly in front of her a man and a woman are seated at opposite ends of the bench, wearing the vacant faces of madhouse tenants let out for an airing. The man ignores a newspaper unfolded on his lap. But Amanda does not pause to look at him; the woman is the striking one, painted like a harlot, lipstick and rouge and mascara daubed so thick that the slightest change of expression, it seems, would crack them like a mask. Yet now she smiles, turning her head slightly toward the man, and lo, the mask is pliable. Amanda too looks at the man and it is Harley Drew. He darts sidelong glances and fumbles with something hidden beneath the paper in his lap, evidently plotting an attack; his face is cruel, crafty. But the painted woman — Florence (even in the original dream Amanda accepted this without surprise, and in the repetitions she looked forward to this moment; 'Now I'm going to recognize her,' she would tell herself) — seems not to fear him, seems rather to welcome the attack, for she is luring him with the painted smile. Amanda looks at the man again, and now she sees the half-hidden weapon: her father's ivory letter opener, she thinks. Then he attacks; the newspaper falls and she sees that the weapon is not a letter opener, but rather a kind of tusk attached down there. His face is the face of a murderer, the teeth bared in a grimace as he flings himself at Florence, and suddenly they are entangled, arms and legs.

As Amanda moves forward to help her sister, whose face is hidden by Drew's shoulder, all she can hear is a growling sound, like a lion devouring his prey. Then she is near them and Florence looks out of the tangle of limbs, panting breast to breast with her attacker. 'Is he hurting you, Florence?' Amanda cries; she stands there, wringing her hands. But Florence only broadens her painted smile. 'I like it, I like it,' she says. Amanda, as she recoils, feels a hand gripping her arm above the elbow; 'Here now,' a voice says, 'Who let *you* in?' and, turning, she sees a guard in a blue uniform with a double row of buttons on his coat. He leads her away without waiting for an explanation — her guilt is only too obvious. Behind her, though she does not dare to look around, she hears Florence giving little throaty cries at regular intervals. Then they are out of earshot; she and the guard are at an iron gate, where he stops without releasing her arm, selects the largest key from a ring at his belt, and fits it into the lock. He wears Major Barcroft's face, but the uniformed body below is much too husky; this is not her father. The face is only a pliable rubber mask, cunningly fitted to answer the play of the different features beneath. 'And dont come back,' he says, pushing her through. This is not her father's voice. What is more, the exertion of opening the gate has caused the mask to slip, exposing part of the face. It is as she has thought. This is not her father; this is a Negro, a black man.

That was her dream; she had that to live with, just as Florence had had hers, except that when Amanda woke there was no one to say, as she had said, 'It's all right. Shh. I'm here: I'm with you. Shh,' for she was alone. Florence had shared her love affair by proxy, verbally. Now she was sharing Florence's — and with the same man, too — but visually. The fact that her sister was dead was not incongruous; Drew was every bit as dead for her. Worse by far, when she looked back on the dream (particularly when she looked back on the repetitions of it) she discovered that, for all her pretended uneasiness and fear, what she really experienced was pleasure — anticipation during the prelude, excitement during the park-bench scene, and a delicious sensation of fear when the black man, wearing her father's face, took hold of her arm. That was where the true horror lay: in just the absence of horror. "I'm some kind of a monster," she said, and she covered her face with her hands and sobbed aloud.

This agitation grew, this commingling of guilt and desire, not only in dreams but in daylight fantasies too. It accounted in a large part for what followed.

△

What followed was that Henry Stubblefield, when he came to work on a Tuesday in mid-May, found that Major Barcroft (whose comings and goings were regular as clockwork, who missed a day for only the gravest reasons: to attempt to enlist in a war or to bury a daughter or suffer a heart attack) was not there. That was strange, and doubly strange, for this made twice; he had not come to the office Monday either. On the Monday — yesterday — Henry had been surprised to find the major's desk still locked when he arrived, the hatrack holding only the bookkeeper's hat. Yet the bookkeeper himself was hunched above his ledger, making entries as if nothing out of the ordinary had happened. Presently (but only when the bookkeeper paused at the foot of a row of figures, for he brooked no interruption) Henry asked: "Did he say anything to you?"

"Not me," the bookkeeper said, and returned to his ledger, the old-time dip pen squeaking.

The morning wore on. Henry half expected to find the major there when he returned from lunch, but it was not so. He stood looking at the locked roll-top desk, upon which a thin film of dust already had settled. The bookkeeper was

back at work, and this time Henry interrupted him. "I'm —
I'm uneasy. Oughtnt one of us go to the house and see if
there's anything wrong?"

For a moment the older man said nothing. Then he turned
on his high stool and peered at the clerk from under the green
eyeshade. "Maybe *you*ll go there," he said. "Not me. Staying
away from that house is the best way I know to keep from
getting your nose shoved out of joint."

"But if he's — "

"Not me," the bookkeeper said. He turned, holding the pen
poised above the pink and faint blue lines of the ledger sheet
like a figure in an allegorical painting, indicating a name in
the doomsday book. He spoke with his back to Henry. "Come
October I'll have been here thirty years, and all the dealings
I ever had with any Barcroft were tended to right here on
Cotton Row."

Henry did not say anything and the pen resumed its squeaking. But at five oclock he tried again. "Dont you think — "

"Look," the other said sharply, as if he had been waiting for
him to speak. He turned from locking his desk. "I told you
once, I'll tell you again. Major Barcroft's old enough to look
out for himself. Even if he wasnt, if he was in some kind of
dotage or something, it wouldnt be up to you to straighten
him out. What you think he's got a daughter for? Quit fret-
ting. It's this war; it's got him all excited. He's probly
busy right this minute shifting pins on that map. I see by the
paper the Nazzies crossed the Mews." This sounded reason-
able to Henry — he had not thought of it before. The bookkeeper took his hat from the rack. "Come on. Lets lock up."

They parted on the sidewalk in front of the office. Henry,
though he had been somewhat reassured by what the other
had said in explanation of the major's absence, felt his doubts
return. After all, people did get murdered in their beds.
Deciding to see for himself, he set off for Lamar Street and
the Barcroft house. He had not been there in almost a month,
not since the brief proposal and refusal, and as he drew closer,

remembering what the bookkeeper had said about getting his nose shoved out of joint, he reached up unconsciously and stroked it. And serve me right, he thought. Then he was there.

The blinds were drawn, the windows all shut in spite of the summer weather; there was no sign of life. He turned in at the walk, the cupolas and tall eaves soaring above him. His footsteps had a hollow echo crossing the veranda, and when he had knocked at the door there was a grim, heavy silence as before. He stroked his nose. As he was about to knock again, leaning forward and listening, fist cocked, he had an eerie feeling that there was someone just on the other side, poised in the same attitude as himself, leaning forward and listening. Standing there in the heat of early summer he felt the hair stir on the back of his neck and a sudden start of cold sweat at his armpits. He rapped lightly; then, without waiting for a reply, he turned and walked swiftly across the veranda and down the steps, not having known a fear like this since the bad dreams of his childhood — a taste of brass at the base of his tongue and a pain in his chest as if an invisible hand had clutched his heart.

That was Monday. Next morning when he came to the office a Negro woman was waiting on the sidewalk. It seemed to him that he knew her or at least had seen her before. "Mr Stubberfield," she said. He stopped and looked at her. She was thin, of medium height, the color of milk chocolate, her hair hidden by a clean and neatly folded headrag. "I cooks for Major Barcroft," she said, and then he recognized her, remembering all those painful Sundays; Nora was her name, the mother of a jazz cornetist who had come home from the North to recover from tuberculosis (— so they thought. But two weeks later he shot a barrelhouse gambler over a woman, and six weeks later was tried for it and sentenced, and five months later died in the electric chair: Bristol's one artist, her one famous man, as they discovered when the musicologists came looking for information. But that was in the future now, both the fate and the fame); "*Did* cook, leastways," she said. She paused. "Captain, they's something you ought to know."

"All right," he said. He said it calmly, so that afterwards, looking back, he could point to this calmness and tell himself that he had known what was coming. Then she told him.

"Yessdy when I come to work Miss Manda was waiting for me at the door. She told me take myself a holiday. It warnt natchel; them folks aint never give no time-off to nobody. Onliest holiday I ever had, disbarring the flood, was three hours back in Twenty Nine when my sister's husband passed. So I been going by there, since. Not up to the house: just walking past and looking. Captain, they's something wrong in there. I could tell by the look on her face. They's something awful wrong."

It came back to him now, the sense of horror that had swept over him the day before, when he stood on the veranda and felt a presence on the other side of the door. Safe at home, he soon recovered from his panic; he believed he had been foolish and he avoided thinking of it, much as a person will put aside thoughts of a previous incarnation or a sense of having lived a particular scene before. But later, as he lay in bed, it returned, and now as he stood in front of the cotton office listening to Nora, it was as strong as ever. "All right," he said, still with the calmness he was later to call prescience. He turned. Leaning through the doorway he said to the bookkeeper, who was hunched above a ledger: "I'll be back," and set off down the street.

This time he did not hesitate. He went up the steps, crossed the veranda, and knocked at the door without pausing. And just as before, the feeling came over him — except that now it was more general, more diffused; the presence was not opposite him, behind the door, but it was somewhere in the house. He knocked again. After waiting and hearing no sound, he turned to leave. At the head of the steps, as he turned again, he caught out of the tail of his eye what he thought was a flicker of motion. It was quick — too quick, like an optical illusion — but he believed he had seen the corner of a lace curtain at one of the front windows drop back into place. He stood facing the house again, looking at the curtain. It hung motionless.

He did not return to the office; he went directly to the police station, walking fast on his short legs, his long trunk leaned forward as if into a strong wind. The chief of police and the desk sergeant sat looking at him solemnly while he told about it. "There's somebody in there," he said. "Somebody was watching me."

"Did you see them?"

"N-no. But I felt it."

"*I* dont feel it," the chief said. He was red-faced and thick-necked, in shiny blue serge. "I cant go busting into people's houses because youve got a feeling. Maybe they took a trip or something."

"A trip?" Henry said. "Major *Bar*croft?" Since this made no impression, he told about the cook. "She knows. She's been working there for over twenty years and *she* knows something's wrong." But the chief still looked doubtful.

Then the telephone rang and the sergeant answered it. "You," he said. He gave it to the chief.

"Hobart here," the chief said. This was his official voice and he narrowed his eyes as he spoke. During the pause that followed, however, his eyes went back to normal. Then they stretched to O's. "Gret God," he said, and Henry could hear the voice at the other end of the line. It was squeaky and indecipherable, like Punch infuriated. The chief's eyes bulged. "Gret God!" he cried. Then: "All right, Mr Barnes," he said, recovering his official voice, "I'll be right over."

He put on his cap and hurried to the door. But there he paused, turning back to Henry. "I guess you better come with me," he told him. "It looks like you really had something after all."

"What?" Henry said. "What is it?"

"Come on." They were outside by now. The chief got into a squad car. "Get in back," he said, and Henry did.

"What is it?"

"We'll see," Chief Hobart said, and he gave the driver the South Lamar address. Henry watched the back of his neck,

194

the bulge of muscle going to fat and the bone-white line at the rim of yesterday's haircut. "Faster," the chief said, pressing the button of the siren till it screamed. It died to a moan, then screamed again. By that time they had lurched to a stop in front of the Barcroft house.

Harry Barnes was waiting on the porch (— as usual; he was always quick to reach the scene when tragedy struck. That was why they called him Light-Hearse Harry); he had just returned from the neighboring house, where he had gone to use the telephone. Behind him the door was open — the door at which Henry had knocked less than an hour ago, without getting any more answer than he had the day before. Chief Hobart got out of the car, moving fast with Henry close behind him; they went up the steps in tandem. "All right," he said. "Where are they?"

"He's in back," the undertaker said. "She's up front, in the parlor, the same as when I got here. But you cant talk to her — she's in shock or something. And you sure cant talk to him and thats a fact."

"Then who called you?"

"Miss Sadie Eggleston. She was passing here about twenty minutes back and she heard somebody call her name. It sounded kind of choked, she said. She looked and it was Amanda Barcroft, right up here on the porch, looking like she was walking in her sleep. Thats what Miss Sadie said. Amanda says, 'Be so good as to call Mr Barnes. Tell him my father died,' and went back into the house."

"All right," the chief said. "Lets go see."

As they crossed the veranda to enter the house, Henry looked over his shoulder and saw a cluster of four or five women on the sidewalk, watching and talking with their heads tipped close together, their hands in front of their mouths. Miss Sadie must have been spreading the word, he thought — and turned back just in time to keep from walking into the chief and Mr Barnes, who had stopped in the hall before an open doorway on the right; ". . . in shock," the undertaker was saying. Henry joined them, looking past their shoulders into the parlor. The room was so dusky behind its curtains that at first, having just come in out of brilliant mid-morning sunlight, he could discern nothing. But presently, his pupils dilating, details emerged as on a photographic print in its chemical bath, and he saw Amanda sitting in her sister's Morris chair. The tabs of lace at her wrists and throat were soft points of light in the gloom; her hands were in her lap, her head slightly bowed above them. Though her face was drawn and pale, there were no tears in her eyes; ". . . since Sunday night," the undertaker was saying.

So now he knew what had been behind that locked door when he knocked on it, first yesterday and again an hour ago — he knew the source of the feeling of dread that had swept over him. The presence had been Death itself. I felt it! he told himself with something of triumph, or at any rate vindication, after the denials by the bookkeeper and the police chief. He stood looking at Amanda but she did not see him; she did not see anything. Then he knew that he must have been standing there quite a while, for he heard a voice say "Gret God" as if from a far distance, and when he looked around, neither Chief Hobart nor Mr Barnes was in sight. "What makes him black like that?" he heard the chief say from beyond the end of the hall.

"Suffocation," Mr Barnes said. "Thats what a heart attack really is: suffocation. Ive had them even blacker. Besides, two days in weather like this . . ."

But he was at the study door by then; he could see for himself the body on the button-studded horsehide couch, with its blue-black, swollen face and staring eyes. Then he began to smell him and realized that he had been smelling him all along, the over-sweet smell of corruption. He turned without having really paused; he hurried back down the hall as fast as his short legs would carry him, out of the door and onto the veranda, where sunlight struck him like a slap across the eyes. For a moment he was blinded. He stood with one hand against a pillar, waiting for his pupils to shrink. At last they did and he saw that the group of four or five women had grown to more than a dozen. They stood as before, their heads tipped close together and their hands in front of their mouths.

By noon all Bristol hummed with it, men clustering on street corners and housewives leaning over backyard fences. They told how the policeman had to hold her when Mr Barnes' assistant came with his long wicker basket. Most of them said she had gone out of her mind with grief and had been sitting there with her dead father because she had not known what else to do. Others, including those who had called her Poor Amanda and were familiar with what they called her scandal, said she had been holding onto all she had left in the world. There was a third group, made up of people who believed they saw still deeper into the matter; they said she had been sitting there gloating over him.

8. Shots in the Dark

For all its intensity, however, the talk of what had happened on Lamar Street would have been even more fervid if it had not had to share the limelight with another outrage of which the news, concerning Harley Drew and Amy and Jeff Carruthers, reached Bristol that same morning, two or three hours earlier, from Briartree down on Lake Jordan. There was less conjecture here but that was because people believed there was less room, or at any rate occasion, for conjecture. The event, though far less common than in the old days — when, as they said, men were men — was not uncommon; indeed it was fairly cut-and-dried, though not without the tinge of humor that usually accompanies such bloodshed. "Why, yes, of course," they told each other, speaking with the irrefutable positiveness which seems at times to be in direct ratio to the extent of error. For they were wrong. They were utterly and ironically wrong.

In the year following that first tourist court assignation, Amy's charm had continued to grow for Drew. He was not only fascinated by her person, he was fascinated by the things that surrounded her person — her clothes, her hair-style, even her cosmetics. He would wake in the night, switch on the bed lamp, and watch her sleeping beside him in the rented room, twenty to fifty miles from Bristol, depending on what point of the compass they had struck out this time. Admiring the texture of her skin, he compared her to those other women, hotel girls like that first Alma ten years back, who had kept the peasant ankles and heavy thighs their forebears brought over from the old world: whereas with Amy, though the blood was basically peasant too, it had thinned to a sort of ichor, actually blue where the veins were near the surface. Cut her, she'd bleed blue, Drew told himself. Or he would cross to the dresser where her overnight bag sat with the lid still raised, a patented model with compartments for everything; he would take out the urn-shaped jars and fluted bottles, unscrew the caps or ease out the glass stoppers, and smell them, the perfumed grease and distillations from the sperm whale, thinking: Ahhh. Then he would lift out the hand-stitched underwear, the pants and slips and petticoats with intricate unreadable monograms, unfolding and refolding them, feeling the whisper of silk against his palms, and to him they felt of money. At last he would return to the bed and sit looking down at her. Even her sunburn represented money, its smooth tan consistency reminding him of the leisure that enabled her to acquire it. He liked the way she smelled, duplicating what was in the various jars and bottles, and the fact that this fragrance could be bought (at as high as fifty dollars an ounce) made it no less enjoyable, no less heady — indeed, that was the pleasure; Fifty dollars a whiff! he thought, and his breath would quicken as he thought it. The fact was, he respected her enormously. It amounted to love, or very nearly love (a relative emotion anyhow, varying from person to person: Romeo and Mercutio, for instance) or as near love, at any rate, as Drew was ever to come.

So it went. He had what he had prayed for, and the tick marks on the calendar, scoring their meetings, were for him what a mounting column of figures would be for a miser. Yet this success — like most successes, no matter how much longed for — bred only further desires, more distant goals. The Memphis and New Orleans visits had not been spent at the Peabody or the St Charles or the Roosevelt; they had not dined at

Galatoire's or Antoine's. They had had to keep to the back streets, the remoter purlieus, dodging recognition. Apparently this was all right with Amy, who had had her share of highlife in her time. But it was not all right with Drew; the memory of that three-year 'look round' was beginning to dim. If originally his desire had been to get her alone, now he wanted her at his side in public. He wanted to wear her like a badge, a panache, her and her expensive clothes, her careless, moneyed manner. "Look what *he's* got; look at that," he wanted to hear them murmur as he entered hotel lobbies and restaurants with Amy on his arm — hotels and restaurants barred to them now because of the dictates of prudence. Not that he was opposed to prudence: he, in fact, was the one who insisted on it. What Drew was opposed to was the necessity for prudence.

He had decided on his goal: his final goal, he told himself, incurably optimistic, still not having learned (and never *to* learn) that his desires were merely steps on an endless staircase leading nowhere. Divorce was no answer; the money was Jeff's. The answer lay in another direction, one that he was waiting for the courage — or anyhow the opportunity — to propose to Amy. He saw himself master of Briartree and all that went with it, including Amy as chatelaine. As for the present master, who would be surprised at anything that befell a blind man? Who would be surprised to hear that the houseboy, coming to work one morning, had found his employer crumpled at the foot of a flight of stairs, dead of a broken neck since late the night before?

Once this thought was in his mind, he would have been hard put to say when it had first occurred to him; it seemed so inescapably the only solution, he came to believe that he must have intended it from the start — as indeed perhaps he had, unconsciously. Yet even now, with it so firmly decided on as the answer to his problems, the only means of fulfilling his desires, he delayed proposing it to Amy: not because he had any fear of moral indignation on her part (he knew her far too well by now to expect any such reaction) but because he was afraid to add a questionable element to their union. He was enjoying himself, and one of his points of superiority over other men — call it that — was that he knew better than to tamper with happiness, a reflex most men find it impossible to abstain from. Whether or not she would agree was another matter, for at times she seemed inordinately fond of Jeff, not from love, of course, or even friendship, but rather from amusement. It was strange.

However, two events brought him to the point of a decision. For one thing, he was offered a job with a Memphis bank, a really exceptional position, and though he did not exactly decline it — he never exactly declined any offer, as has been said — he did not accept it. To his considerable surprise he found that he was not even tempted to accept it. He could not have left Amy if he had wanted to. Thus he discovered that he had lost his freedom, which had been the one thing he thought of himself as prizing highest. The Barcroft business, as he now termed his long engagement to Amanda, had been a different matter: he had felt all along that he could break it off whenever he chose, which in fact was what he had done. But now he thought of himself as a man tied down, and that was bitter.

The other was not really a single event; it was a series of them, more or less alike, modeled after the first one back in July of the previous year when the new bridge over the river was opened to traffic and they went across to Arkansas for a night. They had checked in at a tourist court and were driving along the highway in search of a restaurant, when they saw HANNAHS spelled in lights. "Hey: a nightclub!" Amy cried. Drew turned in, though not without misgivings. The entrance was around at the side, two steps leading up to a closed door, beyond which they heard music and stamping feet. When Drew opened the door it was like looking into a cage of lions and monkeys at feeding time, arms and legs blurred with motion, bodies spinning furiously, skirts flaring, trouser legs flopping. This was the jitterbug, which they had heard of but had never seen before. To them it was reminiscent of the Twenties, like the Charleston gone insane.

A row of booths ran down each side of the room. At the far end a blue-and-gold nickelodeon with moving lights was turned up full, and at this end a long window was cut waist-high into the wall so that you looked over a counter into a room where beer and ice and chasers were kept, and even a pump-up stove for toasting sandwiches. A waitress, dressed no differently from the dancing women except that she wore about her waist a towel with a pocket sewed on it to hold her tips, kept moving between the booths and the counter, crying orders shrilly to be heard above the din. Drew and Amy found a booth in back, not far from the music, which beat against their eardrums.

"Oo! what a dive!" Amy cried happily, her voice as high-pitched as the waitress's. "Break out the bottle, honey lamb. Numb me afore I go deef." Her eyes had an excited glitter, as from fever, and she turned her head this way and that, watching the dancers and the drinkers. "Look at that one," she kept saying; "Look at *that* one." She even pointed, and sometimes the people would look back at her, scowling. Drew's misgivings increased. He could see the headline now: BRISTOL BANKER INVOLVED IN ROADHOUSE BRAWL.

In the booth behind them, nearer the blare of the music, a man and his wife were arguing. Their voices came through during pauses when the machine was changing records.

"I never said I wasnt."

"Ah, *you*."

"Some fun, all right — "

"You think *I* like it?"

"You — "

"Ah, *you!*"

Then the new record would drown them out. But they came through each time the music paused.

"You — "

"Ah, *you*."

Marital bliss, Drew thought, refilling Amy's glass, which she slid across the table at him. That was when the first one came up — a mousy man with a receding chin and claret-colored suspenders. "Say, mister," he said. "Mind if I dance a turn with your girlf she's willing?"

"Thanks," Drew said. "Not yet awhile. But thanks."

Amy watched him walk away. "I *like* this place," she said over the rim of her glass. "I really do."

"A little too informal for me," Drew said.

Then another came up, more positive. "Dance your girl?"

"Sorry," Drew said, watching Amy. The man stood for a moment looking down at him, hard-faced in a damp blue shirt, the sleeves rolled tight above his biceps. Drew still did not return his look and finally he shrugged and walked away.

"Not my type," Amy said, sliding her glass across the table. She had even sucked the ice dry.

"Come on," Drew said. "Lets get out of here."

"*Fill* it," she said. He filled it. This was her third and he was still on his first. "Hats more like it," she said presently. He thought she meant the drink, but when he looked he saw that she was returning the stares of three men in a booth across the room. They wore gabardine shirts with pearl buttons and contrasting yokes, skin-tight Levis bleached sky-blue, and cowboy boots. "Makes me wish I worn my jodhpurs," Amy said.

Looking back across the room, Drew saw that one of the men had risen from the booth and was coming toward them. The tallest of the three, he had high cheekbones and a bleached space at the top of his forehead where he wore his hat. "Dance this next?" he said, standing beside the table. He spoke directly to Amy.

"Be back, honey," she said to Drew before he could decline. She was already standing: had been standing, he realized, since the man first rose to cross the room.

"The name is Tex," Drew heard him say as he put his arm around her waist. He said it solemnly, as if he might have been saying he had a million dollars or tonight was the end of the world. They danced away and Drew was left nursing his drink.

In the course of the next three records he watched them through a haze of smoke and whirling couples. The man was teaching her the jitterbug, throwing her out and pulling her back, showing her how to truck with her knees held close together, pigeon-toed. The hard high heels of his boots made a clatter like hoofs. She seemed to be enjoying it, but in the interval between the third and fourth records — one of those sudden silences which seemed even louder, somehow, than the blare — she came back fanning herself, saying "Woo. Give me a drink. My God." Her upper lip was beaded with perspiration; her eyes were glassy. She drank. "You see him?" she said. "Tex? My God. His hands were even busier than his feet."

"Stay way from him then."

"Well — " The fifth record had started by now.

"Dance?" they heard.

They looked up. It was Tex.

"She's not dancing," Drew said evenly.

"Not?" Tex said. "Aint that kind of up to the lady?"

"It's up to me," Drew said, watching Amy. "It's up to me and I say she's not dancing."

By this time the two friends had crossed the floor; they stood one on each side of Tex, all three looking lean and capable in their cowboy clothes, a little taller than life in their high-heel boots. Amy looked at them, then back at Drew. The music stopped. Eyes glassy, she suddenly leaned forward, patted his arm, and spoke. It sounded loud against the silence. "Go on, Drew boy. Pop him one."

BRISTOL BANKER INVOLVED IN ROADHOUSE BRAWL ran across his mind like a streamer, like a headline dummy across an editor's desk: whereupon he did a thing which, even as he did it, he knew he would never forget, would never remember except with a sense of shame. He looked up at the three men — they stood with their arms held slightly away from their sides, a look of almost happy anticipation on their faces — and smiled;

he smiled broadly. "Sit down, fellows. Have a drink," he said. "Slide over, Amy. Make room for our friends." Yet behind the glibness and the smile there was an ache of shame; he had never declined a fight before. He thought of the DSC in its leather case in the bureau drawer at home, and for a moment he wished he had it here to show them.

They were a party. The whiskey was gone in less than half an hour — bonded stuff, of which the three men showed their appreciation by swishing it around in their mouths before they swallowed. All this time, speculative, bemused, Tex sat looking down the front of Amy's dress like a man on a highdive platform contemplating a jackknife or a gainer. Drew kept as brave a face through this as he had through the loss of his whiskey. Amy, who had had more than her share of the bottle, got more and more glassy-eyed, until finally she went to sleep. "Well —" Drew said. He rose. "Time to go." The others helped him half-guide, half-carry her to the door and out to the car. When one of her breasts tumbled out, Tex leaned forward and with a surprisingly delicate circumspection, of which Drew would never have suspected him capable, stuffed it back. Even then, however, Drew lacked the courage to refuse to shake hands with him. He shook hands all around, for he kept seeing that headline with a subhead: *Millionaire's Wife Was Bone of Contention in Fracas, Witnesses State.* As he drove off he saw the three of them in the rear-vision mirror, silhouetted against the electric sign. Bastards! he thought, and wiped his palm against his thigh.

This was only the first in a series of such incidents, for Amy had an increasing fondness for these places. When he cursed her proclivity for associating with truck drivers, imitation cowboys and roadhouse touts, however, he paused to consider that it also included small-town bank employes; he was forced to reconcile himself to her tastes. Yet as the incidents became more frequent he saw clearly that marriage was the only answer. Then if they went to such places and she said, "Go on, Drew boy. Pop him one," he would pop him one with pleasure.

BRISTOL BANKER DEFENDS WIFE was a headline he could stomach and be proud of.

Then in September, soon after the war got under way in Europe, he received the offer from the Memphis bank, and having refused it he found his position intolerable, being required not only to act the role of a physical coward (for which he was in no way suited) but also to turn down all outside advantages, no matter how exceptional. It seemed to him that he was putting so much more into this thing than she was — in spite of the fact that she would stuff bills of rather large denominations into his side coat pocket as they drove out of town; for what was that but money? while he was giving his peace of mind, his self-respect, his future. A burning sense of the injustice of all this brought him at last to the proposal of murder. The week he received the offer from Memphis he and Amy were driving out of town on a Saturday morning; it had been a year and seven months since the night in the state-line tourist court. "What I dont like is all this waiting," he said, hardly knowing how to begin, in spite of all the thinking he had done. Mainly he was exasperated, but he was also a little afraid; for you could never tell about women. They had stopped at a traffic signal and he fiddled with the steering wheel spokes while waiting for the light to change. "Damn it, Amy — "

He paused, then said it again. "Damn it, Amy — " But she was scarcely listening. She had this ability to blank out when the talk grew serious, just as some people can do when a radio program is held up for the commercial. Sunlight fell in long gold pencilings through the leaves of the oaks and sycamores that grew between the sidewalk and the curb; now was the climax of summer and the nights were perceptibly longer, though no cooler. Maybe the guns in Europe would bring rain — that was how they had explained the rain she remembered falling ceaselessly through her early teens, the long Carolina afternoons with a patter on the windowpanes and the nights when there was a steady drumming on the roof; "It's the guns in Europe," they told her, and now the guns were barking and growling again. A woman dressed in gray stood at the curb, holding a market basket with both hands. The light was with her but she did not move. Then it changed, glared green, and Drew engaged the clutch; the car rolled forward.

He was silent for a time, apparently having decided that 'Damn it, Amy' was the wrong approach. They were well out of town before he spoke again, telling her — to her surprise, for he seldom spoke of the war — a rather tiring story about a man, a friend of his, who got gas in his eyes. Lewisite, he said. It was not very interesting; she was looking out over the fields, alternately green or green-and-white, depending on whether the pickers had passed over them; she only heard snatches of the story. Presently the scene was a hospital behind the lines, the friend in bed with a bandage over his eyes, and Drew was sitting beside him. They were talking; the man was asking for something. He was blind and they were about to send him home. A pistol. "Did you give it to him?" Amy said, interrupting.

"I did."

"Wasnt that kind of risky?"

"Risky? How, risky?"

"The pistol: theyd trace it."

"Mm — no. It wasnt mine. It was one I picked up in a retreat." He kept his eyes on the road, and suddenly for no good reason Amy knew that it was all a lie. He was making it up.

"Did he use it?"

"He used it; he used it that night." Drew kept his eyes on the road. He drove for a while, saying nothing. Then he said, "Dyou think I did right?"

"I guess. If thats what he wanted."

"No: I mean apart from that. He was sort of delirious anyhow — off his rocker. I mean because of the blindness. Wasnt
he better off?"

"*I* dont know. It depends on how he felt about it. Look at
Jeff."

Drew said nothing to this, but he began to glance at her
from time to time, barely turning his head. She wondered why
he had gone to the trouble of making all this up, this rigmarole
about a blind man and a pistol, and suddenly she remembered
something Jeff had said five years ago: *Youre all the way evil,
Amy*. She smiled. 'I'm going to take a little nap,' she intended
to say, but she was asleep before she could form the words.

Then he woke her. They were there. The sun was coming
straight down. It was noon. "I was sleeping so good," she
said. "I dreamed — I dreamed — " But she could not remember; she gave it up. "Where are we?"

"Thats Clarksdale down the road a piece."

He had already checked in at the office. They went into
the cabin. It was neater and cleaner than most; there were
dotted Swiss curtains at the windows and a reading lamp on
each of the twin beds — they had reached the twin-beds stage
by now. Amy looked around. "Why, this is downright *nice*.
Whats our name?"

"Amos Tooth," he said solemnly. They both laughed, for
this was a game they played; Drew signed a different name
on the register each trip. He was really quite ingenious in
this respect. Once he had signed 'Major Malcolm Barcroft,'
which wasnt very funny — being a sort of private joke — but
he made up for it next time by signing 'David Copperfield.'
Amy was always '& Wife.' After the first few times he began
to call her that. "Shall we go eat, & Wife?"

There was a restaurant just up the road. They ate and came
straight back to bed. Later the afternoon sun beat golden
against the shades, which billowed and sighed from time to
time when there was a little breeze. Languid, Amy lay and lis-

tened; the stick at the bottom of the shade made a tapping against the sill; the rhythm of it put her to sleep, and when she woke darkness had almost come. Drew lay in the adjoining bed, a pale naked shadow blowing smoke rings that were steel-gray in the gloom. She watched him through the lattice of her lashes. After a while she said, "Why'd you make up all that business about the blind man?"

"Make up?"

"Yes."

He paused. Caught unprepared he was never a very good liar. "I wanted to see how you felt," he said, and added immediately: "Besides, it really did happen, to a friend of mine."

"The blind man?"

"No: the one who gave him the pistol."

"Oh. Did he really give it to him?"

"Well — he started to. And afterwards he wondered if he shouldnt have."

"I see." She thought a while. "What happened to him?"

"The blind man? I dont know. Somebody said he really did kill himself, on the boat going back. I dont know. There were lots like him."

She watched him light another cigarette, his face dead white in the flare. When he blew out the match the darkness was complete; it was as if night had fallen during that brief spurt of flame. He lay back, the cigarette tip glowing and fading like a signal light. "Were you very scared in the war?" she asked.

"Not very. No. I was what you might call moderately scared. Comparatively speaking, that is." He spoke slowly. "Looking back on it — the excitement and all — I guess it was maybe the best time of my life. I know an old man lives on Lamar Street would sell his soul for ten minutes of what I had almost two years of."

Amy let this pass. The cigarette glowed and faded, glowed and faded. He was thinking. Then he said, "We've all got about the same amount of courage. The difference comes in whether we're willing to use it, provided we get a chance. Take you and me. We want something beyond all this" — he made a gesture, describing a red arc with the tip of his cigarette " — but whether we take it or not is up to us. It's a question of using courage."

"What do you mean?"

"This," he said, and the springs creaked under him. He sat up, flipping the cigarette through the bathroom door. It fell like a miniature comet with a little burst of sparks against the tiles. While he talked it faded and presently it went out. This was what he had been working toward. He took his time; he made it clear. Who would be surprised to hear that the houseboy coming to work one morning had found the blind man crumpled at the foot of the stairs, dead of a broken neck since sometime late the night before? Theyd say he got up for a drink of water or a midnight snack and missed his footing; it was just that simple. Drew spoke in a conspirator's undertone — not so much in fear of being overheard, however, as in an attempt to gauge her reaction to the words. When he had finished he waited for her to speak. She waited too. It was almost a full minute before she replied.

"You want me to hold his legs or something while you trip him?"

In the dark he could not see that she was smiling her slow, down-tending smile; he did not hear the mockery in her voice. He was too delighted with the words themselves to pay much attention to the tone in which they were spoken. "No, no," he said, leaning forward, speaking rapidly; "all I want is — " and was interrupted by a burst of laughter. While she laughed he sat there in the darkness, hating her. It was some little time before she could speak, though not as long as it seemed. Then she said:

"I swear, Drew boy; I swear you take the cake."

This came just in time; for the truth was, she was beginning to weary of him, and not only of him but of the Delta too.

Not that he had failed her in the prime respect: the days of what he, in his artilleryman's jargon, called 'muzzle bursts' were long since past, and she had frequent cause to bless her patience through the trying first few weeks: nowadays in their gladiatorial contests it was quite often Amy who lay sweat-drenched and exhausted, spread-eagle on the mat, and Drew who leaned above her, hawk-faced and triumphant, glaring down — 'There! There, by God!' — victorious after the bitter defeats of the early encounters. She had no complaint in that direction. Paradoxically, what was wearying her of him was what had drawn her in the first place: her essential promiscuity. It was really that simple. She wanted a change.

A year and six months was a very long time, longer than she had been involved with anyone — longer, even, than she had been involved with Jeff — in this particular sense. What kept it going was the clandestine excitement, the conspiratorial air, and the various subterfuges Drew employed. She had been right about the conspiratorial air from the first, and now it turned out that he had been right to adopt it. For that was what held her, that and his skill at subterfuge; he took no chances even with a blind man. Watching his grave demeanor at the Briartree dinner table while he discussed finances or the world political situation with Jeff and turned to her from time to time with the deference any guest owes any hostess: "Isnt that so, Mrs Carruthers?" (or, later: "Isnt that so, Amy?" since he decided that too much formality was itself suspicious) was better than watching a movie. He should have been an actor, she decided. Sometimes she would laugh till tears of mirth stood in her eyes; she had to cover her face with a napkin and pretend to be choking. "Take some water," Drew would say, solicitous; he never so much as smiled at such a time. The most he permitted himself was a twinkle deep in the pupil of each eye, and that would set her to laughing all the harder, until finally she would have to leave the table. All this, together with the series of names on hotel and tourist court registers, from David Copperfield to Amos Tooth — &

Wife — appealed enormously to her simple and somewhat cruel sense of humor.

Some nights when they were stopping only twenty or thirty miles away, Drew would leave her soon after dark and return about three hours later. He would wake her and sit beside her on the bed and tell how he had sat talking with Jeff at Briartree, throwing him off the scent; for otherwise he might have begun to wonder at never seeing Drew when Amy was away, and from there it would be an easy step to assuming that they were together. " 'Where's Amy?' I asked him, and *he* said — you know how he talks: 'Oh she's off to Memphis, shopping. She's buying an awful lot of clothes here lately, seems to me.' " Drew imitated Jeff's voice to perfection, querulous and trembly in the upper registers; he even managed to look a good deal like him when he was quoting, puffing out his cheeks a bit, drawing in the corners of his mouth, and letting his eyes come unfocused. Amy had to laugh. He should indeed have been an actor, she decided.

Even so, there was a limit to how long she could be amused in such a fashion. The jokes were not so funny the third or fourth time around; she wanted a new pair of hands moving nervously over her person, a new voice panting different words in her ear. She had begun to think of a break. This excursion to the Delta — the blind seed swimming home — had long since served whatever vague purpose she had had in mind. (What was his name? Perkins. Was that his name?) She was bored, almost to the point of doing something about it. Then in the quiet September twilight Drew proposed the murder and her interest was revived. "You want me to hold his legs?" she said. She had underestimated him, and even though she laughed there was admiration behind the laughter. Besides, she soon stopped laughing.

She had known from the start what he was really after, beyond the flesh, and it seemed to her now that she should have expected this. From the night of their first intimacy Drew had listened with great interest when she told of her experiences in the world of highlife, especially during the five-year European celebration of the inheritance. He listened, absorbed, while she told of Jeff shooting at the patter of the widow's little Spaniard's pumps; then he roared with laughter, slapping his thigh. But this was unusual. Mostly he listened with quiet pleasure and anticipation, like a child being introduced to history through tales of kings and heroes, for he looked forward to doing such things himself — with Jeff's money and Jeff's wife. So she might have expected the proposal, she realized soon after he had made it, and she stopped laughing. For here was an excitement she had never known before; here were opportunities for amusement beyond anything she had imagined.

Not that she had any intention of going through with it. Jeff suited her too well in too many ways, and she had few delusions as to Drew in the role of husband. What was more, she knew the boredom would return, and later the break. But she saw possibilities for an amusing interim and she worked it for all it was worth, believing that she was in command of the situation. This was the beginning of a more intimate relationship among the three of them — a sort of rehearsal, as Drew believed, for what was to come. Soon after the first of the year, he and Amy no longer went afield for their pleasures; they took them right there in the house, approximately under the blind man's nose. Drew was not entirely without caution, remembering the potshots at the Spaniard, but he came to believe that he would more or less welcome such a scene. For a small risk, even though no plea would be needed before the world — let alone the coroner's jury, whose verdict, if one were called for, would be Accidental Death — it would give him a chance to plead self-defense to his conscience.

This moved swiftly. Amy could sense an approaching climax. Apparently Drew could sense it too, for now their love encounters had the frantic jerkiness of such scenes in the oldtime motion pictures (in the course of which the audience, crouched beneath the lancing beam, kept expecting Valentino or John Gilbert, stigmatized in flickering black and white, to look up from his work and cry with hot impatience — it was part of the illusion — 'Get those cameras out of here!'); yet nothing happened. Then one April night they tried something new. Drew had dinner at Briartree and afterwards the three of them were sitting in the living room. The electric clock hummed on the mantelpiece. For a long time nobody said anything. The servants had left. Then Drew said, "Well" — rising; it was barely after nine — "thanks for the meal. I'd better be heading back."

"Early yet," Jeff told him.

"Hard day tomorrow," Drew said; "Good night," and Amy went to see him out, something she had never done in the old days. "Night," he said, opening the door.

"Good night," she said, and she reached across in front of him and slammed it. They stood together in the hall, facing the closed door. He did not understand until she pointed to the stairs. Then, obediently, he tiptoed up and waited on the landing while she went into the living room; "Good night," he heard her say to Jeff. She joined him on the stairs and they went quietly to her room. After a while they heard Jeff playing the phonograph. He played it until midnight; then they heard him come upstairs and go down the hall to his room. Drew left just before dawn, arriving at Mrs Pentecost's with plenty of time for a bath and a shave before breakfast.

'Hard day tomorrow,' he had said, not meaning it; but it was. He was red-eyed, numb with the need for sleep. Youre not as young as you used to be, he thought. However, he reminded himself that the time was near when he would be delivered. He was upstairs now, familiar with the floor plan; this was all a sort of rehearsal, a dry run, and he continued to labor at it. Twice again in the next two weeks he said good night and stayed, coming to work red-eyed the following day. The fourth time was the second Monday in May and the papers were full of the German break-through; von Rundstedt had crossed the Meuse. After dinner Drew and Jeff and Amy sat in the living room. It was all as before. The clock hummed; the servants had left; nobody said anything. Then Drew rose. "Well. Thanks again. I guess I'd better be going."

"So early?" Jeff said.

"Rough day tomorrow," Drew told him, knowing it was true. Except for this knowledge it was all as before. He and Amy rose. But now Jeff rose too, and the three of them crossed to the entrance hall, where Drew took his hat from the refectory table. Amy went to the front door with him but Jeff stopped in the doorway of the study; he would play some records before bedtime. Drew opened the door. "Night," he said. Jeff raised one hand, waving as if from a distance though he was only fifteen feet away.

"Good night," Amy said, wondering what Drew would do. She had only an instant to wonder, for he slammed the door and they both turned together, watching Jeff. It seemed to Amy that he must hear their heartbeats. He continued to stand in the study doorway and his eyes were fixed on Drew; there was an illusion that his eyesight had returned. Then, as if to reinforce the illusion, he said in a sudden but level voice, still as if looking at Drew:

"Who do you think youre fooling?"

Drew was so taken aback he almost answered. But Amy stepped in front of him, walking toward her husband. "Why should I try to fool you? I havent fooled you yet."

"That I know of, you mean."

"Maybe thats what I do mean. Yes. Good night."

Jeff shrugged and went into the study and Amy stopped at the foot of the stairs. There she turned and beckoned to Drew, who tiptoed past the study door, feet silent on the carpet. As he went by he saw the blind man seated in his armchair, his face toward the hall. Again there was that illusion of recovered sight: Drew flinched. He and Amy went upstairs together.

When they were in the bedroom he said nervously, "You think he saw me?"

"*Saw* you?"

"Knew I was there."

"Oh, he makes all kinds of guesses and stabs in the dark. Here: unhook me."

Apparently she was right, for presently they heard the phonograph. It was Jelly Roll Morton's *Two Nineteen*. At first he talked. "The first blues I no doubt ever heard," he said. He talked some more, hands moving over the keys. Then he began to sing, and it was as if you could see him throw his head back, the drawn ascetic face of a high-yellow monk, the skin fitting close to the skull.

> *Two Nineteen done cared my baby away.*
> *Two Seventeen bring her back some day.*

But Drew was right: Jeff had 'seen' him — meaning he knew he was there. For some time now, since not long after New Year's, he had been increasingly aware of what was going on between them. What was more, he knew exactly where, for he had heard them go upstairs together the week before — Drew had come on from Guard drill, wearing his uniform, and Jeff had heard the creak of his boots and the tiny chink of his spur and saber chains. This was early May; he had not gone to the door with them, and as he sat in the living room he heard the door slam, followed by the sound of what he thought at first was Amy coming down the hall alone. Then he remembered that she was wearing no bracelet, and thus he identified the faint jingling which no one but a blind man would have heard. "I'm going up," she said from the hall; the chinking stopped.

"Good night," he said; it began again, combined now with the creak of boots moving up the stairs.

His first reaction was incredulity, then rage, then incredulity again: he simply could not believe his luck. For more than three months now, with increasing fervor as the conviction grew, he had been plotting, hoping for some move on their part which would place them at his disposal. Now it was here. Yet he did nothing that night, remembering how the incidents involving the Austrian ski instructor and *Mama*'s Spaniard had ended in ridicule; this time he would move according to plan. Besides, this was a new kind of jealousy — double-barreled, so to speak, directed not only at the man but at Amy too, and therefore requiring double caution. She was the alienor and Drew the loved one. Thus on one hand; on the other, she was the property and Drew the thief. On both counts action was required.

Yet he did nothing that night. He went into the study and planned his campaign. Later he went up to his room, put on pajamas, and lay in bed completing the details. Then he got up and rehearsed it, moving quietly down the hall to the door of Amy's room; he could hear them speaking in whispers. He stayed there for perhaps ten minutes, his ear against the panel. At last he came back to his room. He lay smiling in the moonlight. Finally he fell asleep, still smiling, and woke with sunlight warm on his face; he had not heard Drew leave. But that was all right — Drew's leaving had no part in the campaign.

So ten days later, the second Monday in May, he was ready: so ready in fact, so much in the advantage, that he could afford to be sporting about it, like a hunter letting a duck rise off the water. He followed them into the hall and stood in the doorway of the study. "Who do you think youre fooling?" he said when the front door slammed, speaking directly to Drew, eyes fixed on the place where he knew he was standing. He heard him gasp and he felt the thrill that is the reward of sportsmanship, the hunter's consideration for the hunted. This was the greatest intimacy yet; it was like an embrace, flesh touching flesh; for a moment he experienced something akin to buck fever. Then Amy came forward and spoiled it. Jeff replied angrily, going into the study, where presently he heard Drew tiptoe past, his footsteps like so many powderpuffs dropped from a height.

He listened while they climbed the stairs, and that completed Phase One; he had planned it in three phases. Now began Phase Two, which would end when he reached the door of Amy's bedroom. He put the Jelly Roll Morton record on the phonograph, and when that was through he played another — any man to any woman in any dingy hotel room, the man abed, the woman with her hand on the knob of the door:

> *Dont leave me here.*
> *Dont leave me here.*
> *But if you just must go*
> *Leave a dime for beer.*

It was one of his favorites, yet he scarcely heard it. When it was through he wiped it with the complexion brush and put it back. Then he selected a Bessie Smith, and this time he listened in spite of himself.

> *I woke up this morning*
> *with an awful aching head,*
> *I woke up this morning*
> *with an awful aching head;*
> *My new man had left me*
> *just a room and a empty bed.*

Her warm, proud voice soared on though Bessie herself had been dead over two years now. She died after an automobile accident fifty miles from Briartree; they got her to a hospital in time but the authorities couldnt let her in — her color wasnt right and she bled to death.

He listened, head bent, wearing crepe-soled shoes and white wool socks, gray flannel slacks and a polo shirt unbuttoned at the throat. This was a different Jeff from the one who arrived twelve years ago from Carolina or the one who returned from Europe less than five years back. His tan had faded; he had gone to fat. The pectoral muscles, formerly the hard square plates of an athlete, had sagged to almost womanish proportions; the ripple of ribs had disappeared beneath a fatty casing that thickened his torso from armpits to fundament. More than anything he resembled a eunuch, or rather the classic conception of a eunuch — as if the knife-sharp sliver of windshield glass had performed a physical as well as a psychological castration. Yet under that ruined exterior there still lurked, like a ghost in a ruined house, the halfback who had heard his name roared from the grandstand, who had welcomed the shocks, the possible fractures and bruises and concussions, for love (or hatred) of one among the mass of tossing pennants as at the tournaments of old, and who had won her — though not through the football prowess after all — so that now, nearly twenty years later, she waited upstairs, inviting him to another encounter, the chain of flesh relinked. And now, as before, he welcomed the shocks, the fractures and concussions. He took out the pistol.

It was where he had kept it ever since Switzerland, in the nest of wires under the used-needles tray, along with a box containing thirty-eight of the original fifty cartridges. Six were in the pistol; the other six had been fired in the Cannes hotel. He had not fired it since, though every few months he would strip and clean and oil it. Once he had put the muzzle in his mouth to see what suicide was like, but there was such a compulsion to pull the trigger that he took it out in a hurry, badly frightened, and from then on his gorge would rise when he remembered the taste of oily metal. He thought of none of this now, however; he merely sat with the pistol in his lap, waiting for the record to end.

Lord, he's got that sweet something
and I told my gal-friend Lou;
He's got that sweet something
and I told my gal-friend Lou.
From the way she's raving
she must have gone and tried it too.

That was the end of the first side of the record. Jeff was expecting it, waiting with his hand above the tone arm, so that when the final note was wailed he lifted the needle clear of the groove, flipped the record over, and let the tone arm down. For three revolutions it gave a mechanical hissing. Then the music began again: *Empty Bed, Part Two.*

When my bed get empty
makes me feel awful mean and blue,
When my bed get empty
makes me feel awful mean and blue;
My springs are getting rusty
sleeping single like I do.

Bessie said 'blue' with the French *u* language students try so hard for. When she said it the first time Jeff was already at the foot of the stairs; when it came around again he was at the top, walking quietly on crepe soles down the hall, pistol in hand. He moved with the confidence of the blind at home, not having to pause for bearings, not even having to count his steps, but able at any given moment to reach out and touch whatever tables and chairs and doorknobs happened to be within reach, as if the objects exerted some sort of aura, an emanation, or had at least a reflectiveness, twitching the invisible cat-whiskers of the blind. He paused at Amy's bedroom door: Phase Three.

For all his careful planning, however, his rigid adherence to schedule, he was early. Leaning with his ear against the panel he heard the preliminary whispers still in progress, punctuated by the squeak of kisses. Downstairs Bessie sang the blues, indifferent to all misery but her own, and between the lines a trombone throbbed and moaned.

*He give me a lesson
that I never had before,*

*He give me a lesson
that I never had before;*

*When he got through teaching me
from my elbows down was sore.*

Charley Green was the trombone, he remembered. Then he froze, standing with his ear against the panel. Beyond the door the whispering had stopped; he heard the first tentative creaking of the springs. But still he waited, the pistol in his right hand and his left hand on the knob. Downstairs the song was into its final verse, in the course of which the tentative creak from the room beyond changed to a regular groaning, muffled, rhythmic, and profound; he turned the knob.

*When you get good loving
never go and spread the news;
Gals will double cross you
and leave you with them
Empty Bed Blues.*

On the last note, just before the mechanical hissing began, Jeff opened the door, went in, and closed it quietly with a backward movement of his arm. The innerspring groaning was louder now, guiding him to the bed. Though he did not know it, a bedside lamp was burning; as he came nearer his shadow on the wall behind him loomed hunch-shouldered and gigantic. He moved quickly, silently. Halting alongside the bed he placed his left hand in the small of Drew's back, palm down, rested the base of his other fist upon it, gripping the pistol, and walked the left hand up Drew's backbone like a tarantula. This was all according to plan; the backbone guided the pistol to the brain; this time he would not miss. Drew, if he felt the hand at all, must have thought it was Amy's. However, it is unlikely that he felt it, for he was approaching that brief ecstasy which is characterized — as is no other sensation, except perhaps extreme pain (and maybe nausea) — by a profound indifference to the world around him; whatever feelings of warmth and tenderness may lap the shores of these tiny timeless islands in the time-stream, no man is ever more alone than in this moment of closest possible contact. Amy, though, feeling something brush her knee, opened her eyes and saw Jeff with the pistol. She gave a yelp and a start of surprise. But here again Drew, if he noticed at all, must have taken her cry of alarm and her sudden writhing as evidence of a gratification similar to his own. Yet it was no matter — he had so little time anyhow; for then Jeff pulled the trigger.

He fired twice. At the first shot Drew merely jerked spasmodically, but at the second he gave a leap that raised him clear of the mattress. He fell back, tumbling sideways, and rolled to the floor at Jeff's feet. Meanwhile Amy, freed of his weight, scrambled out of bed in the other direction. Then she made her first mistake: she ran for the far corner instead of the door. Her bare feet made thudding sounds on the carpet and Jeff turned, coming toward her around the end of the bed. Neither of them spoke. Amy, crouched in the corner as if ashamed of her nakedness, watched him coming nearer; she had terror in her face. Jeff advanced with his arms outspread, like a man catching a turkey in a barnlot. The closer he came the less room there was left to go around him; the sooner she tried to reach the door, the better her chances were. She decided to make a rush for it, and that was when she made her second mistake; she went to the right, away from the hand that held the pistol. As it was, she almost made it; she was almost past when his free hand grazed her hair and suddenly clutched. He caught her. "Jeff!" she cried, but he dragged her inexorably across his hip, his left hand still grasping her hair — they posed thus for an instant, motionless, like dancers performing a deadly Apache — and slashed at her twice with the pistol, once at her right cheekbone and once across the bridge of her nose; then, chipping her teeth, he shoved the muzzle in her mouth. Downstairs the phonograph hissed and hissed. There were four shots left.

9. Miss Amanda

They gave Major Barcroft a military funeral. Colonel Tilden, flanked by what was left of his staff, stood at the salute while a bugler faltered through *Taps* and six National Guardsmen from the local battery, in lace-up boots and khaki breeches, o.d. shirts and dishpan helmets, fired three ragged pistol volleys across the grave. The cemetery was crowded, spectators pressing close about the funeral canopy and trailing back in thinning queues toward the gate through which the hearse had turned with its flag-draped burden. There were veterans among them, some of whom — the grizzled few with walking canes, trembly mouths, and eyes gone blear, come to honor this old soldier who had made so long a march toward death before them — had been members of his company in the Second Mississippi more than forty years ago, but mostly they were Legionnaires wearing snug blue bobtail tunics and jaunty caps with yellow piping cocked above one eye. Some had passed through the fire which their overseas caps and ribbons and fourrageres implied, had lived with bullets humming above them like the plucked strings of a gigantic musical instrument; others, like the man they had come to bury, had never seen battle.

Craning and insistent, they milled about, elbowing each other and stepping on graves, disappointed at having been denied the main attraction, the feature which had drawn them in the first place. For Amanda was not here — she was in the isolation ward of the hospital, where Dr Clinton had had her confined the day before. She was dazed; she took no interest in what went on around her, spoke to no one, and did not seem to realize what had happened or even where she was. She lay on the iron cot, staring straight ahead, and her eyes were dry and vacant. A group of women, including those who had been first to reach the scene on Lamar Street yesterday, stood in the corridor with fresh-cut flowers in their fists like tickets of admission. There would be a steady buzzing, as of bees, until the door came open from time to time, the nurse or doctor passing in or out, and for a moment it would hush; they saw her lying there, her face in bleak profile. Then the door would close and the whispering resume: "Did you *see* her? Did you see her *face*?"

Three stories above, in a corner room with a private bath and a telephone and a No Visitors sign upon the door, Harley Drew was convalescing from his wounds. Downstairs the women talked about that too, about what had happened at Briartree night before last: how Jeff, with Amy across his hip, the muzzle of the pistol in her mouth, one bullet left in the chamber and three more in the magazine, had suddenly lost his nerve or changed his mind or anyhow had dropped her, had relented, and had gone around Drew's body to the bedside phone and put in a call for a doctor in Ithaca, five miles to the south. He sat on the bed and held his head in his hands, beginning to weep. Then he took up the phone again and called a Bristol clinic. "Tell him I said quick!" he shouted into the mouthpiece, as if long-distance required a louder voice. "Tell him I said bring a nurse and all his instruments. She's banged up pretty bad I think." Amy lay battered and barely conscious, one cheek laid open and the bridge of her nose crushed almost flat, her lip split and bits of teeth like sand and gravel in her mouth. She wanted to crawl to the dresser and look in the mirror but she was afraid of what she knew she would see.

The Ithaca doctor was there within fifteen minutes. His name was Kidderman, an elderly country doctor who worked as much with mules as he did with men. He did what he could for Amy, disinfecting the cuts and dabbing at the bloodstains while waiting for the other doctor and his nurse to arrive. This was at Amy's insistence: she took one look at him, the greasy tie, the frayed collar, the gray crescents under his fingernails, and decided that the Bristol clinician would do a neater job. Meanwhile Dr Kidderman, who was not at all offended — who, rather, was relieved at not having to attempt such a delicate performance — went over to the body lying naked beside the bed in a welter of congealing blood and seed; he bent down for a perfunctory examination before covering it with a blanket, and suddenly he cried in a startled voice: "What do you mean, dead? This man's not dead."

He spoke in anger and reproach, as much at himself as at anyone. Then he went to work, moving deftly with an unexpected skill. This was more in Dr Kidderman's line, who for better than forty years had spent the last half of almost every Saturday night and the first half of every Sunday morning patching up the variously shot and cut survivors of the razor and pistol arguments that exploded in and overflowed the Negro dancehalls and barrelhouses down around Ithaca. When he had swabbed away the coagulated blood matting the hair around the wounds he found that both bullets had grooved the skull. It was as if Drew had been rapped smartly twice across the back of the head with a red-hot poker. The deeper groove was from the second shot; that was the one that gave him the concussion. If this had been one of the doctor's barrelhouse patients he would have stitched in a couple of dozen sutures, wrapped his head in several yards of gauze, and sent him home on a stretcher. As it was, he put in a call for an ambulance, which arrived soon after the clinician and his nurse had started to work on Amy, and Drew was taken, still unconscious, to the hospital in Bristol.

He did not regain consciousness until that afternoon. Shortly before five oclock his eyelids fluttered, lifted, lowered, then lifted again; he looked at the nurse beside his bed and the gray plaster walls of the hospital room. For a moment he said nothing. He seemed quite calm. Then he said, "What hit me?"

It was certainly the natural, indeed the expected thing to say. The laughter that followed whenever this was repeated around town was out of all proportion to the words themselves; 'Where am I?' would have served as well, would have provoked as much hilarity and as many digs in the ribs — considering where he was when he was shot. Drew was in the position of some favorite comedian whose appearance on the stage is greeted with uncontrollable laughter before he speaks or even grimaces, whose very picture on a billboard calls for smiles. The humor lay in the expectation of humor; they listened with their mouths all shaped for guffaws. Some, however, shook their heads with mock-serious regret: "All I got to say is he certainly missed a chance for a lovely death. I hope when my time comes I go like that."

Besides, it provided a sort of counterpoint to the outrage on Lamar Street. Try as they might they could find no humor in that occurrence, only horror. So they swung from topic to topic with the agility of trapeze artists. When they grew weary of brooding they could laugh, and when they grew weary of laughing they could brood: Bristol had not been so fortunate since 1911 when Hector Sturgis, son of old Mrs Sturgis, hung himself in his mother's attic after his wife was found asphyxiated in a hotel room with a drummer. Gossip had a field day — a field week. By the end of that time, however, distortion had made its inroads; the smallest fact in either event was taken as a theme for variations, until finally by the end of the week the original themes had disappeared, as happens in certain stretches of Brahms. People no longer believed anything they heard or told. In each case they had killed it, talked it to death.

Now all that remained to look forward to was the reading of Major Barcroft's will, the announcement of the extent of his estate. There was considerable difference of opinion about this, mainly because of his banking out of town since 1928 when Harley Drew went to work at the Planters Bank. Estimates ran from half a million — the amount he started out with when his young wife's father died — to three or even four millions, depending on whether you believed the rumors of loss (such as the one concerning the purchase of Reichsmarks after the war) or the rumors of stupendous coups and 'straddles' engineered by long-distance telephone across the board in Memphis. The latter were more widely believed, however, for the major had been a quiet one, never discussing his business transactions with anyone, and it was a general observation that men might be quiet about their successes, content to radiate a glow of satisfaction, but no man yet had managed to be quiet about his losses, if only for the sake of cursing aloud or unconvincing himself of his shortcomings. Exaggeration did its work here too: by the end of the week they were telling themselves that they had had a financial wizard among them. Meantime, waiting for the reading of the will, they told and retold the manner of his death and shuddered and re-shuddered at his daughter's strange reaction.

Some of it percolated up to the third-floor hospital room where Drew lay face-down on the iron cot while the two longitudinal wounds at the back of his head began to heal; primary intention was under way and there was a constant itching worse than pain — or so he thought now that the pain had abated. When he heard of Major Barcroft's death, the morning of the funeral, his first reaction was grief (grief for himself) and regret that this death had not come a year and seven months sooner, any time before that final interview in early October of year-before-last when he flung 'I wont marry you!' back over his shoulder as he hurried past Amanda, down the steps and down Lamar Street, out of her life. She was downstairs now, his nurse informed him; the hall was full of women clutching flowers and crowding each other aside for a better view each time the door came open. Thus he was kept posted on her condition. Next morning she ate breakfast; that afternoon she asked what there was for supper — she seemed to be coming out of it; in fact the doctor had said she might be going home in a couple of days. The nurse told him also of the speculation as to the size of Major Barcroft's estate, and Drew lay face-down feeling regret along with the itching at the shaven back of his head.

But wait. Wait, he thought. All is not lost, he told himself like Milton's fallen angel. Amy was lost — no doubt about that: but Amanda? no: he could make it up. If he knew women (And I know women, he thought) her love was stronger after the separation, for since when did mistreatment do anything to love but strengthen it where women were concerned? She was waiting for him now, downstairs — had been waiting ever since the night of the renouncement — and now that her father was out of the way she probably was wondering, even in her dazed condition, why Drew had not come running. Doubtless, though, she would hear about the shooting. That gave him pause. However, having paused, he moved on. Being shot in a lady's bedroom by an irate husband was no serious drawback. He would work the old Cynara excuse: 'Between her breast and mine fell your shadow' — something like that; 'Between the something something and the wine' — he would look it up and quote it properly if it didnt turn out too randy. Thus he remembered his old resolve to be romantically bold but never brash, as in the very beginning he had said "I intend to see you," remembering to add: "with your permission." As far as the involvement with Amy went, he could say he was trying to drown his remorse with a gesture of despair, a sort of spiritual suicide, a flirting with death. Which was what it damned well was, he thought, feeling a tingling in his wounds.

He was back in stride now and he figuratively rubbed his palms and chuckled from relief at having ended the three-day hiatus when he lay planless on the narrow cot without an aim in life, with only the pain and itching at the back of his head to occupy his mind, to turn it from consideration of his double failure and the bootless dozen precious years invested here in

Bristol. He moved on, thinking rapidly, back in the old familiar groove, rehearsing the speech of reconciliation. 'I couldnt pull you into poverty, I told you. But I see now I was wrong. Wrong, Amanda. Youre all there ever was or ever will be, and anything is better than being apart.' He thought he might even kneel as he spoke; just as he said 'Youre all there ever was' he'd sink to his knees and hold his arms out. It couldnt be too maudlin, he decided, considering how much there was at stake. For the next two days he worked at it, expanding, revising, polishing. At what he judged appropriate points he jotted in stage directions, such as: *Kneel; Hold out hands; Squeeze a tear if possible; Here a sob.* This was to be his masterpiece, and his spirits rose in ratio to the estimates of Major Barcroft's fortune.

Amanda went home Saturday but Drew was kept in bed, chafing at the delay; he imagined young men hurrying by the hundreds to Lamar Street to avail themselves of all she had to offer. He staged quite a scene that night, demanding to be released tomorrow morning. The doctor was firm, however: Drew was past all danger as long as he was quiet, but any sort of blow on the back of the head might prove serious indeed, even fatal. "You think I care?" Drew cried. But he did care; he cared considerably. This sobered him. He got through Sunday, chafing. Then Monday when his second-shift nurse came on duty she was frowning.

"Whats the matter?"

"Oh that mean old man!"

"What mean old man?"

"That Major Barcroft. You know what he did?"

"What?" Drew said, and felt a sinking at his heart.

Then she told him. The whole town had been waiting for the reading of the will, but there turned out to be no will. Wills could be broken. And besides, there was no need for one — for when, with Amanda's permission, they opened the safe in the major's study (this was on the Monday morning after the Saturday she came home; they were searching for the will) they found in a drawer, the key to which he had carried in his bottom left vest pocket, four thousand dollars in hundred-dollar bills and a deed to a quarter interest in a downtown office building. The forty crisp new greenbacks and the deed had a rubber band around them and a slip of paper tucked under it on top. Across this he had written in a neat, soldierly script with a hard-lead pencil: *For Amanda. This is All.* It was dated *11-11-39*, six weeks after the first heart attack.

They could not believe it. For the past week all the arguments had been as to whether there would be three or four millions, and by this time some were expecting five or six; they had been prepared to be surprised at how large a sum it was but they were unprepared for a surprise in this direction. Two of the men ran next door and put in a call for the major's bank in Memphis. They were calling for Major Malcolm Barcroft's daughter, his heir: what was the amount of the account? A hum came over the wire, the same hum Harley Drew had once identified with chuckling, except that perhaps this time it was — a ghostly chuckling — for then the banker's voice, urbane and silky, came down the line. Major Barcroft no longer had an account; he had cleared it out seven months ago, at the time of the donation. For a moment they did not get the word, and then they did: Donation? What donation?

Well, it was supposed to be a secret — he had given in the manner of a gentleman, without fanfare; but now that he was dead . . . And then they heard the worst. Something less than a year ago he had begun to liquidate his holdings, converting everything to cash. In the end it amounted to a little over one hundred and fifty thousand dollars, all that was left of the inherited half million; the rumor about the Reichsmarks was true, and there had been other investments as unwise. A check for a hundred and fifty thousand dollars was sent to endow a library of military history and tactics at the Tennessee school where he had been cadet captain fifty years ago; he had never been back, the major said in the letter inclosing the check, but he had always remembered his school years as the happiest of his life. This left four thousand, which he directed the bank to send him by registered mail, forty crisp new hundred-dollar bills. That closed out the account, and that was what his daughter got, four thousand dollars in cash and a quarter interest in the office building — the same one Henry Stubblefield owned part of; it would yield her a bit under two hundred dollars a month. *For Amanda,* he had written. *This is All.*

The nurse had most of it right; she had the figures right at least, and as Drew lay listening he grew paler and paler, even under the hospital pallor; "Isnt it just a sin and a shame?" she cried. But he said nothing. He lay there almost fifteen minutes, subdued and morose — the major had foiled him here on earth and now he had foiled him from beyond the grave. Then he said, "Would you mind stepping out a minute? Ive got a business call to make." She left and he took up the phone. He called the Memphis bank the men had called from Lamar Street that morning; he even talked to the same banker, the one with the urbane, silky voice.

"Mr Easely: Harley Drew, down in Bristol. Fine, and you? Fine. Mr Easely, Ive been thinking. That offer you made me a while back — Ive been thinking; Ive reconsidered. If the position is still open I'll take you up on it."

Next afternoon the doctor removed the stitches, and Wednesday morning he was released. Downstairs in the office when they handed him the bill he considered saying 'Send it to Jeff Carruthers down at Briartree,' thinking how much he would enjoy watching his face when Amy read it to him. But this was impossible in more ways than one. So he paid it and walked out into the sunlight of a Bristol that was no longer bright with promise and desire; even the trees looked ugly. That night at supper when he told Mrs Pentecost he was leaving she just nodded, prim and distant, like a wife beginning to get accustomed to evidence that her husband has been unfaithful, has betrayed her. The following morning, in Tilden's office, he gave notice of his departure from the bank and resigned his commission in the Guard. "I sure hate to see you leave us, Harley," Tilden told him. He said it without conviction, though, and the handshake was almost as brief as the one with Major Barcroft that first afternoon on Cotton Row. Drew spent the rest of the day closing out his affairs. He sold what he could, including his Ford, and gave the incidentals to the cook.

Friday he caught the noon train for Memphis, arriving at the station after it was already in. He boarded it in a hurry. Except for the golf bag he had no more luggage than he had brought to town twelve years ago. In fact he looked almost the same, still wearing the urban-cut tweeds; he had hardly aged at all. The biggest difference was the big white bandage across the back of his head — that and the paleness due to the loss of blood and the week spent indoors convalescing. He came down the aisle and took a seat just as the train jerked and began to roll; he did not look back. That was the last time Bristol saw him in the flesh.

For a lurid but briefer period Amanda was in the public eye again, moving once more among the turning heads and darted glances, leaving a trail of furtive, hand-cupped whispers. A practical nurse had come home from the hospital with her, on twenty-four-hour duty, but this was only a precaution on Dr Clinton's part — Amanda kept her a week and let her go. By that time the cook's son, the jazz cornetist who had returned from Harlem to rest up from t.b., had got into his trouble, had shot the gambler and been put in jail, awaiting trial, and Nora moved in with her mistress on Lamar Street. 'Them folks aint never give no time-off to nobody,' she had said, and now more than ever it was true. She slept on a folding canvas cot in the kitchen with a big mail-order nickel-plate revolver on the floor beneath her head, thrown down like a gauntlet in the face of all the prowlers in the Delta, black or white, man or beast.

Amanda was more removed from the life of the town than ever. This was not only because of the bulwark of her history (especially the latest chapter, the death watch) or Nora's pistol, cocked and ready on the kitchen floor: it was just that she had never had any friends, and had none now. She lived all but alone in the big house, its lofty rooms filled for her with memories of the dead, whose shapes were yet preserved in the sagged chairs where they had sat and the worn places on the carpets where their feet had scuffed. They returned to her now, the stern father and the invalid sister. Sometimes in the night she would come awake with the sound of her sister's screams in her ears; she would be out of bed, already knotting the sash of her robe, before she remembered that Florence had been dead almost two years; then, shaking her head in self-reproach, she would get back into bed. Nor was it only in her sleep they came. Occasionally as the afternoon wore on toward five oclock, the shadows lengthening, she would remind herself — speaking aloud in the big upstairs bedroom, her voice a bit reverberant because she was alone in the house except for Nora downstairs in the kitchen — "I must get my hat and go meet Papa." Then she would stop, remembering. She would chide herself for being absent-minded. "Youre getting *old*," she would say, half joking and half serious; for in her mind, using the eyes of children when they look down the long stretch of time between themselves and middle-age, she saw herself as old at forty-two.

Her only outside interest was the church. Florence had found the ritual exciting, taking the white Christ in her mouth and sipping his red blood, but Amanda found it soothing. What she enjoyed most was the sense of belonging, of making one among those who kneeled with their heads on the backs of the pews ahead, then rose all together like some many-legged animal to murmur the responses or confess their manifold sins and wickednesses. Where previously she had attended only the regular Sunday morning services, now she began to go to Wednesday vespers. She never missed a Sunday or a Wednesday; Mr Clinkscales was delighted. This was the path that led back to the world: so that toward the end of that first summer, when she was invited to become a member of the Altar Guild, she accepted. At first she was frightened; it was all so new to her, the society of women her own age — they were like nothing she had ever known before. Seeing thus at first hand their flashing teeth and bright flimsy dresses cut to feature instead of hide their bodily appointments, their lipsticked mouths and powdered arms, Amanda was like some puritan tourist who, lost from her party, strays in innocence about the grounds of an Eastern palace until at length, fairly desperate, panicky, she finds herself in the seraglio, a vaulted apartment littered with silken cushions, wreathed with incense, and dedicated to sin. She was startled; her first instinct was to run. But after a few meetings she became accustomed to them and began to understand that what she had mistaken for voluptuousness was just modernity.

By then the talk had diminished; it had flared too high to be lasting, and though Bristol still remembered all the tragedies of her life, it had become too worn a topic for conversation, let alone gossip. When she had moved among them for a while, wives began to tell their husbands, "Amanda Barcroft was at Altar Guild this afternoon. You know, she's not as strange as I used to think. Of course she's had any number of perfectly weird things happen to her and she's got that awful haunted look around her eyes, but I declare she's really kind of nice. At least you can see she *wants* to be. You know?"

Besides — as always — there were other things to talk about. News of Jeff and Amy Carruthers had filtered down from Baltimore. That was where they went for plastic surgery after the doctor from the Bristol clinic, despite the neatness of his appearance and the glittering array of instruments, turned out to be not so skilful after all; she might as well have accepted the services of Dr Kidderman, who had done such a fine preliminary job on Harley Drew. They had stayed at Briartree while the cuts healed, one at the point of her right cheekbone, the other almost through her upper lip, running diagonally down from one wing of her nose. Both scars were an angry red, puckered at the edges by a herringbone pattern of stitches like the seam on a baseball, only not so neat. The bridge of her nose, as the soreness left, got flatter every morning in her mirror until finally she would have stopped looking but could not, fascinated as she was by the wreckage of her face. She kept to her room, the shades all drawn, and had her meals served on a tray. Jeff brought them, for she would allow no one else to enter the room, not even the servants; she would not be seen.

She stayed up there a little better than two months, by which time the room had attained an almost unbelievable degree of squalor. Then they went to Baltimore — Jeff made the appointment by telephone. They left in mid-July, summer approaching its climax, but Amy came downstairs heavily veiled and the shot-silk blinds were drawn at the rear windows of the car. Two chauffeurs took turns sleeping; they drove straight through. Their meals were sandwiches at roadside places that advertised curb service, and Amy took a minimum of liquids because the only rest-rooms she would use were at dimly lighted filling stations in the dead of night.

The doctor, a specialist who had repaired and rebuilt some of the nation's most famous faces — screen stars who had gone through windshields or dived into empty swimming pools or fallen on whiskey bottles or, like Amy, provoked a violent man — examined her under a strong light, his nurse moving white and silent in the darkness beyond his shoulder, and Amy sat there feeling horribly ashamed; he was the first to look at her since the Bristol doctor came back down to Briartree toward the end of May and removed the stitches. "Hm," he said. His eyes glittered like the eyes of the Mad Scientist in the movies. He touched her face. "That hurt?"

"No."

"Hm. That?"

"No." But she winced.

"Hm." He mused. "Top light," he said, impersonal again. A switch clicked and the ceiling light came on. He rose. "All right, Mrs Carruthers. Tomorrow. You want to get this over with tomorrow?"

Next morning in the operating room the five masked heads around the table were like a whole stadium full of people; she was glad when the anesthetist brought the cone down over her face. Then she woke and she was looking out through slits in a bandage like a visor. Jeff sat in a chair beside the bed. She felt sick and was going to ask for something — what? — but fell back to sleep before she could think. Soon afterwards she woke again and he was still there. "You smashed my face," she said, but Jeff said nothing. He was asleep.

"There now," the nurse said. "It's all right. The doctor says it's going to be all right."

And it was, nearly. When she and Jeff came down to Briartree two months later on a flying packing trip, though she still wore a veil it was not the heavy one she had worn when they left, and only the closest examination showed the thin pink scars like three short strands of scarlet thread that had been washed in too-strong soap so that the color had not held, one at the cheekbone, one at the lip, and one down the bridge of her now patrician nose; her teeth were as straight and even and dead-white as piano keys. Then they left, and Bristol later heard that she had discarded the veil. Pancake make-up had come into style by then; it covered the faint scars and now she had a beauty beyond all her former claims; she resembled Nefretete and that one model — apparently one — who looks out at you from page after page of *Vogue*. Not that the cuts had really changed her face. The difference lay in the absence of expression, or rather in the absence of any change of expression, for there was none; the slow, down-tending smile was gone.

All this was hearsay, however, as far as Jordan County was concerned. Their visit was only a short one; they were there less than two days, gathering up a few personal odds and ends. Then they were gone for good. They had sold Briartree, lock, stock and barrel, to the Wisten brothers, owners of a Bristol department store advertised in both the county papers as 'the finest merchandising bazaar between Memphis and New Orleans' — which it was, though it had once been one of those near the levee at the foot of Marshall Avenue and their father had been an expert at cajoling Negroes inside off the boardwalk; but the 'boys,' now in their fifties, had turned this skill to better account and now they owned Briartree. As for Jeff and Amy, though they never came back to Jordan County, Bristol continued to hear of them in one place or another round the country, Jeff with his record collection, his polo shirts and crepe-sole shoes, his pistol, and Amy with her beautiful cold immobile Max Factor death mask.

The sale was in September and by that time Nora's son, Duff Conway, had been tried and sentenced. All through the summer and into the fall whoever passed the county jail heard the cornet playing sweet and clear. Then in October the state executioner brought the portable electric chair ('My old shocking chair' he called it) and installed it in one of the ground-floor cells; wires ran from the electrodes, through the window bars, to the generator in the truck parked in the outer darkness of the yard. Amanda was alone in the house that night. Nora hired a drayman and waited down Jail Alley with a pine coffin that lay in the bed of the wagon like an elongated, pale six-sided shadow. The body was turned over to them not long after midnight; they buried him early that afternoon, and Nora was back on Lamar Street in time to prepare the evening meal.

Amanda was in the parlor; when she heard the front door come open, she got up and went to the hall and it was Nora. They stood within touching-distance, looking at each other. Amanda wanted to touch her, at least lay her hand on her arm, but she did not; she just stood there, conscious of belonging to the white conspiracy. "I'm sorry," she murmured, hesitant, inadequate.

"Yessum," Nora said, and went back to the kitchen.

They were two women of sorrow, cook and mistress, but just as Nora had her kitchen and the preparation of food to occupy her mind, Amanda had the church and her duties in the Altar Guild. No one had ever done such a careful job of polishing the brass angel that stood barefoot on the base of the lectern, a caryatid balancing the Bible on its head; she even removed the green, acid-smelling traces of polish from the grooves between the feathers on its wings. It glittered in the Sunday morning sunlight or reflected the glimmer of candles at Wednesday vespers, and Amanda would look at it and feel possessive. She had this. And sometimes Mr Clinkscales would glance at her, then at the angel and back at her, and smile congratulations.

The year went into November, nearing the anniversary of her meeting with Harley Drew. The local battery of the National Guard was mobilized and half the town turned out, lining Marshall Avenue to wave goodbye. Colonel Tilden rode up front in his command car, looking pudgy and severe, and everyone cheered when the howitzers rolled past, the cannoneers sitting at attention, forearms up, looking proud and balancing their heads like eggs, all alike in freshly blocked campaign hats. Amanda watched from the porch of the library; the Battle of Britain was in full swing and she came here to follow it in the papers, having canceled her subscription to the Memphis paper for economy's sake, all but the Sunday edition which she read before and after church, almost as intensively as Florence once had done. She had never been much of a reader, but now she was — and not only of the paper; for she had been watching people coming and going, taking books down and putting them back, and one day on the way out she stopped at the circulation desk. "Could you suggest something you think I'd like to read?"

Startled, the librarian looked up. "Read? A book? ...
Well —" She appeared to think, tapping her teeth with a
pencil. "I think *Jane*," she said at last, and rose and went into
the other room. Amanda remembered a large blue volume in
her father's study, *Jane's Fighting Ships*. But the librarian
returned with a small arsenic-colored book which she stamped
and slid across the desk: *Pride and Prejudice*. Amanda took it
and hurried home.

After lunch she went into the parlor and settled down in
the Morris chair to read. But with every turning page she sat
a little straighter, horrified; finally she had to give it up — the
book read like a series of dispatches on the war between men
and women, viewed from the women's camp. Next morning
when she put it back on the desk the librarian smiled. "You
like it?" Amanda shook her head. "Oh," the librarian said. She
stopped smiling. "Well. Want to try something else?" Amanda
nodded doubtfully, and the other woman (they were about of
an age) took a thick pink book from the shelf beside her desk.
"Try this," she said.

It was *Vanity Fair* and after lunch Amanda went into the
parlor. She was still there when Nora called her to supper;
Becky Sharp seemed much less immoral than the Bennets —
the Bennet women, anyhow. After supper she came back,
and she was still reading at ten oclock when Nora made her go
to bed. Next morning after breakfast she was in the Morris
chair again. "You ghy put your eyes plum out," Nora said
when she came to tell her lunch was ready.

"Wait till I finish this chapter," Amanda said.

That afternoon she was back at the library, checking out
The Newcomes and *Pendennis*; she went straight through
Thackeray in a week and within another week was half
through Dickens. Thus began a year of omnivorous reading.
By the end of that time the librarian was toying with the idea
of recommending Proust. "That ought to hold her," she said.
She smirked. "But I dont believe she really reads them. Not that
fast. Or pays much attention to what she's reading, anyhow."

This last was at least partly true, in a sense; for in time, and in widely spaced installments as it were — Balzac, James, Faulkner: Eugenie Grandet, Catherine Sloper, Emily Grierson — she read her own story without recognition. She did not think while she read; she lived. Nothing *there* applied to anything outside, and she preferred it so. If some author, up to the tricks of his trade, attempted to increase the verisimilitude of his book by having the narrator insist that the story was 'true,' had really occurred, Amanda was not impressed. It seemed to her that real people just had things happen to them; that was all. They lived along as best they could, never really comprehending either their triumphs or their setbacks. Reality was mostly numbness (and in ratio: the deeper the tragedy, the deeper the numbness) whereas in books the characters actually understood — the deeper the experience, the deeper the perception; they suffered or exalted on a comprehensive scale, and the proper emotion was always there, on tap. She read on, coming and going between Lamar Street and the library with her armloads of books, and in her case the law of diminishing returns did not obtain. Except for the trips to market, her duties in the Altar Guild, and the hours in bed, she spent as much time in the Morris chair as Florence once had done.

She read the war news only on Sundays now, and then only as a sort of memorial to her father. In early summer, a little over a month after the anniversary of the major's death, the Russians were attacked; they joined the fighting and were overrun; German armor clanked across the steppes; thatch-roofed huts burned fiercely. Amanda hardly looked up from her book. Summer wore itself out, declined into fall; the nights were cooler now, and another anniversary of her meeting with Harley Drew went past. She read on. Then one morning in early December, a Sunday, she got up, put on her robe, and went downstairs for the paper. It was on the veranda, at the head of the steps with a bottle of milk beside it. She took them up and went back into the house, reading the headlines: RED ARMY LAUNCHES COUNTER-OFFENSIVE; JAP ENVOYS SEE HULL.

As she came down the hall, hearing the coffee percolating in the kitchen, the thick inky-smelling center section of the paper slid out and fell to the floor, the Society section, and when she bent to pick it up she saw the photograph.

A three-column cut of a wedding party, it obviously had been taken immediately after the ceremony, bride and groom flanked by the bride's attendants whose painted mouths and eyes and nails stood out black against the newsprint. The bride, a large matronly woman with an unmistakable aura of wealth — diamonds on her hands, pearls at her throat — was looking not at the camera but at the groom; she watched him, fiercely possessive. The groom, who smiled directly into the lens, was Harley Drew.

△

That afternoon — our time — the bombs fell on Pearl Harbor, and now the women had cause to appreciate Amanda even more. The energy that had gone into making the brass lectern angel one of the prides of the Episcopal church was directed into other channels too; there were bandage-folding sessions and gatherings where they mended clothes for refugees and packed dusty books and magazines for shipment to the soldiers overseas. At first all the women were enthusiastic, but gradually this particular fervor waned, especially when the new air base was established north of Bristol, after which most of the women Amanda's age (and older too: in fact the most active ones in this respect were crowding fifty) preferred to advance the war effort by entertaining the cadets, many of whom had nervous stomachs as well as rosy cheeks and wavy hair; 'fly boys' they called themselves, and afterwards, after Ploesti, Schweinfurt, and the Hump — after the roses had paled (or yellowed from atabrine) and the wavy hair had straightened (from lack of attention, or maybe just from fright) — they were to look back on these few weeks in Bristol as a sort of misty, all-providing second childhood in which no metal screamed at them nor flak bloomed blackly to the left and right, and their greatest worry was some crank instructor. Though Amanda did not attend the teas or supper dances staged to help the fliers past the rigors of war, she was always willing to make one among the bandage folders. Thus she was a godsend (they used that word, godsend) to the women responsible in turn for recruiting workers.

They convened in the armory, vacant more than a year now since the Guard had mobilized. Drawn up to long tables made from sawhorses overlaid with planks, they performed intricate folding motions with their hands and thickened the air with chatter and cigarette smoke. This was Amanda's first real contact with gossip as a participant, or at any rate a listener, rather than as a subject. She enjoyed it, the bright chattering voices, the odd stories about the secret triangular lives of people you saw every day on the street — that was what it mainly concerned: whose wife had been seen with whose husband the week before — and in time she even learned to add an occasional bit to the sibilant hum of the place. So that at last, toward the end of this first year of the war, those members of the Altar Guild who formerly had said to their husbands, 'At least you can see she *wants* to be. You know?' would come home from the bandage foldings and say without explanation or extenuation, without any marvel at all: "Amanda Barcroft was telling me today . . ."

And yet her life was not really so very different. All this was merely extra, an entering wedge not even recognized as such. She went on with her reading, her trips to market, and her duties at the church. Nora — who, with three empty bedrooms in the house, still slept on the hard, drum-tight canvas cot in the kitchen; each time she moved it squeaked like a box full of frightened mice — continued to be her only real companion; they lived alone and there were never any visitors, white or black. Then something developed that changed everything. In late November (another anniversary) a contractor's representative called on her and offered what she considered a large sum for the house and lot on Lamar Street. Her first reaction was to say what Bertha Tarfeller said in a similar situation some years back: 'Oh I couldnt do that.' But then she thought, Well: why not? and told him, "I shall have to speak to my attorney, Sir." She talked that way now — bookish. Next morning she went to the office of the man who had handled her father's legal affairs in the old days, Judge Nowell. He was dead now but his son was there, a rising politician, a leading light in the state legislature despite the handicap of a Harvard education.

"Why, certainly, Miss Amanda," he said, speaking across the polished top of his father's walnut desk. He called her Miss but that was nothing; he was five years younger, and even people her own age had begun to call her that. She wore her Sunday dress and sat with her hands in her lap. "It will do you good to get away," he told her. "We havent felt right anyhow — the town I mean — about you living there alone with tramps and millhands roaming past at all hours of the night. Certainly sell it."

So that evening when the contractor's representative called again she said that she would sell. This was Monday; Nowell made the arrangements. Amanda moved out on Thursday, having made a selection of what furnishings she wanted, and the rest was sold at auction the next day by a man who drove down from Memphis with a little wooden hammer in his pocket. It lasted all day; half the women in Bristol were there, and even some of the men. Though this time they had not had to wait for a funeral to gain admission to the house, there was still that air of feverish haste, as of vandals engaged in the rifling of a tomb, and most of them continued to speak with their hands in front of their mouths. First they made tours of inspection, visiting all the rooms, including some they had never seen before. In the major's study they found the map still on the wall, its pins showing the positions of the armies in early May of 1940 just before the 'phony' war erupted. They even climbed the dusty stairs to the attic where they once had told each other Florence was kept behind bars. The auction, which got under way at ten oclock and continued on past sundown, was held on the veranda to accommodate the crowd that overflowed the lawn and sidewalk in both directions down Lamar Street. The bidding was intense, for the auctioneer — a big, jolly-looking man with a ducktail haircut and a double-breasted vest — knew how to pit them one against another; quarrels were begun that day that lasted through the decade. They bought everything he offered, the heavy, overstuffed ball-and-claw furniture, the china and silver, the carpets and drapes, even the cut-glass chandeliers. It all went under the hammer.

Over the weekend the house stood empty, gutted; someone even came at night and rooted out the shrubs and iris bulbs. Children threw rocks at the windows for the pleasure of hearing the crash and tinkle of glass, and wrote with chalk on the steps and doors the old four-letter Anglo-Saxon expletives. Sunday was cold and rainy. Early next morning the wreckers came with machines, like a tableau of some mechanistic future in which these, the only survivors after the Bomb, turn on the world with destruction. Pulling and prizing at the walls with ropes and crowbars, they razed the house in just four days. When the sound of the airhammers stopped and the dust had cleared, there was only the vacant lot strewed with rubble and marked in places by the paler scars of flower beds; the house had disappeared like the fulfillment of a prophecy out of Isaiah.

For three days it stayed like that, like photographs of London during the blitz. Sunday was cold and rainy, as before — it was December now. Monday morning, even earlier than the wreckers had arrived, the contractor broke ground for the foundation of a new building. Within six weeks it was completed, a modern structure with sharp, uncluttered lines and a cavernous mouth at one end to swallow automobiles as they rolled up the concrete ramp. The broad low façade of garish brick had a sign with foot-high letters slashed across it: MAXEY'S GARAGE. ONE STOP SERVICE. All that remained of what had been there in the major's time was one of the four original oaks; the garage man built a circular seat around it and on fine days off-shift workers would sit there watching cars go by. The Barcroft oak, it was called, one of Bristol's landmarks, even after most people no longer remembered how it got its name.

There was so much else to talk about, especially now with the war moving toward a climax. And not only the war: the old topics still flourished too, sometimes with the same characters, as long as they supplied food for conversation. Amy and Jeff Carruthers for instance. Ever since they moved away Bristol had been hearing various things from various sunny corners of the nation — Florida (something about a thrown drink in a Miami nightclub; but they never got the straight of that, neither who had thrown it nor even whom it was thrown at) and Southern California (this in a movie magazine: 'What young male lead is head-over-heels about what tobacco heiress?' and several pages further on, a photograph with the caption: *Elsa Maxwell with Jeff and Amy Carruthers, the charming Carolinians (he is blind). That's Gary Cooper in the background. Paulette Goddard is dancing with her Buzz*) and Santa Fe. Santa Fe was where the fullest report came from — too full in fact, full of exaggeration and contradiction, for by then the legend had begun to acquire a somewhat mythic character. They had bought a house out there, a two-story adobe affair with Mission furniture, Indian rugs, and idols squatting in niches. You could park a car in the living-room fireplace and there were a dozen bedrooms, most of them continuously occupied according to the report; people dropped in from everywhere, the international set, kept on this side of the water by the war. Then followed the same involvement — Amy must have gotten bored again. This time it was a real cowboy, a wrangler off a ranch, not one of the imitation Arkansas varieties, and this time there was shooting too (but no blood-shed; the cowboy lost no blood as Drew had done; all he lost was one heel from a pair of forty-dollar boots, shot clean away) and Jeff and Amy sold the house and moved on: to South America, the report said hazily. In fact there was a good deal that was hazy — one version even said Amy did the shooting. When people in Bristol heard this last they began to understand that they might have been mistaken as to the direction in which Jeff's jealousy had been pointed down at Briartree. It opened new fields for speculation.

But not for Amanda, who listened and put it out of her mind. She preferred the stories she found between the covers of books; for her the Carruthers couple were just two people who shot Harley Drew, and that was that. Taking a few pieces of furniture — her bed and two silk-shaded lamps, the Morris chair and a rosewood chifforobe — she engaged a room on the top floor of the new hotel, a towering eight-story building twice as tall as any other in Bristol, where she had the steel-and-plastic sticks of furniture removed and replaced them with the things she brought from Lamar Street. Now that she had no household cares or marketing trips to distract her, reading took up more of her time than ever. She had no responsibilities, no ties: not even Nora, whom she had presented with a check for one hundred dollars as severance pay. This was probably the most expansive free gesture any Barcroft ever made, not ex-cluding the major's bequest to the Tennessee school; for that had not been exactly open-handed — he was more or less ma-neuvered into that.

She liked it there, the breath-taking elevator rides, the atten-tive desk clerk with his waxed mustache, the bustling transients, the long dim carpeted corridors with so many doors and all kinds of secret exciting things going on behind them, like the night a man and his wife in the adjoining room called each other such vile names and finally, when dawn came through, began to throw things at each other; Amanda hugged her pillow and listened and regretted it when someone down the hall complained and the night clerk brought a policeman and made them quit. There were other incidents, less violent but no less interesting, like the businessmen in the dining room, leaning their heads together and whispering, or the high school couples coming home from the malt shop, holding hands — they also leaned their heads together and whispered. Soon she began to sit for a while in the lobby before going out or after coming in. She liked it there. Sometimes she had little exchanges, almost conversations, with transients who asked for advice about restaurants and picture shows and what there was to 'do,' even the traveling men ('drummers' in the old days, 'salesmen' and 'representatives' now, though in either case Amanda knew a girl was ruined if she went out with them) who thanked her and, strangely enough, were always civil. Many of them reminded her of Harley, smelling like him of bay rum and tobacco and paying a great deal of attention to the grooming of their fingernails and hair. Thus gradually Amanda was drawn away from her reading and into the orbit of the day-to-day life of Bristol; she too became a watcher.

Best of all she liked the closing hour of every day, when she sat in the Morris chair at her high window and saw the town spread out beneath, with people moving along its checkerboard pattern on the way from work. She sat there while the light failed, watching them; she identified their small, foreshortened figures one by one, gave each its name, recalled its history, and traced its path along the sidewalk to its home. It was as if, brooding there like a gargoyle, her image had been imprinted on the public retina so long that now, at last, she had been absorbed by it, had now herself become a part of the enormous eye, and was looking out as all those others had done.

She also took an interest in her food. Seated in the glass-and-marble, somewhat reverberant dining room, she would study the menu carefully and with much deliberation while the waitress stood by, pad and pencil poised; it was always thus, but the waitresses had become so accustomed to it that they did not even get impatient any more. She always ordered the full

table d'hôte, and as a result she had begun to put on weight —
she was not willowy now; she was almost plump, and when
her gray, lace-appointed dresses no longer fitted her, she replaced them with new, tailored ones in softer grays and
browns. They became her. "*My*, Miss Amanda," the women
said at Altar Guild and at the bandage foldings. "Youre really
looking well these days." And though at first she was flustered
by the compliments, later she would preen herself a bit while
thanking them and settle her pince-nez more firmly. The
glasses were a recent addition, a result of eyestrain; they were
rimless, like her father's, and like him she wore them with a
fine gold chain that drooped in a cobwebby glistening parabola to a button at her bosom. Taken in conjunction with the
gray that had begun to streak her hair, they caused people to
remark how much she had come to resemble Major Barcroft.

Half an hour before time for the evening meal she would
come down in the elevator and claim a seat in the lobby near
the dining-room doors in order to be among the first to enter
when dinner was announced. In this way, sitting there with
time on her hands, she reacquired her sister's newspaper habit;
she felt that she could afford it now that her income had been
boosted by the sale of the house on Lamar Street. Every evening, between six-thirty and seven, she sat there with the
Memphis paper spread comfortably in her lap. From time to
time other hotel residents would arrive and speak to her, wish-
ing her good evening. She would nod decorously, the pince-nez
glinting, and return to her paper. In the Society section she
read frequent notes that told of the comings and goings of
Harley Drew.

He had married well. His wife, the widow of a cosmetics
manufacturer and twelve years older than Drew, had brought
him not only wealth but also high social position, and now —
though his wife, they said, kept a grip on the purse strings and
held him strictly in line — he bloomed exactly as he had said
he would do when money came his way. The social notes re-
ferred to him as 'sportsman, socialite and cotton broker,' and

there were photographs of him at all the best affairs. In the last summer of the war, for instance, Amanda saw a three-column cut that showed him surrounded by debutantes, leading the grand march at the annual cotillion. He wore the uniform of a colonel in the Tennessee Home Guard.